To Julia —
Thank-you for being here
to share the magic —

xo
Lise

The Between

LJ Cohen

!?*Interrobang Books*

The Between
LJ Cohen

Published by Interrobang Books
Newton, MA
First print edition: January 2012

ISBN-13: 978-0-9847870-1-2
ISBN-10: 0984787011

Copyright 2012 by Lisa Janice (LJ) Cohen, all rights reserved

Original cover art by Jade E. Zivanovic
(http://www.facebook.com/artofjez), 2011

For Neil, Philip, and Eric

My sounding boards,
my first readers,
my personal cheering section.
Without you, my stories could never have been written.

Chapter 1

LYDIA GLANCED AT HER PHONE and jumped down from the edge of the sink in the girl's bathroom. Ten more minutes before the late bus. She could risk leaving now. Cracking open the door, she looked up and down the hallway for any sign of Clive. So far, so good. She'd kept her backpack and jacket with her all day so all she had to do was escape outside without being seen. Then she'd have the whole weekend without him following her around. The way he seemed to know where she'd be at any given time was more than a little creepy. It wasn't right. He wasn't right. Lydia couldn't figure out what Clive wanted, but whenever he looked at her she felt unsteady, like the ground was tilting under her feet.

For once she'd timed it perfectly—the halls were empty. Shouldering her pack, Lydia sprinted down the stairs to the side exit where she could see the bus loading zone and had a clear view of anyone coming in or out of the building. A few other students and several of her teachers passed by as if she were invisible. If only she were invisible, then Clive wouldn't be her problem.

She waited until everyone else boarded before jogging across the field to the bus. There were a few other kids she knew, but no one spoke to her. It had been a long week and Lydia didn't want to talk to anyone, either. As they pulled away from school, she let her breath out in a long sigh, shoved her backpack under an empty seat, and slumped against the window. With Monday off, she had three days to work on her college essays and get her history paper finished. Three whole days without having to dodge her personal stalker. "Thank God it's Friday" had never seemed more appropriate.

"May I?" a deep voice asked, full of exaggerated politeness.

She jerked her head up, heart pounding. It couldn't be. Clive was standing, leaning over her seat, staring at her with his odd emerald eyes. He shouldn't even be here—as far as she knew, he didn't live anywhere near her side of town. As usual, no one even glanced her way. She wondered if anyone would react if she screamed. If Clive tried to touch her, she sure as hell would. He sat down beside her and she inched closer to the window.

"It's the glamour," he said.

All that effort avoiding him for nothing. How did he even get on the bus? Lydia was sure he hadn't boarded before her and she was the last one on. Maybe he would just go away if she closed her eyes.

"That's why they don't really notice you."

Lydia could hear the perfect smile in his voice. Ever since he came to school in September, most of the girls and even some of the guys had practically drooled over him. But no one else seemed to catch the odd things he said to her. Not the kids who orbited around "Planet Clive," not the teachers, who somehow never called on him or collected his homework. Not the guidance counselor, who didn't seem to register her complaints about him. No one.

"But it's thinning," he said.

At least her stop was next. Then she could go home and pretend there wasn't anyone named Clive Barrow following her around at school. And in seven months, she would graduate, then head off to college. With any luck, she would never, ever see him again.

"Once it's gone altogether, you won't be safe here anymore. Even Oberon couldn't keep you hidden forever."

She opened her eyes. He was staring at her, smiling. Oberon. Shakespeare. He was talking nonsense again. And she was pretty sure he was mocking her, too. They just finished reading *A Midsummer Night's Dream* in English class. "Taking the in-character exercise pretty seriously, aren't you?" Lydia said, irritation making her sarcastic.

"Where do you think he stole his ideas from?"

"Who?" she asked, before pressing her lips closed. She shouldn't have opened her mouth. The last thing she wanted was to encourage him. In a few minutes, she would be home. Surely he wouldn't follow her there.

"Shakespeare." Clive shook his head, his straight, black hair falling to frame his oval face. "Never mind."

"What's wrong with you? Just leave me alone," she said, tugging her backpack free from under the seat in front of her. The bus groaned as it turned the corner of her street. Lydia glared

3

at Clive, but he didn't budge, effectively trapping her there.

"Excuse me," she said, not even trying to mirror his formal tone. Her mom's Subaru was parked in the driveway. Good. She stood up and shouldered her bag, cursing as the bus accelerated past her house. Freaking driver wasn't going to stop. Again. "Hey, that's my stop!" she called. He slammed on the brakes and the bus squealed to a halt. The door hissed open.

Clive stood up and swept his arm in a bow that should have seemed weird and awkward in the confined space of the bus, but somehow didn't. "After you," he said.

Lydia pushed past him into the aisle, trying not to think of what she'd do if he followed her. Yell? Call the police? Run? She smiled. There weren't a lot of kids who could outpace her when she poured it on. "Whatever," she said.

As she turned toward the front of the bus, a shadow fell over it, darkening the afternoon to instant dusk. Thunder rumbled in the distance.

"Thorn pierce it," Clive said, his voice a low growl.

She glanced back at him, not sure why the strange things he said bothered her, why she couldn't just ignore him. He was staring out the widow, his face chalk white. Something had ruffled his perfect composure. Lydia followed the line of his gaze to her house. Her brother Marco's bike was leaning on the railing of the front porch, his muddy soccer cleats draped over the handlebars, as usual. One of her neighbors was walking a yapping Corgi. The sky that had been threatening rain all day let loose with a spray of fat droplets. It was all utterly ordinary. So why was her pulse pounding in time to the beat of the rain on the roof of the bus?

The door closed. They lurched forward. "You idiot, you made me miss my stop," she said, reaching out to shove him in the chest. He muttered something under his breath.

A flare of lightning turned the other kids on the bus into distant silhouettes. Lydia squeezed her eyes shut against the searing brightness. Thunder roared like a freight train, rattling windows and leaving her ears ringing. She had never seen a storm hit so hard or so fast. Tornadoes weren't common around here, but that didn't mean they couldn't happen, right?

The hair on her arms fanned out and a wave of pressure thrummed against her chest. The bus skidded to a stop, throwing Lydia against the edge of a seat. Its high back caught her in the stomach, leaving her gasping for breath.

Screams and shouts competed with the eerie harmonics of the wailing horn, making her skin crawl. She blinked, trying to clear the afterimages from the lightning strike. Her ears still buzzed. The bus was complete chaos. Kids were scrambling to get to their feet, climbing over scattered backpacks and one another, shoving their way toward the door.

It all seemed so far away. Lydia stared out the windshield, her mouth falling open, as a torrent of water rushed down the street. Flashes of lightning pierced the dark sky. Pain burned like a stitch in her side, making it hard to breathe. She had to get out. She had to run. Lydia shivered, pushing her way through her panicked classmates to the front of the bus.

The driver was slumped over the wheel, blood running from his forehead. Outside, a huge maple tree lay across the road. It was a miracle they hadn't hit it.

"Come on!" Clive said. "They're looking for you."

"What? Who?" Lydia shuddered, his words like the cold rain lashing the bus. She reached for the door release.

"Not that way, you fool!" he shouted. "Look!" Clive pivoted her shoulders around toward the windshield.

The next flare burned a nightmare into her memory. The darkness outside was moving, like a sky full of insects. Each lightning strike erased huge swaths of wriggling blackness. As she watched, more of the swarm poured in to fill the gaps and ate their way closer to the bus. Her arms broke out in goose bumps. She couldn't look away. "What the hell is that?" The sounds around her faded and all Lydia could hear was a low vibration from outside, pressing against the skin of the bus.

"Darklings. Let's go," Clive said.

"I don't understand!"

He grabbed her wrist. "Come on, Lydia."

"Let go of me," she said, pulling away and cradling her hand.

"I can't let them find you."

The kids around her were crying or shouting, but it was as if she were in a sound-proof bubble. Only Clive's voice and the buzzing darkness felt real. Some part of her recognized this sense of floating as shock. Like the time she fell out of the apple tree and fractured her arm when she was six. She remembered the thump of her body hitting the ground, and the snap of bone, like a tree branch breaking. The pain had been a distant thing. Lydia frowned and took a deep breath. Something was happening here. Something important. She took an uncertain step toward the bus driver, trying to shake off the numbness. "What about him? We have to call 9-1-1."

"It's you they're after. We have to get you away from here.

Now move!" She had never heard that note of panic in Clive's smooth voice before.

She looked from the driver to the writhing shadow outside. As she watched, she knew whatever the darkness was, it saw her. Her mouth dried and she couldn't swallow. Something deep inside her was being slowly unwound like a spool of thread.

"Lydia!'

She couldn't move. He grabbed her arm again. There was a tug near her heart. She gasped, her free hand grappling for what was tearing at her chest. "No, stop!" she cried. The pressure built and built until Lydia was sure she was being turned inside out. Just when she thought she would collapse, there was an abrupt snap like a rubber band recoiling, and she lurched backward into an open seat, her lungs burning.

"Shut your eyes," Clive warned.

"What was that?" she whispered. "What are you doing to me?"

"We don't have time for this," he snapped. Still holding onto her wrist, he pulled her to her feet and flung himself toward the emergency exit window. Lydia was too shocked to flinch.

Rainbow-colored ripples moved through the glass, slowly liquefying it. She tried to yank free, but his long fingers clamped down like the jaws of an animal. He dragged her along with him through the spreading waves of what had once been a dingy bus window. She could still read the placard below the window frame—in case of emergency, push glass out. There was no glass left to push. They were swimming through air as dense as sea water. Warmth and color lapped at her skin.

This couldn't be happening.

Craning her neck, she tried to look back the way they'd come. The inside of the bus was a swirl of colors and far away, as if she were seeing it through the wrong end of a kaleidoscope. People moved in a jerky, freeze-frame kind of motion. A vibration like the low twang of a bass string shivered through her bones. Lydia clawed at Clive, struggling to break away.

"I told you to close your eyes!" He pulled sharply and she wheeled around him, a skater at the end of the line in crack the whip. He shoved her farther into the strangely thick air, his body blocking her view of the bus. The painful buzzing eased. She fell, rolling to a stop on solid ground.

"It's okay," he said, breathing hard as if he'd been running. "You're safe now."

Safe? He had to be kidding. She pressed her hand against her chest, expecting to find a bruise or cut. Something. There was no pain under her probing fingers. What just happened on the bus? Where was the bus? She looked back the way they had come. The rainbow window constricted like a pupil in bright sunlight. Where the hell was home? Lydia scrambled to her feet, her heart pounding in the sudden absence of pressure and sound.

"Really, it's all right," Clive said. "They can't follow you here."

"What was that? What did you do to me?" Keeping watch on Clive, she backed away slowly. Lydia blinked, her eyes tearing under a harsh, blue-white sky that reminded her of the glaciers they had studied in science. The rain had stopped. They were standing in a clearing filled with clashing shades of green. Trees jutted out at impossible angles. The horizon was much too close. She tried to swallow, but her throat was too tight.

"I've brought you Between," he said.

"Between? Between what?" The thunderstorm was gone, but so was her house, her neighbor and the dog and the bus. "This is crazy." Fear squeezed Lydia's chest. It was hard to breathe. She closed her eyes. *I'm dull. Boring. Nothing interesting ever happens to me.* When she opened them again, she was still in a strangely flat landscape.

The perspective was all wrong. She tried to fix her eyes on the trees and grass nearby. Leaves the shape of butterfly wings flapped in the light breeze and the grass looked more like seaweed than any lawn Lydia had ever mowed. But at least they stayed in focus. If she looked even slightly to the right or left, the edges of the landscape moved away from her.

"Try to keep your head still," Clive said.

She whirled around to face him. The world warped in the blurred lines of a movie camera panning too quickly. Lydia gagged, falling to her knees, fighting to keep down the remnants of school lunch. Saliva flooded her mouth and she swallowed reflexively, staring at a single frond of the odd grass. Rainbows swirled in the drop of water on its tip.

"Are you all right?' Clive asked.

"Fine," she said through gritted teeth. Damned if she was going to lose her cookies while he stood there. Her stomach stopped trying to turn itself inside out and she got up slowly, keeping her eyes fixed on the horizon.

"Between what?" she repeated.

"Between Faerie and the Mortal world," Clive said. "A way

station of sorts. A place to catch our breath."

"Faerie." She shook her head and instantly regretted it. Colors dripped and ran in this strange tie-dye place. "This isn't happening."

"We'll just rest here a minute and I'll take you the rest of the way. King Oberon . . . "

Lydia took a step back and Clive cocked his head, his eyebrows coming together over bright green eyes.

"Oberon. Faerie," she said. The words sounded silly on her tongue. Lydia took deep breaths though her mouth. Her stomach settled.

"Is it so hard to believe? Have you not always wondered why you felt out of step? Why it was so easy to stay unnoticed?"

"What the hell are you talking about?" Lydia had never run with the popular crowd, but that didn't mean she was some kind of freak like Clive.

He met her gaze with his, wide and unblinking, like a cat's.

"I told you. On the bus. The glamour. Oberon sent me to bring you to safety."

The intensity of his stare made her want to disappear. It was like being trapped by a spotlight on a bare stage. She narrowed her eyes and squared her shoulders, lifting her chin. "Oberon." He was clearly insane, but she couldn't figure out why she'd be trapped in his delusion. That's what this had to be. A minute ago, there was some kind of freak storm. Did the bus crash? Maybe she'd hit her head. She felt through her hair, but nothing hurt. There was no bump, no blood. Not a concussion, then.

"Lydia, there's nothing wrong with you."

The strangeness started with Clive, so it had to end with him, too. She had to humor him, find out as much as she could, figure this out. "So you're a Faerie," she said. A Faerie. This was crazy. She swallowed a laugh. That wasn't something you said every day in high school, at least not without getting the crap kicked out of you.

"Fae," Clive said. "We are the Fae. Where we live is Faerie."

"We?" Lydia took another step back.

Clive nodded. "Oberon hid you in the Mortal world when you were a babe, but you are one of us. The Fae."

"Right. You and me. We." It made as much sense as the wigged-out world around them, or the rabbit hole they fell through to get here, or Clive being practically invisible to all the teachers at school. Lydia looked down at her ordinary jeans and t-shirt and laughed until she started coughing.

"You don't believe me. Look around you."

She raised her head to meet his eyes. They certainly weren't in Kansas anymore. She put her hands to her mouth to stop another bout of uncontrollable laughter. "You've obviously made some kind of mistake. I'm Lydia Hawthorne. I live back there." She waved her hand behind her. "What the hell did you do with my house? My family?"

"They are not."

"What?"

"Not your family."

"Right," Lydia said, stepping farther away from him. The more distance, the better. "It's been real and you're definitely different. Faerie, Fae, whatever, but I need to go home now." It was time to fall out of whatever storybook she had fallen into.

"You can't go back. The darklings are still hunting for you."

If nothing else about this was real, the seething blackness and the bus crash definitely were. "Darklings. What are they?"

"Trackers."

"What, like Faerie ninjas?" She said it to make a joke, but Clive didn't laugh.

"More akin to hunting hounds."

"Why are they after us? Who sent them?"

"Titania. And you, not us. They search for you," Clive said.

"Titania. Oberon. You've got to be kidding."

"Lydia, Titania set the darklings after you. They won't stop. Not ever. Not until they bind you and take you to Shadow."

What the hell was Shadow? Whatever it was, it didn't sound good. "No. You're not making any sense." A wave of dizziness almost took her to her knees. Lydia rubbed her hand in small circles over her heart. She felt bruised. Something happened on the bus. Something about that swarm of darkness.

"I swear, I'll explain it all to you when we get to Faerie."

"Everything was fine. Until you showed up. You've done something." He must have drugged her, but how? She should have told her parents about him. She should have called the police when she had the chance. How was she going to get out of here?

A flicker of annoyance distorted his perfectly symmetrical features. "Lydia, we cannot delay here much longer."

She wasn't going anywhere with him, but she wasn't going to tell him that. If she kept him talking long enough, maybe whatever was causing this would wear off. "Why? Aside from the vomit-inducing scenery, this place has the distinct advantage of lack of bus crash and killer bugs." It was all wrong. She shouldn't be here. The thought of home tugged at her as if she were a needle in a compass.

"Time. Time moves differently here, Lydia."

"I don't need this." She shook her head and started to walk away. It didn't matter where.

"Lydia."

She turned back, despite her unease. Clive stared at her with his peculiar eyes. They were as weird as the rest of this place. She couldn't exactly fix their color. One moment they were brilliant green, the next emerald flecked with gold.

"Okay. So say this is real and not some hallucination." She glared at him, daring him to contradict her. "Once we're sure the darklings are gone, you could get us home, right?"

He stood silently.

"Clive?"

"Actually, no," he said.

"No?"

"No."

Lydia fought a rising panic that threatened to close her throat. "You mean you can't or you won't?"

"I am bound to Oberon and his will," he said. "He is waiting for you."

He could keep on waiting, as far as Lydia was concerned. "I didn't ask you to drag me here," she said, feeling a familiar twitch in her shoulders and a building pressure bubbling up in her chest. Anger. Anger was good.

"So I should have left you to the darklings?" He smiled as he shook his head. "I can see the Bright magic in you, Lydia. It makes you as Fae as I, whatever you believe. And you belong in Faerie."

"Right," she said. It was better not to argue with him, but she'd be damned if she was going to let him make any decisions for her. "I'm going back now." She grabbed her cell phone. Its reflection sent rainbows skittering across the rippling landscape. The plastic cover was cool and smooth and real in her hand.

"I doubt your phone works here," Clive said.

Lydia scowled at him, more annoyed than scared. "Okay, then." She flipped up the phone's cover and the picture of her cat was missing, replaced with an out of area message. "Great, well that's just great," she muttered.

"I told you," Clive said.

Lydia set her jaw, refusing to give in to panic. It was easier just to go with the dream logic of her bizarro day. She slipped the phone in her pocket.

Clive stood with the patience of a tree, watching and waiting, close enough to her that she caught the scent of wood smoke and pine needles rising from him.

The air was wrong, the trees were wrong. Clive was most definitely wrong. This morning, it was early fall. She began to sweat under her jacket and not only from the heat. Rainbow-tinged leaves rustled without any hint of a breeze. Something told Lydia the trees were laughing at her. She took a step backward. "You're crazy. This is crazy." She could hear her voice rise in pitch, like a distant siren.

"When you are ready, I will take you into Faerie."

He was wild. Elemental. He crackled with the energy of a

lightning bolt. Her heart raced as if she were running. The landscape looked the same in every direction. Empty aquamarine sky and tangled trees. Not even a single bird flew overhead. The silence smothered her. There was nowhere she could go.

She thrust her hands in her pockets to keep them from shaking. Her right hand brushed her house keys. They were a link out of this strangeness. The fob was shaped like a decorative cat with pointed ears. She slipped her fingers into the cat's eyes with the ears pointing outward like they had taught her in self-defense class and the comfortable coolness of the metal eased the tightness in her chest.

Clive reached for her. Lydia was suddenly certain that if he touched her again, something in his insanity would spread like a virus and she would never find her way back into her normal life. "Don't," she warned.

"It will be fine. I swear it." He took a step forward.

Lydia's heart sped up even faster. She whipped out the key fob and jabbed it at him, catching his right forearm with the tip of one of the sharp ears. He jerked his arm back and cradled it against his body, hissing in pain. Clouds boiled overhead. A thin scream that seemed to rise from the air around them tore the clearing's peace. Clive was silent, his eyes narrowed, his face sculpted into an expression of fury. The fob had cut a neat line through his sleeve and into the flesh beneath.

Blood welled up from the cut, a wet stain against the dark material. Her hands shook. The key chain fell to the ground, burning a patch of brown in the grass.

He stared at her, the thin, green ring of his eye nearly swallowed by the black. He staggered back to a tree trunk and slid to the ground.

"I'm sorry," she whispered, her body shaking with cold as if she'd been plunged in a winter lake. She hadn't really meant to hurt him, not like this.

His face was gray. "What have you done?"

The sky went dark.

Chapter 2

THE METAL SEARED CLIVE'S SKIN like a brand. *She cut me! Thorn and weed, she cut me!* Clive pressed against a willow tree, wincing as the movement jarred his arm. The willow's roots sunk deep into the earth, drinking Fae magic along with cool, clear water and Clive borrowed some of its strength. The pain eased, but the damage was already done.

His arm burned clear down to the bone. The wrongness of the iron leached like poison from a thorn. They had to leave before it was too late. He lurched to his feet, hissing at the shock running the length of his arm. He pointed to the key ring lying on a spreading patch of death. "Pick it up," he said. She looked at him with blank eyes. He had no time to coddle her. "Now." Leaving the metal here would only speed the decay.

Even with the tree's borrowed vitality, Clive could sense how close he was to collapse. He cradled his arm next to his side.

Lydia reached for the key ring like it was a venomous snake. Little did she know how true that was. He stared at her as she tucked the metal back in her pocket. How could she handle it with her naked skin? What kind of magic filled her? "We need to leave now," he said.

"It was an accident," she whispered. The scattered freckles on her cheeks and nose stood out against her shocked white face. Her brown eyes were open wide and she stared past him, unblinking.

He set aside his fury. Their safety, her safety, was more important than consequences right now. She was used to the Mortal world and needed explanations. Something to anchor herself to. "Look around," he said. This part of the Between was falling into full twilight. The sky was smoky, turning a translucent gray as the horizon receded. "This place is going to collapse on us like a big soap bubble. We have very little time." Measuring time was a Mortal construct, but it was a factor right now and not in their favor.

"I don't understand."

"I don't have the strength to take us through now. And we can't stay here." How had something so simple gone so wrong? "So you get your wish." He swallowed his anger. The delay would be costly, no matter that she hadn't intended it. "I need you to take us back to the Mortal world."

A tinge of color crept back into her cheeks. "How?"

"This is a place your mind helped build. You have Bright magic. Use it." She had been cut off from her Fae heritage for so long. What if she couldn't do it? His wounded arm throbbed. That wasn't something he wanted to dwell on. "Picture your room, imagine yourself opening the door."

"What do you mean?"

He had borrowed the rainbows from her wallpaper, the

trees from a painting of butterflies hanging in her room. "You have to take us back there," he said. In the distance, Clive heard a crack as sharp as the thawing of winter ice. "Now, Lydia."

She stared at him, unblinking. "So I just click my heels together?" Her voice broke and her whole face flushed. "You've got to be kidding."

"Magic is harnessed by belief," he said. This wasn't the time or place for a lesson on Fae magic and the building of bindings and glamours. "Look, if you expect to get home after clicking your heels three times, it will happen."

She backed away from him. "This isn't *The Wizard of Oz.*"

He didn't know what she was talking about, but if it was something she had faith in, then it would work. "Lydia, we have no time for your denial." The trees nearest them were shivering in a non-existent gale. Further away, all the green had smudged into gray. "The longer you wait, the more distorted time gets." There was no telling how much time had passed in the Mortal realm already. Maybe only hours, maybe as long as a day or two.

"You got us here," she said, "why can't you get me home?"

"The metal. You . . . it poisoned me," he said, working hard to keep his voice steady. Her cheeks colored. She was so ignorant, yet she had the strength to wield iron on Faerie's doorstep. How much did Oberon truly know about her? "And until I can cleanse the wound and recover my strength, it's up to you."

Lydia frowned, looking at him square in the face. "Can I really believe us home?"

Clive paused, not wanting to look too closely at the wilting

19

grass beneath his feet. "That's the question," he said. "Can you?"

Her hand fluttered to her mouth. "I don't think . . . "

Clive shook his head. If she said it out loud, if she really believed they couldn't get out, it would be true and they would be trapped here.

"I feel kind of silly," she said, looking down at her feet.

He shrugged, trying to remain casual. It wouldn't help to frighten her any further. "Get over it."

"I'll try," she whispered. She closed her eyes and the silence stretched out until it felt brittle.

Wind chilled his skin with the memory of snow. "Lydia, hurry."

"Okay," she said, "there's no place like home." She touched the heels of her sneakers together. One tap, two taps and she paused. "I can't . . . "

"What? What's wrong?"

"Nothing. Wait," she said.

He took a deep breath. The sky was split like a cracked egg. Soon he and Lydia would spill out. She tapped her heels a third time. For the span of ten heartbeats, nothing happened. Blood pulsed in his injured arm. He imagined the iron being driven deeper inside his body. He tasted metal on his tongue.

Then it was if he were spinning in space, his body impossibly large or infinitesimally small. A door slammed in his mind and the scent of freshly cut grass rose up around them. Stumbling, he sprawled to the ground, and reached his hands out to break his fall. Pain shot up his arm and knocked the breath out of him.

Darkness had fallen. In the distance a dog barked. The porch light snapped on.

"Lydia? Lyds is that you?" a woman's voice rang out.

She had done it.

*

A SLOW STEADY RAIN WASHED down the kitchen window. Lydia stared out at the muted landscape. Since her side trip down the rabbit hole with Clive yesterday, everything was different. She rubbed her chest, but the ache in her heart wasn't something she could reach. Nothing kept its true color anymore, not the trees, not the grass, not even her parents. Her mother just looked worn away like a chalk drawing that some careless thumb had rubbed across. Lydia turned to the breakfast dishes piled in the sink.

At least the house was quiet. Her father had taken Marco and Taylor to the movies since their soccer games were washed out. It was just Lydia and her mom. Her mom. Except Clive said this wasn't her true family. She wanted to believe everything he said was wrong, just the product of a deranged mind, but she couldn't shake the sense that she was changed somehow by that darkness yesterday.

"What's wrong, sweetheart?"

Lydia jumped, splashing water along the counter top. Her mother reached over with a towel and blotted it dry.

"I'm good, Mom." How could Lydia even begin to tell her what happened? She didn't understand it herself. Her mom had accepted her explanation that she'd missed the late bus and had found another way home from a schoolmate. She'd been so relieved that Lydia hadn't been on the bus when the driver collapsed. At least he was going to be okay. Lydia was feeling guilty enough already.

It was the truth, if not the full story. At least she didn't have to explain Clive. He'd vanished as soon as her mom stepped off the porch.

"You're so pale," her mom said. "And you hardly ate anything for dinner last night or breakfast."

Lydia busied herself drying dishes. It was easier than looking at the washed-out version of her mother or explaining that the food just tasted gray.

"Your father and I were talking. If you can save up half the money, we'll help you pay for the car."

It seemed like a lifetime ago they had that argument. Less than two days had passed since Lydia's life and happiness hinged on having her own car. She even remembered her impassioned arguments, but that girl and her concerns were distant now. Besides, who needed a car when you could pop through doors from here to there and back again? Wherever there was. Lydia didn't know whether she wanted to laugh or cry.

She turned to her mother. And despite what Clive had said, this woman *was* her mother. That hadn't changed even if everything else had. "It's okay," she said. "The car's not that important."

Her mother's eyes widened. She placed a cool hand on Lydia's forehead. "Are you sure you're feeling all right?"

Lydia nodded, finding a smile for her mother.

"Okay, who are you and what have you done with my daughter?"

She couldn't laugh at the familiar family joke. Changeling child. Something out of faerie tales. How could she be what Clive said? This was crazy. "I'm going for a run."

"You'll get soaked, Lydia."

"I'm not made of sugar and spice, Mom."

"Well, leave your muddy shoes in the laundry room."

"Yes, Mom." It was one thing to be planning to leave in a year. No matter how far away college was, she would still belong here. But this was different. Whatever Clive had done to her yesterday had already started to tear everything apart. Even if he disappeared forever, Lydia knew her life would never be the same.

*

CLIVE LEANED AGAINST A TREE, fuming. The skin over his forearm itched beneath the bandage. At least the Mortals understood how to repair their fragile bodies. Flexing and extending his fingers, he felt the pull across the rapidly healing scar. The metal had been completely flushed from the wound, but he still felt washed out, weak.

He watched Lydia emerge from her house in sweats and a t-shirt, her hair pulled back into a ponytail. How could she just pretend everything was back to normal? And how was he going to get her to Faerie before Oberon lost his patience? He knew Oberon as well as any member of court. Maybe better. Powerful, charming, and utterly ruled by his whims. The Mortals had that word totally out of context. They used whimsical as a synonym for harmless. Clearly, they had never met Oberon.

Clive was weary, but he slipped between raindrops as he followed Lydia, making no more sound than a shadow might. Her sneakers pounded against the pavement. She made no attempt to avoid the puddles, smashing down in them hard enough to break glass. The rain slicked her bangs against her face.

It was simple to let the rain bend around him. No use both of them getting soaked and these small magics didn't strain his resources, even on this side of the barrier. He ran along and beside her, hidden in plain sight. Fae she might be, but her untrained eye saw no more than any Mortal would. She would never notice him.

A peal of thunder rumbled in the distance. Darklings? Or maybe something more? Clive jerked his head up and stared across the park. Lydia swore and swerved off the bike path towards an enclosed field. She slammed the gate open with her hip and ducked into the scant cover of a shelter as the skies let loose.

Still breathing hard, Lydia paced around the shelter, keeping her leg muscles moving. She didn't really need to do that. Well, as long as she saw herself as Mortal, she did, but that wouldn't be for much longer.

The tang of ozone teased his tongue. Someone was definitely crossing between the worlds. He searched the horizon, but couldn't see anything. It had to be someone from the Shadow court. For all of Oberon's faults, mistrust wasn't one of them. Clive was pretty certain that as soon as the Faerie king had sent him here, he moved on to other plans and plots. It wasn't as if he didn't care, only that he expected success. It was a boon and a burden. He scanned the sky and the trees. Nothing.

Not that he figured he would find anything or anyone unless Titania willed it. Where Oberon's Bright magic was overt, aggressive, the Shadow Queen was an expert in subtlety and concealment. He expected no less from the Fae who served her court. Clive would watch and wait. Unless the darklings returned or Titania's emissary presented a clear threat to Lydia, he could not directly intervene. This was a matter between the courts and Clive knew his place and the law.

So Shadow was here, as well. He settled into the silence of old trees and watched Lydia pace.

Chapter 3

LYDIA SCUFFED THE DUGOUT FLOOR, trying to kick-start her brain. Running had always been her sanity. It was something that came easily to her and the steady rhythm of her feet on pavement usually helped her work through whatever problems life threw her way. But this. This was something else. She collapsed on the bench, dropping her head in her hands. Clive. Faerie. Fae. What was happening to her?

"This is not your fault."

Lydia jumped to her feet. "Who the hell are you?"

The girl standing at the edge of the dugout was what the emo wannabees tried for and failed, ending up with badly over-dyed hair and zombie makeup. This one was the real deal. Hair so black it looked wet and eyes a blue that bordered on purple against a backdrop of flawless pale skin. And she stood a head taller than Lydia, perfectly dry as the rain fell in sheets around her.

Lydia shivered.

"I can fix that," she said.

"Fix what?"

"This," she said and gestured to the rain beyond the dugout's shelter.

Goosebumps chased one another down Lydia's arms. The attack on the roof stopped. Lydia's ears rang in the sudden silence. Her teeth stopped chattering.

"Better?"

The air in the dugout carried the scent of burning leaves and the warmth of an Indian summer day.

"Did Clive send you?" Lydia asked.

The girl laughed and a momentary chill swept through the dry space. "He really knows how to charm a girl." She shook her head and her unbound hair swung in an arc around her shoulders. "No. I am Aileen, emissary of the Shadow Court. I bring greetings from my Queen, Titania."

Aileen bowed, her lithe body folding and unfolding in one continuous movement that reminded Lydia of a tree swaying in the wind. She looked down at her ratty sweat pants and would have traded anything to be invisible. "Great, another Faerie. Look, I already told Clive I wasn't interested in the tour and time share pitch. Life is confusing enough right now. So why don't you ask Tinkerbell for a ride back to Neverland and leave me the hell alone?"

"Titania was right. You do have spirit, even under the remnants of Oberon's glamour."

"I'm leaving." Lydia brushed past Aileen and into the perfect ring of sunshine surrounding them. Beyond a circle of three feet, a wall of gray marked where the rain began again. "Is this real or one of your Faerie tricks?" Was she still soaked through under the illusion of warmth?

"Does it matter?" Aileen asked, her head cocked to one side.

"Yes. Of course it matters."

"You have lived amongst the ephemerals for too long. They have such a narrow view of reality." Aileen shrugged one shoulder. "A glamour is not a trick. Nor is it a costume you put on." She waved her hand indicating the little cone of sunlight they stood in. "The air is warm. It is dry here. A simple matter of persuasion," she said, smiling.

Lydia recognized that smile. It was the smile that held just a hint of pity and disdain. The popular girls smiled like that. "Persuasion?" That sounded like hypnosis or something.

"Have you studied physics in your schooling?"

"Some. I'm not a science nerd or anything."

"The ephemeral physicists have come closest to seeing to the heart of things, as much good as that will do them."

There was that flash of superiority again. Or dismissal. Lydia began to tap her foot. Of course, they were mere 'ephemerals,' how could they hope to understand anything?

"Reality shifts depending on how you look at it," Aileen said. "And sometimes, with the right leverage, you can shift it yourself. Like I did with the rain. Like Oberon did. With you."

The breath caught in Lydia's throat.

A glint of triumph lit Aileen's smile. "As a measure of our good faith, Titania has bidden me to remove the glamour entirely."

Lydia stepped back one slow footfall at a time, never taking her eyes off Aileen. She hit the edge of the circle and felt rain drops spatter across her back and shoulders. "Don't. Touch.

Me." The hairs on the back of her neck lifted like a dog's hackles.

"My dear child, I can easily remove the ephemeral taint. Beneath Oberon's handiwork, you are one of us. Let me uncover your beauty. You no longer need this limited shell."

"This is who I am," she said, jutting her chin out. She'd be damned if she let some perfect Elf Faerie chick stand there and judge her.

"So be it." Aileen added a ritualistic tone to the words that made Lydia take another step back into the pouring rain. Her t-shirt molded itself to her spine. Aileen laughed and took a step forward. The weather shifted with her. "I think you will regret wearing this human seeming when you meet my Queen." She shrugged. "But it is your choice."

"Take your pocket of sunlight and leave. Stay away from me."

Aileen frowned, the perfect arches of her eyebrows moving toward the bridge of her nose. "So you have chosen Bright?"

A dangerous quiet spread out from where they stood, silencing even the distant beat of rain. Lydia shifted forward and back on the balls of her feet. It was at least a fifteen minute flat-out run home. She took a deep breath, weighing her words carefully. "I didn't choose anything. I didn't ask Clive to drag me to the other side of the looking glass. I didn't ask for you to come waltzing in and wave your magic wand. Just leave me alone."

Aileen cocked her head and stared at Lydia like a cat might study a mouse. Then she burst out laughing. "Titania will have her hands full civilizing you." She bowed again, holding an exaggerated, mocking pose. A peal of thunder shook the dugout. Lydia blinked in the lightning flash and Aileen was gone.

*

Clive exhaled into the gray morning as Lydia kicked over the bench. He hadn't known her long and the depth of her anger surprised him, just as she had surprised him yesterday. But then again, she wasn't truly Fae. At least not yet. She wore her humanity like a second skin and perhaps that was Oberon's fault. He'd let her stay here far too long. Clive wanted to kick something, as well, but giving emotions free rein wasn't something that came easily to his people. In Faerie, magic made stray wishes or undisciplined thoughts manifest. Any Fae who couldn't exercise control lived an uncharacteristically short life.

Lydia would have to learn how to channel her passions if she wanted to survive in Oberon's court.

He followed her as she ran back into the wet morning. Her feet churned the saturated ground to a thick clay. Without stopping to think, he firmed up the ground beneath her soggy sneakers, but he held himself from diverting the raindrops around her. That she would notice and given her state of mind, would definitely not be a good thing.

Lydia ran with the grace of the Fae. Even Oberon's glamour couldn't inhibit all of her true nature. Her legs seemed to float over the uneven terrain and he had to push himself to keep pace with her.

Clive wasn't sure how it all went so horribly wrong. He had been certain she would have embraced her Fae nature. As much as even he liked the Mortal world, he could not imagine always being so aware of the end of things. But at least she had rejected Aileen, too. Regardless of what Lydia thought she wanted, she was going to have to choose. Him or Aileen. Oberon or Titania.

So it was a race between Bright and Shadow courts. So be it. For as long as Clive could remember, there was no conflict in Faerie that wasn't somehow a struggle between Oberon and Titania. There was a time when they were lovers, when there was only one royal Fae court, but that was more than his lifetime ago. Even the Fae who lived through that time rarely spoke of it, lest they incur Oberon's fury.

Since then, things between the two courts had never escalated to overt war. No, that wasn't their way. The Fae fought through sniping and skirmishes, battles of words that shifted the balance from one court to another. Now Oberon held most of the openings between the worlds and most of the power.

Most, but not all. Else Titania's emissary would never have been able to so much as dip her toes here. But thanks to the darklings, she had found Lydia easily enough. More easily than she should have. It must have cost Titania half the tithe of her court to send them.

Lydia was nearly home and Clive hesitated under the cover of an old maple. Although its bare limbs looked almost dead, he could feel the sap running beneath its skin. Clive knew better than to trust the surface seeming of things.

He waited as Lydia slammed the mud room door behind

her. This task was turning out to be far more than the simple retrieval Oberon had led him to believe. But if he had to face Oberon's displeasure, Aileen would have to deal with Titania's. Well, Lydia seemed to have handled Aileen just fine. Clive smiled. She couldn't have known how annoyed his Shadow court counterpart had been.

Lydia shed her muddy shoes just inside the door. Clive hesitated, watching her strip off the sodden t-shirt to the tank top beneath. He could see beneath the edges of the glamour. She was lovely, all the shades of brown in Faerie, from her eyes, to her hair, to her bronzed skin.

"If you don't turn around right now and leave, I'll call the police and have them slap a restraining order on you."

Lydia stood in the doorway, her hands on her hips, her voice simmering with suppressed rage.

Clive smiled and stepped away from the tree. "You knew I was here. There are few Fae who could break through my glamour." It was true and he didn't say it to brag, though he was pretty certain Lydia wouldn't see it that way.

"I've had enough of you and your friend Aileen today. Can't you leave me alone?"

"Aileen and I are not friends." Though friends didn't exactly translate between the realms of Mortal and Faerie. "I told you. Her Queen is the one who sent the darklings."

Lydia shuddered, her anger collapsing back in on itself to find its true shape—fear. Her face paled and her voice dropped to a whisper. "I tried to pretend it didn't happen. That this was all some weird joke."

"I'm sorry." With the openings between the worlds narrower

than they once had been, and with the sheer amount of iron everywhere, Clive couldn't shield her from the darklings. And it didn't help that Lydia stubbornly held to Mortal limitations. "It's no joke. Darklings aren't a joke. Once they latch on, they will hold until whoever sent them calls them off. Or until they have drunk their fill of power." He stared into the distance as if he could see into the heart of the Shadow court. Oberon wanted Lydia. Titania would risk anything to make sure he didn't get her. But using the darklings here was risky. "They would drain your magic dry, but I have no idea what they would do to a Mortal."

She crossed her arms over her chest. "What do you want from me?"

"I want to take you home."

"I am home."

The sound of slamming doors and the high-pitched laughter of a child interrupted them. Clive glanced toward the driveway. A little girl, not much older than six, skipped over to them and threw herself at Lydia.

"Lyds!"

Lydia glared at Clive before scooping up her little sister and swinging her in an arc. Peals of the child's laughter rang out in the overcast afternoon. He watched them, a strange bubble rising in his chest, an emotion he didn't quite have a name for. Driven by more than the need to remain unnoticed in this world, he cloaked himself again, careful not to focus his attention on Lydia this time. Her eyes swept over the spot where she had last seen him and slid past the concealing shadows, frowning. She turned back to her sister.

"Taylor, get inside before you get soaked!"

The little girl hugged Lydia and turned to look directly into Clive's eyes. She smiled and waved before bounding into the house.

She sees me.

A chill moved through him.

She sees me.

Chapter 4

"LYDDIE'S GOT A BOYFRIEND, LYDDIE'S got a boyfriend."
Taylor twirled on her tiptoes, spinning around Lydia in the living room.

"I do not, you little monster." Lydia grabbed her sister and tickled her until she screamed. It was the best way to distract Taylor. Clive, her boyfriend? Not hardly. Besides, how did Taylor even see through his invincible Faerie magic?

"Mom!" Taylor squealed. For a kid with pint-sized lungs, Taylor could really shriek.

"Lydia, I'm trying to do some paperwork."

"Sorry, Mom."

Taylor stuck her tongue out. "Lyddie's got a boyfriend," she whispered.

Lydia pulled her sister's ponytail. "Come on, Tails. Let's make some cookies."

The girl's face lit up. She grabbed Lydia's hand and pulled her into the kitchen without even complaining about the nickname. Maybe Lydia could get some answers using a chocolate bribe.

Taylor dragged over a small stool as Lydia pulled out the mixer and measured ingredients for chocolate chip cookies. She let Taylor push the button to mix the dough. It was a universal cure for the rainy day blues and annoying Faerie incursions. She smiled. It was hard to worry with Taylor around. She had a way of making everything around her sunny. Taylor's happiness spread a warmth that was one hundred percent real. She hugged her sister until she wriggled out of her grasp.

Taylor helped her roll the dough into small balls. Lydia flattened them slightly on the waiting cookie trays.

"Can I lick the bowl?" her sister asked.

"Rock, Paper, Scissors."

"Okie dokie," Taylor said.

Lydia watched the look of concentration in Taylor's eyes. She always started off with scissors. Lydia threw the sign for paper and Taylor let out a whoop of triumph. She took the bowl to the kitchen table as Lydia popped the cookies into the oven. Taylor could make licking the batter a full-body contact sport.

"He's cute," she said, her face smudged with melted chocolate.

"Who's cute?" Lydia hoped she'd forgotten about seeing Clive earlier.

"That boy."

Lydia watched Taylor out of the corner of her eye. Could her sister be a changeling, too? Clive said she wasn't Fae. That no one else in her family was. But that assumed he was telling her the truth. Trying to work through it all was giving her a headache. "Tails?"

"Hmmm?" Taylor was still immersed in the batter.

"He's in my class at school and he kind of likes to surprise me. If you see him again, will you let me know right away?"

"Sure."

"It's like a game, Tails. Like Hide and Go Seek. Don't let him know when you find him. Just tell me, okay?"

"So you can win?" she asked.

"Yeah. Something like that." Taylor hated to lose at any kind of game.

The kitchen warmed with the oven's heat and the cookies were working their particular wizardry on Lydia's mood. It didn't matter what Clive or Aileen wanted. This was home. The only place she would be leaving it for was one of the colleges whose glossy brochures were sitting on her desk upstairs. And it would be her choice.

*

"So she refused you, as well," Aileen said.

Clive gave her the shallowest bow that propriety dictated. Aileen narrowed her eyes, but he hadn't slighted her. No, there was nothing in his actions to cause a grievance. He made sure of that. He turned back to Lydia's house. The little girl, Taylor, was swinging her legs at the kitchen table, talking and laughing with her sister. "What are you doing here, Emissary?"

"Such formality." She laughed with a low, throaty purr. "What? No kiss for your cousin?"

Technically, Clive supposed they could be considered distant cousins, at least the way the Mortals named such things. He hadn't expected her to know that.

"You are not the only one of us who has studied the ephemerals, cousin."

Clive nodded. "But I don't mock them."

"Why is that, do you suppose?" Her tone was light, but Clive knew she was mocking him. It was no secret he had Mortal blood. Almost everyone in Faerie did, including Aileen herself, but his grandmother's disgrace was unique amongst the Fae. "They do not need our scorn, Aileen, nor our pity." In their limited lives, the Mortals still managed to create more beauty than any of the Fae. And without Mortal fertility, there would be few Fae left in Faerie.

"You are an odd one, Clive Barrow. Perhaps my Queen would enjoy your company as well as our little changeling's."

"I am sworn to Oberon, and I have sworn to bring her to Bright." The echo of the formal promise he had made at court rang in the air even here. Aileen took a step back.

"So we are enemies, then," she said.

Clive stared at Aileen for a moment, letting himself enjoy the loveliness of her classical Fae features, the lithe line of her body. "No, not enemies," he said. "Adversaries."

The smell of baking cookies wafted through the air.

She laughed. "You even play with words like they do. Amongst the Fae, cousin, there is no difference." Her eyes glittered like cut sapphires. "It's a shame we could not come to an understanding. Your death will accomplish nothing."

"I think you have overreached, Aileen," Clive said. She

couldn't tap enough power here to pose a threat to him.

"Do not underestimate the strength of need," she said. "When we have the Trueborn, we will break Oberon's hold in Faerie. Too long has he starved Shadow. Did he believe our Queen would crawl back to him begging forgiveness? That as our numbers dwindled, we would forget his cruelty?"

"There is nothing to be gained here, Aileen. She has rejected you." Clive put as much certainty as he could in his voice and his bearing. Yes, Lydia had rejected Shadow, but she had also rejected Bright.

"She is destined for our court. My Lady has so pledged."

Clive answered her with silence and she vanished, leaving the scent of night blooming cereus and jasmine in her wake. He stared at the place where she had been standing, a smile spreading across his face. "Destined? I think not." He rubbed his arm lightly where Lydia had cut him. If she was destined for anything, it was to become something Faerie had never seen before.

Chapter 5

LYDIA SPRAWLED FACE DOWN ACROSS her bed, books and papers scattered around her. It was no use. She couldn't concentrate to read and math was a joke. Its precise world of rules and logic didn't have room for magic or invisible doors into Faerie. She slammed the books shut and watched as one thudded to the floor.

"Lyds? You okay?" her mother called from downstairs.

"Dropped a book. Sorry."

What was happening to her? When her friend, Emily, turned sixteen, she had discovered she was adopted. She'd been seeing a therapist for over a year now and still wasn't speaking to her mom. But this? This was different. Lydia shook her head. She sat up, reached for the scrapbook she had made with her mom years ago, and hugged it to her chest.

She flipped through the pages, some going back to her baby pictures. Everything was so much easier back then. From the time she was little, everyone said she had her mother's eyes and her father's hair. But if what Clive was saying was true, then that couldn't be. First Clive, then Aileen. Lydia shivered, still chilled from her run. If it had only been creepy Clive, then she might have been able to reason away the whole darklings and between thing. But now? They both said Oberon's magic had changed her, somehow, and she couldn't deny that something, something deep inside her was different. She closed the scrapbook and stared out the window.

The rain had stopped and the late afternoon sun brightened a cloudless sky. Downstairs, Marco was squawking his clarinet. It sounded like a cross between a pissed off goose and the neighbor's hound dog. She usually had more patience for her brother's practicing, but today his sour notes left a metallic taste in her mouth and made her head throb.

Lydia grabbed her messenger bag and slid her phone and the scrapbook inside. "Mom, I'm going to Emily's, okay?" She and Emily had known each other since grade school. Half the pictures in her scrapbook had Emily in them. Maybe her friend could help her make sense out of all this.

"Be home by six. Dad and I are going out with the Sloans for dinner and a movie. I need you to watch Marco and Taylor."

She sighed. Maybe she could convince Emily to come back home with her.

Lydia cut through her old elementary school playground. She stopped to watch the swings sway in a light breeze. When she was little, she loved to pump the swing as high as she could, close her eyes, lean her head back, and pretend she was flying. Her mom had always said she had an overactive imagination.

If only she could believe this was her imagination.

She pulled the scrap book from her bag and sat down on a

swing. The first page had a picture of her mom and dad holding a swaddled baby in their arms. Was it her, or the Lydia she must have replaced? She squinted, trying to focus. The baby had a shock of dark brown hair and a little fisted hand fighting free of the blankets. There was no way to tell. All babies looked pretty much the same.

"That was their first born."

"I told you to stay the hell away from me," Lydia said. It was Clive. She didn't look up from the album. Maybe he would leave if she ignored him.

"She was born damaged," Clive said. "Something was wrong with her insides. The doctors said she wouldn't live to see her first birthday."

"You're lying." She didn't want to listen to him. It was too painful to think about.

"Oberon knows. He can tell you the truth of your history."

"I know my history."

"The baby you were named for died."

She shivered and stared down at the photo, her eyes blurred. "I was supposed to be their miracle," Lydia whispered. "They said I proved the doctors wrong. I was a stubborn girl. A fighter."

"You were the miracle Oberon gave them."

"I don't believe you." Except, she did. Somewhere deep inside, she heard the truth in his words. She was a lie. Her whole life was a lie. She stood and swatted the swing away from her, listening to the chain squeak and groan. Clive stepped away from the arc of its movement. Lydia closed the distance between them and thrust the scrap book into his chest.

"When? When did he switch us? What did he do with their child?" A flare of anger burned through her. Their baby died and they never knew. They would never know.

"I think you were a few months old." He closed the book gently. "Does it matter?"

Yes. It mattered. It mattered to her. "Where is she buried?"

"In Faerie, I think."

"You think." She turned on him then, snatching her scrapbook back. "You think? What gave him the right?" Lydia was shaking. "They deserved to know. Oberon gave them a lie."

"Oberon gifted them with the child they desired."

"They deserve to know the truth!" Lydia stumbled away from him, tears blurring her vision. A chill snaked through her. What if Clive were lying? What if the child would have lived, but Oberon snatched it away to hide her in its place? What if he'd killed it? "Why? Why me?"

"I cannot tell you, Lydia."

She stared at him. "Can't or won't?"

Clive's face flushed and he turned away.

"Why does he want me now? What's so special about me that you and Aileen are fighting like a dog over a bone?" Lydia paced a small square back and forth in front of the swing set.

"You must ask Oberon."

"So I just go with you to Faerie? Why should I trust you?" The same strange fury that came over her in the Between made her head pound.

"The Fae do not lie."

"Everyone lies," Lydia said.

Clive let silence hang between them for a few seconds. "Not

you," he said.

No, she didn't. That didn't prove anything. It was just simpler to leave out details than to make up outright lies, that was all. "So I'm a lousy liar. So what."

"Lydia, I told you, you are Fae. And you do not belong here."

"You have no idea who I am," Lydia said, snatching up her bag and walking toward Emily's house. She refused to look back.

*

BY THE TIME CLIVE SCRAMBLED after her, she was halfway across the park. The echo of her pain thrummed through him like the lowest string of a harp. "Lydia, wait," he called out. She stopped and he walked toward her. "I promise, if you come with me to the Bright court, I will help you find the answers you seek." It was an oath and his words bound him to a course of action he feared he would regret. Yet, he didn't regret having made the pledge.

She turned around. "And what will Titania promise me?"

Clive shrugged. "Power. Standing in the Shadow court. Vengeance."

"And Oberon? What about him?"

Power. Oberon would promise power, too. And prestige. That is what the Fae vied for. They would offer her what they themselves would desire. And she would reject their gifts, with all the consequences that followed. Clive's mouth dried. As much as Lydia didn't understand, the Fae wouldn't understand her. How could they? For all her power and her birthright, she belonged more to the Mortal world than Faerie. Fear crawled up his spine like tendrils of wildweed. Cold certainty shook him. This was going to end badly for Lydia and the rest of the Fae.

"You should run." The words shocked him even as he said them.

She laughed then, a strangled, hopeless sound. "Where can I go?"

"The Between," he said, his heart pounding with impossible emotion. They couldn't follow her there. She would be safe. But if she chose to flee, Clive would be trapped by broken vows. He was oathsworn now, twice over. The enormous power of his promises writhed and seethed within him.

Lydia's eyes widened. "You work for Oberon. Why are you telling me this?"

Clive shook his head. Confusion strangled him into silence. He had never been cursed with foresight, but he knew, with a burning clarity, that if she set foot in Faerie, nothing would ever be the same.

"How can I run away?" Lydia said. "I can't do that to my family. They would never understand."

Relief and guilt flooded him. He shook his head to clear his confusion. Those were Mortal things. Not Fae.

"Besides, I'm going to college," she said. "In less than a year. I have a life. I have the right to make my own choices."

"You cannot return to the way things were." He had known that the moment he set eyes on her. What was he thinking? She was a pawn in Faerie's war just as he was. "You must declare for either Bright or Shadow," he said, staring. She rocked back and forth as if ready to flee. "There is no middle way. Reject me and Aileen will find a way to trap you, to bring you to Titania."

"And you? You would let me go?"

"It's not me you need to worry about," he said.

"What do you mean?"

Clive fidgeted, rubbing his forearm where she'd cut him. "If I fail, Oberon will send others. He will have you at court, no matter what you wish or where you run to." He knew how ruthless the Bright King could be and regretted his earlier words. "But if you pledge to Bright, I will protect you. At Oberon's court." He was surprised by the pleading in his own voice. What was happening to him? "They will only see you as a prize."

"What do you see?" She stood with her hands on her hips.

He shivered. Nascent power swirled through her like a rainbow in an oil-slicked puddle. Had Oberon foreseen what she would become? He thought not. She was Fae, yet not Fae. He rubbed his forearm again. Lydia could do things no Fae should be able to do.

"I see you, Lydia Hawthorne," he said, wondering if Oberon had chosen her foster family simply for their surname. It wouldn't have surprised him. The hawthorn was a hardy tree. Adaptable. Like Lydia would have to be to survive in Faerie.

"What about my family?"

"You were never really theirs." He saw the pain cloud her eyes. "If you truly care for them, return to Faerie, or our war will spread here, too. In the end, they will not be spared."

She blinked rapidly and looked away. Clive took a step toward her, wrestling with the urge to comfort her.

"And if . . . if I chose to come with you?" Lydia swallowed and Clive waited for her to finish her question. "What would I have to do?" She wouldn't meet his gaze.

"Speak your choice. Say it three times."

"That's it?" Her eyes narrowed. "You're making fun of me."

"I swear I am not. There is power in the word of a Fae repeated thrice. If you make your oath public beneath the sky, it will be binding." He stared out into the distance. A line of black spread across the horizon, blotting out the blue. They were running out of time. "You need to decide," Clive said. "Aileen's bloodhounds are sniffing around for you."

As if he conjured her by using her name, she strode into the playground. "How touching, Clive. You are showing your ephemeral side."

*

LYDIA FELT A WARNING PRICKLE on the back of her neck. The Fae woman ignored Clive and stepped within inches of her. "My dear cousin, he is trying to confuse you. You will only find mockery in Oberon's court. My Lady Titania is ready to welcome you back in your rightful place as kin."

Cousin? Kin? "What do you mean?" Lydia asked, looking from Clive to Aileen and finding nothing in their delicate features but more questions.

"Why Lydia, did he not tell you?" She smiled at Clive, the triumph written on her face. "Your father was a noble of My

Lady's court. You, my dear, are Fae royalty."

"My father? My father is an architect and coaches my brother's soccer team." She glared at Aileen, irritated by her confidence and her assumptions.

"Being raised by the ephemerals does not change your lineage."

She also hated the mocking tone in Aileen's voice when she used that word.

"As a trueborn Fae, you must take your place at court. And my Queen wishes to be your patron."

Lydia glanced over to Clive. Nothing in his expression changed from his usual watchful waiting, but she sensed the deep unease moving below the surface. She didn't exactly trust him, but he had saved her from the darklings. He'd also given her a lot of information about the Fae. Maybe she could use it to her advantage. "And what does your Queen offer me?" she asked.

Aileen smiled. "You are as unprepared as a sapling for a winter storm. My Lady Titania will help you find your strength. At her side, you will be honored."

That was power and status. Two of the three things Clive had predicted. "And what does she want from me?" Aileen was too beautiful, too perfect. And too arrogant. Clive had the same physical intensity, but at least she didn't hear the mockery in his voice when he spoke of the human world.

"Why, my dear cousin, she wants to help you." Aileen paused, as if considering her words. "Help you find justice."

Out of the corner of her eye, she saw Clive clench his jaw.

"Justice? For my parents?" Even if there were a Fae equivalent of a court of law, how could her parents be compensated for their loss? What about her loss?

"Their deaths deserve an answer," Aileen said.

Lydia's heart lurched. "What?" The two Fae were watching her with predators' eyes. She took a deep breath. Aileen must be talking about her parents in Faerie. She hadn't even stopped to wonder who they were and why they had let her get taken away. Now she knew. They were dead. "They're not my parents," Lydia said. Until a day ago, she never knew the Fae existed. Thinking about them made her feel disloyal to her own parents somehow. "I don't want to hear any more." She took a step back, the cool metal of the climbing structure supporting her spine.

"But my dear, you need to know," Aileen said. Clive stepped closer, his eyes narrowing. "Know what?" Lydia asked, trying to keep them both in her field of view.

"About Oberon." Aileen said. It was clear she was enjoying this.

"Aileen," Clive said, his voice a low growl.

"What about him?" Lydia asked, shivering even though the late afternoon sun was warm in the small playground.

"He had them put to death."

The breath caught in Lydia's throat. "I don't believe you," she whispered. Aileen stood still, watching her, waiting. Clive's face blanched, his eyes smoky with anger.

Clive said the Fae didn't lie. What was the truth? Had Oberon killed her Fae parents? But then he hid her, protected her all those years and now he wanted her at his court. It didn't make any sense. She whirled on Clive. "Did he? Did he kill them?"

He wouldn't meet her eyes. "I was not there," Clive said. "Oberon will give you a true account. You have that right."

He didn't deny it. Again, she caught a flash of triumph in Aileen's eyes. "Why should I care? Bright or Shadow. You both want something from me." Her anger was a runaway train. "I don't know what it is, but I don't appreciate being manipulated into caring about two dead strangers." A pang of guilt twisted her insides.

"You don't know jack shit about me," Lydia said, forcing thoughts of her murdered Fae family from her mind for now. She pressed forward, ticking off her points on the fingers of her right hand. "I don't want you. I don't want your Queen, and I don't want your promises." Confidence settled on her shoulders like a heavy, warm blanket. If Clive was right, there was power in saying something three times. It wasn't the same thing three times, but it was three related things and she said them with conviction.

"Do you think Oberon will reward you for your service?" Aileen asked. Lydia was confused until she realized she was talking to Clive.

"It hardly matters," he said. "I made a pledge."

Aileen turned back to Lydia. Her eyes glittered, but her voice remained controlled. "You are considering a dangerous path, cousin."

Clive was right, at least about one thing. They would never stop hunting her. And there was no going back to the way things were. No matter what she did next, her world would never be the same. What if someone got hurt the next time the darklings came after her? It would be her fault. She had to protect them. Her parents, Marco, and Taylor. Goosebumps broke out across her arms. There was nothing her family could do. Nothing. Not against Fae magic. If she stayed, she would just be a danger to them now.

Lydia's stomach churned. Graduating high school and leaving home. That was a choice she understood. But this. This was different. Whatever she decided, she would lose everything in her life she loved. "What gives you the right?"

The two Fae were watching her. Aileen's face was alive with a hunger, an eagerness she didn't trust. They didn't care about her or what she wanted. "I choose Bright," Lydia said, her throat tightening on the words. Clive stiffened. Everything stilled. A cloud drifted over the sun.

"Are you certain, cousin? Truly certain?" There was a desperate edge to Aileen's voice.

Lydia swallowed against the lump in her throat. "I choose Bright," she repeated. Her heart began to pound. She wanted to run.

"It is not too late," Aileen whispered. "Come back with me. Come back to Shadow."

Lydia turned to Clive for some sort of assurance and found none.

"Oberon is not your friend," Aileen said as the moments ticked by.

"I know." Lydia wasn't sure Clive could be trusted. She wasn't even sure she trusted her own feelings anymore, but she remembered the hunger of the darklings, how they had tried to yank something out of her. And Titania had sent them. "But neither are you," Lydia said.

Their attention was a weight on her chest. The sky, too, seemed to press down on her. Dark clouds roiled in the distance. Aileen leaned forward, reaching out to her. "I choose Bright," she said for the third time.

Aileen cried out, vanishing between one breath and the next. Lydia didn't know what she'd expected, but there was no sudden crack of thunder or flash of light, only an unnatural silence that threatened to suffocate her. Even the wind had died and the swings stilled. Lydia hung her head in her hands.

Chapter 6

Cʟɪᴠᴇ ᴄᴏᴜʟᴅɴ'ᴛ ᴜɴᴅᴇʀsᴛᴀɴᴅ ᴡʜʏ ʜᴇ felt no triumph. The choice was made and Oberon was waiting. "We need to go," he said.

She nodded, but made no move to get closer to him.

"Lydia?" Clive took a step toward her. She lifted her face and something cold and hard in her expression stopped him.

"Is it true?" Her voice was weary, stripped of emotion.

"Is what true?" he asked, as gently as he could.

"My parents. Oberon. Everything."

"You will find your answers at court," Clive said, hoping he was not making yet another promise impossible to fulfill. "Are you ready?"

"Wait. What does trueborn mean?"

"We have no time for the history of Fae politics and society. Oberon is not a patient man."

"Make time," she said.

He read anger in the slight narrowing of her eyes and the set of her shoulders. She was as immovable as stone. If she chose to fight him, he would never get her across to Faerie. He glared at her, muscles tensing at his jaw line, and forced himself to relax. "All right," he said. "You are trueborn because both of your parents were Fae. Furthermore, your mother was from Bright court, your father from Shadow. It's rare." She would find out soon just how rare. "If Shadow court had claimed you, it would have shifted the balance of power in Faerie toward Titania. With you at Bright, Oberon consolidates his rule." And his control over the future of the Fae bloodlines.

"This is crazy," Lydia said. "First I fall into *A Midsummer Night's Dream*. Now it's like something out of *Romeo and Juliet*. Don't tell me. They were star-crossed lovers, right?"

"This is neither a story, Lydia, nor a joke." Urgency was making Clive irritable. In Faerie, plots and plans took decades to unfold. Here, it felt as if time was sweeping over him. How did the Mortals stand it? They had so little of it as it was. "The Fae are not like Mortals. Our families are nothing of the kind you grew up in." His own mother could not have been more different than Lydia's. "It certainly was not love that brought your parents together."

"Then what was it?"

"A chance at power." There was little else that motivated the Fae. At least since the courts split.

"Whatever Oberon thinks, I'm nothing special," Lydia said.

Clive met her eyes with his. "No, you are trueborn Fae and you are needed." There was more to it than that, more than what Oberon had said. But he didn't know exactly what. Only that Lydia was more than anyone had bargained for.

"Right. After you abandon me for seventeen years." She

paused, considering him. "What's so important about a true-born, anyway?"

Her accusation, he could not answer. As to why the courts would be fighting over her now, that was simple. "The Fae are dying out. We cannot create children together anymore."

"Big deal. Half the kids I know were probably born in a test tube or a petri dish or something. So Oberon needs a fertility specialist."

An intoxicating rush of anger sent heat pulsing through his body. "You cannot understand how pointless this is." He was Oberon's errand boy, plain and simple, and it was past time to deliver his charge.

"Then explain it to me. So I can understand."

"What do explanations matter? You have made your choice." Though perhaps this had been decided long before Lydia had been born. Certainly, he had never had the luxury of choices. "The more you struggle against the King, the more difficult it will be for you." He would do her no kindness by giving her a false sense of life in Faerie, but the confusion and hurt in her expression pained him and he relented. "You were the last trueborn babe in Faerie. Your parents were powerful Fae, sub-ordinate only to Oberon and Titania. Why you were hidden here, I cannot know, but now that you are found there will never be peace in Faerie as long as you remain unclaimed by either court."

"Wait. What about Aileen? What about you?" she asked.

"Me? Trueborn?" Clive laughed and there was no humor in it, only pain. "That honor is not mine. My mother refuses to name my own father, but he is certainly from the Mortal world." There was no shame in that, only expediency. But that wasn't what galled, what kept him from rising higher at Bright. It was no secret that most of the upper echelon at Bright did not trust him and his easy comfort with the Mortal realm. Why would they? Crossing out of Faerie would bleed them of power to spin their precious glamours or twist their way to status at court. The only reason any one of them would set foot beyond the barrier was if Oberon granted them leave to take a lover. Then they would flee back to Faerie as quickly as they could. "Lydia, the only reason the Fae haven't faded entirely from the world is that we breed true."

"What's that supposed to mean?"

"It means that any child of a Mortal and a Fae will produce a Fae child. It means that Oberon chooses which bloodlines may thrive. If he wishes to favor one of his court, he allows that Fae access to the doors between worlds. Access to a Mortal lover. Access to create a child. A child who will be one of us."

Her face blanched. "What if the baby is born here to a Mortal mother?"

"It is taken."

"And what about the mother?"

"A seeming is made. The mother has a baby for a short time and then it dies."

"You have no right." A slow fire glowed in her eyes.

"We have no choice." He forced himself to lower his voice. "The court that holds the doors between the worlds controls all. Right now, the balance favors Oberon. Bright court thrives while Shadow is in decline. Do you understand now why Titania sought you out?"

Lydia frowned and shook her head. "Whatever or whoever you think I am, you're wrong."

"You are a trueborn Fae. Through your children, our blood lines will be strengthened." No longer would they be dependent on Mortal lovers. And with Lydia at Oberon's court, Bright magic would rule over Shadow.

"You've got to be kidding. Oberon wants to use me as some kind of Faerie brood mare?" Her eyes flashed with anger. "I'm done." Lydia turned away. "I'm going home."

Clive's breath caught in his throat. "You cannot," he said.

She whirled back to face him. The air between them stirred the playground grit. He had to hold himself from stepping away.

"You made a thrice witnessed oath. You are Fae and thus bound."

"You tricked me," she said, red spots blooming on her cheeks.

"No. I have given you only truth. The Bright court seeks to honor you, to protect you."

Lydia crossed her arms over her chest. "And if I don't want your honor or your protection?" She made the words sound like curses.

"This is not about what you want. You have a duty to your people." Bringing Lydia back to court would justify Oberon's trust. He didn't know what he had been thinking. Of course, she had to return to Faerie. There was no other path for either of them. But Clive was not looking forward to presenting her to the Fae. She was something Oberon could not have planned for and it had been a long time since something or someone had surprised his King. "Lydia . . . "

She looked him directly in the eye and he faltered. Where the sun touched her hair, it brought out gold highlights in the warm brown. Her features seemed sculpted, the bones of her face more angular, her eyes larger, the pupils ringed with fire. Even without Oberon's intervention, the last of the glamour was falling away. Magic thrummed around her, power that would be obvious to all but the least talented of the Fae. Oberon couldn't fail to see it.

Something in his expression must have alarmed her. Her gaze darted all around the playground. "What is it?"

Clive swallowed past the lump in his throat. "Do not trust him."

Lydia folded her arms across her chest.

"Do not trust any of us," Clive said. There was so much more he wanted to tell her, but there was no time.

"You said the Fae don't lie," she said.

"It is complicated." He pushed his hair away from his forehead. "Not lying is not the same thing as being trustworthy." He glanced across the playground to a thicket of trees. It was past time to go.

"What about you?"

He felt his face heat up and stared at the ground. "I am an instrument of Oberon's will. Bound to his word."

She touched him lightly on the arm she had injured. The healing cut tingled. "You made a promise to me. Will you keep it?"

He looked up into a face that was familiar and alien at the same time. His stomach knotted. "Yes."

*

"THEN LET'S GET THIS OVER with," Lydia said, looking every-where except into his face.

"Take my hand." Clive extended his arm toward her.

Her hands were shaking. When would her parents realize she was gone? They would be annoyed when she wasn't back at six like she promised. After fifteen minutes' grace, they would call her cell phone. She could almost hear the lecture about re-sponsibility and trust. When she didn't answer, they'd try Emily's house and find out she'd never gotten there. Then the worry would start. Would they think she'd run away? She'd moved through the usual teen angst and, for the most part, had a pretty solid relationship with her folks. They would be devastated. Taylor would never understand.

Lydia shivered in the afternoon sunshine. She closed her eyes, not wanting to look at Clive. What would happen to her parents? Could Oberon make them forget about her altogeth-er? Then Lydia Hawthorne would be truly dead and whoever she was, she would be nameless and alone. Taylor would never have had a big sister. A bubble of pain burst in her chest. She couldn't imagine not holding her baby sister's chubby hands or brushing her silky hair after a bath. Even Marco's smelly soccer cleats and his terrible clarinet lessons were part of her.

"Why me?" she asked again, not really expecting an answer.

"Lydia, we must go."

Part of her knew it would come to this. Why else would she have left home with the scrapbook? She swiped at her eyes with her shirt sleeve, hating to lose control in front of Clive. Clenching her jaw, she stood as straight and tall as she could, though he still towered over her. "Don't let Oberon hurt my family again." Lydia couldn't bear the thought of simply being erased from their lives, but she loved them too much to see them in pain.

"I will do what I can," Clive said.

No matter what he believed was or wasn't possible, she was going to find a way back and reclaim her life. Taking a deep breath, Lydia turned full circle to look at her old playground. This was the place she had met Emily on the first day of Kindergarten. They had made a train on the slide. Emily planted her feet down on the metal surface and the two of them had tumbled off the side. Lydia had split her forehead on a rock. Emily had bitten through her lower lip. They both needed stitches.

Clive waited, his body like a dancer's holding a pose, without effort or thought. His inhuman grace made her shiver. Fae. We're both Fae.

She slung the bag across her shoulder and stepped toward him.

"Wait. Where are your keys?"

She pointed to the messenger bag before she remembered. Her face flushed. The Between. Her key fob. Clive's arm.

"You have to leave your metal here," he said.

She lowered the bag to the ground and took her keys out. They felt cool and solid in her hand. She gripped them tightly, her earlier resolve wavering. "I'm not coming back, am I?"

"I cannot say," he said.

There was sadness in his eyes. It was the answer she feared.

"Are you ready?"

"No," she whispered. "I told my mom I was going to Emily's house." Clive looked confused. "She'll think I lied to her." She glanced at the keys in her hand. If anyone found them, her parents might think she'd dropped them in a struggle or that she'd been kidnapped or something. The pain that would bring them was unimaginable.

"Wait," Lydia said. There was a hollowed out tree stump at the edge of the fence. Lydia dropped her key ring inside. Rummaging through her bag, she pulled her phone out and turned it off, laying it beside the keys. "I guess I won't be needing this in Faerie, either." She covered them with some wood chips from the playground. It was the best she could do. "Okay." She took a deep breath as if she were about to jump into the cold lake at her grandparents' summer cottage and reached out for his hand. It was warmer than she expected, no different than any ordinary hand.

"Close your eyes," he said. "It will be easier. If you pull away, I might miss the right door."

How could there be a right door when they all led away from her life?

"Lydia?"

She closed her eyes.

"Just walk with me. It will not be as jarring as it was on the bus."

He led her forward, walking slowly. To anyone watching, if they could see them at all, it would look like two friends out for a stroll. The wood chip playground surface gave way to a gravel path and then the ground shifted beneath her feet. Springy moss replaced the asphalt sidewalk. She jerked to a stop.

"You are almost there, Lydia. Keep going," Clive urged, gently squeezing her hand.

The sound of their footfalls faded. Birds whistled urgently. A gust of wind brought the scent of pine and damp earth. Trees rustled as they passed. The trees were mostly bare back home. Had they gotten to Faerie already? She pulled away from his hold.

"Wait. This is the boundary. A forest where the two worlds overlap a little. We need to keep going."

She opened her eyes and gasped. She'd been here before. She could swear it. This was a place she and Emily used to play as children. They had called it the magic forest. It had long ago faded into a memory of her imagination, but they had been able to enter here, pretending to be characters from the Narnia books or enchanted princesses from an old Faerie tale. She shook her head. Some Faerie tale.

The trees were fully leafed out and glistened a deep, moist green. Sunlight pierced the canopy in slants of light that illuminated tiny patches of mushrooms and colored moss. Shadows danced between the trees like the echoes of children. Had Emily seen it like this? Or was it just the stand of trees beside the elementary school playground to her?

Lydia turned her head to look back the way they'd come. The forest faded out, a green mist obscured the old playground. Etched in the mist was the faint shape of a doorway, smudging away as she watched.

"We cannot stop here," Clive said.

The shadows took on greater weight and truer shape. Lydia smiled, watching children dance and dart around the tree trunks.

"Lydia. Come on." He jerked on her arm and she turned to him, annoyed.

"I want to stay here." The words felt thick on her tongue.

"I told you to close your eyes."

She wished he'd stop bullying her. There was no reason to be rude. Two girls skipped past her, laughing. One tossed a silver ball toward her. It caught the light and flashed like a firefly. She lifted her arms to catch it. Bells rang at the edge of her hearing. The ball spun and she stared at it, her heart slowing to match its pulse. Her feet pressed into the litter of leaves and moss. The sun touched her face and hair. She turned to it, thirsty.

Hands shook her, but she felt the sway of her body as a distant thing. It didn't matter. There was no urgency when time was measured in seasons.

Chapter 7

THE FARAWAY LOOK IN HER eyes should have warned him, but Clive had been more concerned about Oberon and the court then about how Lydia might respond to her first glimpse of Faerie. Or Faerie to her.

"Lydia." He tried to keep irritation out of his voice. She ignored him and wrapped herself into a glamour like she'd been manipulating magic all her life. Her outstretched arms elongated and her fingers branched into small, fully leafed twigs. Her legs fused together and grew a thick covering of dark, twisted bark. As he watched, stunned, her face vanished. Where her eyes had been were two symmetrical knots in the tree trunk. The glamour was utterly complete. If he had come upon her in the forest, he would only have noticed a lone tree growing on the path, a bag lying on the ground beside it.

A ripple of fear moved through him, like the wind through the hawthorn's leaves. It wasn't possible. Very few Fae could work a glamour that strong that quickly. Oberon and Titania, certainly, maybe some of the older nobles. None in his generation could channel that much raw power. How had she done it? And how was he going to break it? Oberon was waiting and the longer Clive made him wait, the more uncomfortable their homecoming would be. For Lydia's sake and for his own, he couldn't leave her here.

He sighed and glanced up, looking for inspiration. All around him were ordinary trees from Lydia's adopted world, long grown tangled in the ground of Faerie and imbued with Fae magic. There was plenty of ambient power here, if you knew how to tap into it. Though there was danger in it for the unwary. Lydia might have been able to sense it, but she shouldn't have had the skill to use any of that power. In truth, she was defenseless here. He struck his head with the palm of his hand. Defenseless and with the waking power of a trueborn. Why had Oberon not warned him? Faerie must have recognized one of its own and embraced Lydia. Literally.

He clenched his hands into fists. There was no break in the transformation. Lydia was now a hawthorn tree. Clive may have had a moment's fantasy of protecting her from Oberon's reach, but that was as unlikely as he being a trueborn. Arriving at court without her was simply not an option. Circling the tree she had become, he was uncomfortably aware of time, as if his weeks in the Mortal world had set a clock ticking in his head.

"Lydia, you have to help me," he said, without any expectation that she could hear him. If she had persuaded reality that she was a tree, then not only did she look like one, she actually was one. There were stories about Fae children lost forever to glamour. The mockingbird was supposed to be a Fae trapped in the Mortal world retaining only enough magic to mimic every sound it heard. Clive was certain there was at least a glimmer of truth to it. Unless he did something, Lydia would be rooted here, neither fully in Faerie or the Mortal world until the hawthorn itself died.

How could he persuade a tree? He kicked at the dry leaves and pine needles lining the path. Maybe she was more clever than he thought. More clever or more desperate. Did she think she could hide from Oberon forever? "It's not so simple, Lydia," he said. "Oberon has the power to claim his own." He could return to court and lead the Bright King here. Oberon would tear out the hawthorn's roots and gouge the very earth itself to force Lydia back to her true form, heedless of the damage done. And what would Clive's oaths mean then? He was as trapped as she was.

"If I had a tenth of your power, Lydia, then we could both be trees." He laughed at the childish urge to hide. At least then he would have fulfilled his promises; return to Faerie with Lydia and protect her from Oberon. But if he'd had the power to shape Faerie thus to his will, he would not be Oberon's message boy.

He placed a hand on the hawthorn's bark. "I'm sorry. I have no choice." Perhaps he could create a glamour to wrap around hers. Something that would threaten a tree and force her to change back. A forest fire might break through to the girl hidden within.

It was risky, and he would have to be prepared to counter it if the wind shifted, but he couldn't think of what else to try. Kindling a fire in his mind, he let a tiny flame dance in the palm of his hand, feeding it with the memory of heat and light and smoke. Setting his hands down on the forest floor, he urged the fire to spread. The trees around him shivered, branches tossing wildly in the still air.

Clouds boiled overhead, racing with impossible speed to blot out the sun. He fed more power to the struggling flames as the temperature plummeted. A damp breeze chilled his bare skin and the fire guttered. Rain spattered upturned leaves and dripped down the collar of his shirt. He had nothing left to feed the glamour with. In his palms, the flames flickered and died.

Not that way, he thought, breathing heavily. He should have known better than to directly challenge the forest. He turned to face the trees, his back to Lydia's sturdy trunk. "Nothing personal, you understand," he said. Clive brushed ash from his hands and paced, trying to warm his body and think. The clouds shredded and the sun's rays chased the cold out of the air. The lone hawthorn tree stood illuminated in a shaft of light as if to mock him.

If the forest wouldn't let him shock Lydia back to her true form, he wasn't sure what he was going to do. Asking Oberon for help would only earn him ridicule at best. Banishment was a real consequence of failure. Though at this point, maybe that would be a gift. Oberon had vastly crueler ways of showing his displeasure. And even if Aileen hadn't been smug and superior, going to Titania would be a violation of his oath. He was back to where he'd begun. On his own and out of ideas.

He collapsed down under the hawthorn's spreading branches, his back pressing into its trunk. Closing his eyes, he lifted his face to the sky, feeling the dappled light on his skin. Now what?

What would rattle Lydia without threatening the trees and Faerie itself?

Darklings. They had terrified her on the bus. He could create the seeming of a darkling swarm. Not quite a glamour, but it might just be enough. If he could only capture Lydia's attention, it might break the magic's hold. As soon as she started to transform back, he could dispel the illusion. With any luck, she wouldn't even know what he had done.

Clive scrambled to his feet. He would just have to recreate the sight and sound of the swarm. Lydia's own mind and memory would provide the rest. He pulled an image of darklings from a childhood encounter and let fear take shape around him. A cloud coalesced between them, smudging the air gray. The sound began as a vibration deep in his chest, expanding until thunder rumbled inside him and throughout the grove. He exhaled and sent his illusion spinning toward Lydia. It had substance and menace, circling the tree as if looking for a place to breach its bark.

The other trees around him stood silently in the fake twilight. Even true darklings wouldn't be a threat to them. They only had the power to harm living Fae who channeled the ambient magic of Faerie.

The branches of the hawthorn quivered as the darkness surrounded her. Clive let out his trapped breath. It was going to work.

"Lydia!" he called. "Lydia, we need to go."

Leaves shook as the glamoured darklings pressed closer.

The trunk wavered, bark thinning out. Her body fought to form itself. Dark hair, freed from the tree crown, whipped around her head in the freshening wind.

"Hurry, Lydia." Clive was afraid to pull apart the seeming too soon, but there was only so long Oberon would wait. He had to know Lydia had entered Faerie. Clive took a step closer to her, straining to see through the swarm. It seemed more menacing that when he had loosed it; somehow his urgency had given it more power than he had intended.

An opaque mist cut him off from the trees around them. He winced as the hawthorn's limbs creaked. A hand covered with leaves reached out toward him. The darklings vibrated hunger and eagerness. Clive shivered, gooseflesh prickling his arms. This wasn't right. Something wasn't right.

He plunged between Lydia and the darklings. The cloud gathered into the shape of a fist. The hum rose to a high-pitched whine that resonated deep within Clive's bones. That shouldn't be. It was just a minor seeming. He loosed his hold on the illusion. Nothing happened.

The darklings hammered towards him.

"Thorn and weed!" he swore. This was no illusion. Titania's darklings had found them again, slipping beneath his glamour. He had given the swarm perfect cover.

Heart pounding, Clive moved as close to Lydia as he could get. He had to risk tapping Faerie itself for enough power to protect them. Oberon would take it back tenfold in tithe, but he had no choice. He gathered magic, pulling it from the ground beneath his feet in a desperate gulp and feeding it to a shield he drew around them both.

He would be an irresistible target to the darklings. It didn't matter. He had to fulfill Oberon's charge and his oaths, even at the risk of his life. Besides, it would be hard for Titania to command the swarm for long and she was far from her court's power. It was a matter of waiting. Clive was gambling he could hold his shield longer than she could keep the darklings here to threaten them.

He had been a fool. Until they set foot in Bright court and were taken into Oberon's protection, they were still vulnerable. The hum of power buzzed and circled around them, creating a wall of dark he could not pierce. He looked up as shadows shifted overhead.

There was a tickle at the back of his neck. He snapped to attention before the darklings poured through a crack in his shield. Sweat dripped down his forehead and into his eyes. Clive struggled to hold his shield, the muscles across his shoulders burning with the effort.

The swarm thinned and vanished.

Clive dropped the shield, breathing hard, his body shaking. At least something was working right. Leaves rustled on the hawthorn tree beside him. Thorn pierce it—he was no closer to getting Lydia back. He slumped to the ground.

Her carry bag was lying upended on the ground, the book of photos she had taken open to the sky. He reached over to pick it up. This was the life she had known. There were pictures of her parents, younger and less careworn than they were now; smiling at what they thought was their baby. Clive flipped through the pages, not even sure what he was looking for. In one, a two or three-year-old Lydia was sitting in a stroller. Her foster mother was smiling down at her, but Lydia was looking at something she held in a chubby fist. He squinted, holding the book up to take a closer look. It was a beam of sunlight, the dust motes trapped within it dancing like fireflies. To her parents, it probably had looked like Lydia was just waving her arms, but even as a babe, she had been able to see behind and beyond their reality into the heart of the world.

Clive blinked and stared into the distance where the door out of Faerie was hidden. Lydia's sister saw, too, but she was fully Mortal. That shouldn't be. Perhaps it was because she was so young or because she had been around the trueborn all her life. He shook his head. That was a puzzle for another time. First he had to free Lydia.

Threats didn't work, but what if he used her own memories? He had to remind her of who she believed she was. It didn't matter that she was Fae if she saw herself as Mortal. And Mortals didn't just magically turn into trees.

There was an old photograph of a family picnic from when Lydia's mother must have been pregnant with Taylor. Lydia was probably eleven or twelve at the time, her brother maybe four. Pushing off his fatigue, Clive created a seeming of her family from that picture, adding details from his observations and adding Taylor to the picnic. He built up the image in his mind, looking at it from all sides until it felt full and true. As weary as he was, to make the seeming real enough to fool Lydia, he would have to coax even more power from Faerie itself, a tricky thing when it seemed the place wanted Lydia just where it had her. Clive let some of his fear and his need trickle over his tight control. His emotion was like water sinking into thirsty earth.

Static played over his skin, the hair on his arms standing up in the sudden stirring of air.

Lydia's family came to life around him. At first, they looked like projections of the photographs, but as he concentrated, their faint outlines filled in. Laughter brightened the shade beneath the trees. Taylor skipped around the hawthorn tree, calling out her sister's name.

*

"LYDIA . . . LYDIA."

The voice seemed very thin and far away, but Lydia recognized her sister. She drew breath to answer, but felt as if there was a great weight pressing in on her chest. The pulse of blood through her body was all wrong. She couldn't feel her heart beat.

"Taylor, where are you?" She listened hard, but all she heard was the rustle of leaves in her outstretched branches.

Branches? Arms. Her arms felt stiff and numb and her neck wouldn't turn. Forcing her heavy eyelids to open, Lydia saw a welter of green patched with blue. The sun warmed the bark wrapped around her limbs and she tapped the earth beneath her feet for cool water.

What an odd dream.

"Lydia?" Taylor cried out her name again.

She'd never dreamed she was a tree before.

"Mom? Where's Lydia?"

"I don't know, dear," her mother said, "but I hope she'll come home soon."

She sounded worried. That was odd. Why should her mother be worried?

"I'm right here," Lydia said, wondering why they didn't notice her. There was no sound except the scrape of branch against branch.

Her dad and Marco were dragging a picnic basket between them. Taylor and her mom were holding hands as they threaded through the nearby trees. "How about over there?" her mother asked. They moved past Lydia as if she didn't exist.

They're not going to wait for me, she thought, and turned to follow them. Her legs weren't working right. She tried looking down at her feet, feeling like she'd stepped in concrete. Her head wouldn't bend.

"Mom?" Lydia's voice was the warble of a bird in the topmost branch. Her family was still walking through the woods, moving further and further away from her. If she didn't catch up with them soon, she would be left behind. "Wait, wait for me!"

She could barely see her dad's head through the trees.

"No! Don't go," she called.

Pitch flowed down the side of her bark.

This was crazy. She couldn't be a tree. What would her mother say?

Her blood ran warmer and flowed more easily. The steady thrum of her heart beat against her chest. She opened and closed stiff fingers and slowly lowered her arms to her sides. Something shifted in her legs and she could move again. Lydia shook and leaves flew from her hair to shower the ground.

"Mom!" She turned to run after her family, but she swayed

on legs that felt rubbery and too thin. Forcing one foot in front of the other, she lurched a few steps forward before stumbling to the ground.

"Let me help you," Clive said.

"You!" She glared at him. "What did you do to my family?" He held out his arm to her and she swept it aside.

"I am sorry. It was only an illusion."

It had felt so real. Her hands balled into fists. She didn't want to cry; she wanted to slug him. The pain of losing Taylor and the rest of her family again was like ripping off a scab on a barely healed wound. "You tricked me," she said, blinking back tears. "Why? Haven't you tortured me enough?" She had done what he wanted.

Clive sighed. "What do you remember?"

"What do you mean?" she asked, squinting in the distance, hoping to catch a glimpse of her family. Even if it was some Fae trick, part of her still wanted to chase after them. "Why are you doing this to me?" If she went back home now, how much time would have passed for them? It was hard to breathe past the hurt. She grabbed the scrapbook from Clive and clutched it to her chest.

"Lydia. After we left the playground. What do you remember after that?"

She looked at him, her head tilted to one side. "You took my hand and we started walking. And ended up here." She frowned. "Something weird happened. I was . . . I dreamed . . . I was a tree." Then her family was here, but they left without her. It didn't make sense. She scowled and looked at her hands. The fingers felt clumsy.

"It was no dream," Clive said. His quiet voice sent shivers down her spine.

At the edges of the path, a silent forest of birch and pine waited. Lydia felt the breath catch in her throat. "Why are you doing this to me?" she repeated. Wasn't it enough that she agreed to return with him? What else did he want from her? Her gaze darted from tree to tree, but unless she sprouted wings to fly, she wouldn't be able to find her own way out of wherever they were.

"I'm not. I didn't," Clive said. "The tree, that was you, Lydia."

"No. No. I don't believe you." She backed into a tree at the edge of the path and shuddered.

He spread his arms wide. "Then I have no way to convince you," he said. "I am Fae. The Fae do not lie, least of all to themselves. It's how we are able to harness the power of glamour. You can only change what you know and we know of our own true nature. It's long past time for self-deception. You are Fae. You have power. This is the truth, Lydia."

Something in his voice cut through her fear. There was still a core of arrogance that defined him, but concern twisted around it, like a vine around a tree. She shook her head, wanting to hold onto her hurt and her anger. It was easier that way. Better not to trust him.

Lydia stared at her fingers again, remembering the scrape of bark instead of skin and the warmth of sun on upturned leaves.

"Do you not see?" Clive asked.

"It's not possible," Lydia whispered. A crow streaked overhead, his call mocking her. She looked down at the soft earth beneath her feet. It was waiting for her to sink roots here and drink from the clear underground springs that fed the forest. For an instant, Lydia saw herself as both girl and tree, the one image melding effortlessly into the other.

"Lydia," Clive called.

He startled her out of the slow rhythm of sap and season.

"What is happening to me?" she asked and covered her face with her hands.

"Faerie is calling you home," Clive said. "And unless you particularly liked being a tree, you will listen to me next time."

Lydia's cheeks blazed.

"Oberon is waiting for us," he said. "We have to go."

He handed her the bag and she stuffed her scrapbook inside it. No matter what Clive believed, that was her true family. She wasn't going to let them go. He offered her his hand once more and she took it reluctantly.

Clive tugged her after him and she stumbled, feeling as if each step brought them closer to a danger she couldn't name.

"Hold fast," he said. Clive stopped and traced the shape of a door in the air. It shimmered in front of him.

"Ready or not."

"You had best be ready," Clive warned, tightening his grip on Lydia's wrist. She suppressed a shudder as he called the door into being and pulled her through it.

Chapter 8

WARM AIR BRUSHED THE HAIR from her forehead. Lydia kept her eyes tightly shut. She heard Clive sigh.

"You can open your eyes now," he said.

Lydia blinked, her eyes watering as the light hit them. They had stepped into the heart of a summer day in the midst of a wild garden. Hedges, overgrown with twisted vines bearing trumpet-shaped flowers formed the tangled walls of a maze. The sweetness of honeysuckle and mock orange flavored the air.

"I think Oberon needs to fire his gardener," Lydia said, trying to ignore the feel of eyes staring at her.

Clive laughed. "Not very likely."

She turned in a slow circle. Tall trees stood sentry at the garden's edge. There was no one there, but she knew she couldn't trust her ordinary senses. A Fae army could be concealed here and she would never know it.

"Now what?" Keeping her voice steady was a triumph of self-control. She wasn't going to let Clive know how scared she was.

"Through there," he said.

She lost her bearings just looking at the green riot. She hoped Clive knew how to find their way.

The entrance to the maze was flanked by two statues nearly swallowed up by moss and vines. Lydia stared at the crumbling stone figures. It was hard to make out what they were supposed to be. They looked like children, but the faces had been mostly worn away. Empty eye sockets seemed to follow her. She stopped just inside the maze, suddenly certain that if she took one more step into the tangle of greenery and hedge walls, she would never be able to find her way back.

Clive urged her forward. Lydia gripped the strap of her messenger bag with both hands. They walked along hedgerows that stretched higher and higher until Lydia could no longer see over them. The maze hemmed them in. At the end of the path, they had a choice to turn right or left.

Clive stopped and turned to her. "Which way?" he said.

"You've got to be kidding," Lydia said. "This is your gig. You're the guide. I follow you, remember?"

"The path changes for every crossing. Only visitors Oberon wants to see find their way through."

"I thought you said he was expecting us," Lydia said, her voice fading to a whisper. The hedge walls seemed to narrow the further they went in. The light changed inside the maze. Outside, it had been a full summer day. Now they were standing in smoky twilight.

"He has tangled the way for me." She felt his eyes studying her face. "It's a glamour. One of Oberon's masterpieces," Clive said. "Can you not feel it? The whole maze is drenched in magic. Close your eyes."

Not again.

"You can do this, Lydia."

She heard the pleading in his voice. "Okay, I'll try."

Clive stepped closer to her and she had to force herself to close her eyes and not to flinch. "The true path will feel like a thread of sunlight," he said, his voice falling into a whisper, as if he was afraid of being overheard.

"Right," Lydia said. She turned her face to the right and then to the left, but felt nothing.

"You can do this. Bright Court is waiting for us."

She stopped, opened her eyes and hugged her arms around her chest. "Bright and Shadow. That's like white magic and black magic, right?" That's the way it was in all the stories. Light was good. Dark was evil.

"It's not that simple, Lydia," Clive said.

What kind of choice had she made? "Then what's the difference?"

"Once you meet Oberon, you'll understand." Clive looked away.

"Well," Lydia said, shrugging, "if I can't get through the maze, I won't have to worry about it."

"That is not an option," Clive said. "You carry Bright magic in your blood. You must guide us both."

"What about you?"

"I am an afterthought," Clive said. Lydia stared at him. There was no bitterness in his words. It was just a simple statement like he was saying it was a nice day, or that he was in the mood for pizza. She shivered, his lack of emotion more alien than his magic.

"It is a challenge, Lydia. If you bring us through, it will enhance your standing in Oberon's eyes."

"And if I get us lost?" she whispered, not sure she wanted to know the answer.

Color tinged Clive's cheeks and Lydia wondered what he was thinking. "Do not get us lost."

She studied the branching path. So Oberon wanted to test her. It was like all the petty games her classmates played that Lydia had no patience for. "Who does he think he is?"

Clive went completely pale. He gripped her wrist with his long-fingered hand. She tried to pull away, but his arm seemed to turn to stone. "He is Oberon, master of Bright magic, Lord of the Fae. And he can do as he pleases."

"Maybe to you." She shook him off.

"Lydia," Clive said, his voice low and cold, "remember, you chose Bright."

"Some choice," she snapped. "Your Oberon backed me into a corner."

"This is Oberon's court," he said. "His rules, his whims, his power." Clive stood inches from Lydia. "He will keep you to your promises." He held her chin and tipped her face up toward his. "I cannot act against his direct commands and neither can you."

She couldn't stop her body from trembling. What the hell had she gotten herself into?

"Do not goad him, Lydia," Clive warned. "He is much more dangerous than he appears."

Clive let her go. Her face tingled where he had touched it.

"Pick out our path, Lydia. Right or left."

She looked up at him, fear of failure keeping her silent. An invisible breeze played with her hair as she studied the maze. The air around them was hazy with power. The path to their right suddenly bloomed with a carpet of tiny yellow flowers and the air on that side of the maze brightened to midsummer gold. Lydia turned in a circle, her mouth falling open.

"Did he . . . did Oberon do that?"

Clive frowned.

"What's wrong?" she asked.

"Nothing. I don't know," he said.

Cold washed through her. This had to be Oberon's doing. If she had somehow altered Oberon's maze, that changed the game entirely in ways Lydia didn't want to think about. It was easier to believe that something had turned her into a tree. That Oberon was using his magic to lead her to him. But what if it wasn't? What if Clive was right and she was the one who did all this?

Then she was really not normal. Not Lydia. Not human.

She took a step back, but there was nowhere to go. A faint wind brought the scent of lilacs. It was like her mother's favorite perfume and she clung to its reassurance.

Clive stared into the thick hedge walls and said nothing.

The deeper they walked into the maze, the jumpier Clive seemed to get. He kept stealing glances at her when he thought she wasn't looking. She hoped he wasn't mad at her about the path. When he had pushed her to lead them, all she could think of were the words to "Follow the Yellow Brick

Road." And then the flowers had blossomed at her feet. It was a little freaky, but it was the second time something from *The Wizard of Oz* had rescued her.

It was belief, Clive had told her.

Too bad she couldn't believe herself right out of this weirdness.

At each branching, there was a clear path to summer. A breath of warm air caressed her just before the flowers spread out ahead of them. Oberon must have wanted them to get through the maze, or it wouldn't have been this easy.

But then why was Clive so worried?

She couldn't have said what she sensed, exactly, but she knew they were at the end of the maze. The air was brighter and the scent of flowers deepened without being cloying. They turned a corner and the exit was marked with two statues just like the entrance. But these were cut from stone so white it was practically translucent and the detail was almost painfully vivid. Two marble Fae, captured in their haughty glory, looked out from the maze toward a formal garden that had more kinds of flowers and colors than Lydia had ever seen.

A handful of Fae in clothing that rivaled the flowers' hues waited as Lydia stood between the carved sentinels. Frowning, she looked down at her jeans and sneakers before straightening her shoulders and standing as tall as she could. They sought her out. They wanted her here. But it was hard to feel welcomed when they stared at her, a mix of curiosity and hostility in their guarded expressions. Maybe she would be as tough for them to read.

At the far end of the garden was a white, domed pavilion

with open sides. A single throne carved from what glittered like gold sat on a raised dais. Oberon sprawled across the throne looking as permanent and as chiseled as the marble statues. From the moment she saw him, it was as if none of the other Fae existed. Only Oberon mattered.

She gasped as Clive touched her shoulder.

"You must kneel before the throne. And keep silent until you are given leave to speak," he warned.

They walked through a gauntlet of Fae. From the time she and Clive had stepped out of the confines of the maze, no one broke the silence. Lydia struggled to keep her breathing even and her heart from racing. She wasn't going to let them rattle her. Or at least she would make damned sure they couldn't tell.

"Off to see the wizard," she muttered, fear sharpening her sarcasm. Clive frowned her to silence. The path to the center of the pavilion seemed to stretch out endlessly in front of them. Lydia couldn't tell if that was magic or her nerves, but she kept her head up and her eyes on the King. He rivaled his own throne in gaudiness. His hair was gold and his robes must have had gold thread woven through the red and orange designs. His skin glowed with a dusky bronze cast. The sun touched him and glinted off the crown, his hair, and his robes. He dazzled and Lydia knew that was intentional.

He was like all the popular kids at Central High. Everything about him was calculated to impress. It was a piece of something familiar in the strangeness, and it calmed her jitters. It took a lot more than flash to impress Lydia. That was one of the benefits to being invisible at school.

She turned to peek at Clive. His teeth were clenched and his spine stiff. Clearly, he hadn't spent enough time in high school.

They finally reached Oberon and the throne. Lydia stared at the Faerie King, meeting his haughty gaze with her own stubborn one. That was something she was very good at. Out of the corner of her eye, she saw Clive kneel, bowing his head. There was a sound like the wind through summer leaves. The Fae attending the king stared at her. Their scrutiny made Lydia stand even straighter. Oberon's expression was unreadable. His eyes blazed like the desert sun.

Lydia swallowed, her mouth suddenly dry. When she was Taylor's age, she'd found a pack of matches and burned her fingers playing with them. Oberon was as dangerous as an open flame. She dropped to one knee, mirroring Clive's bow. The tension in the room eased as Oberon rose, towering over them.

He was standing on the throne's dais and she had to look up to meet his eyes. Lydia was annoyed all over again. She hated games. Clive seemed to sense her mood and he shot her a warning look. She clenched her jaw and waited, feeling ridiculous and exposed.

Oberon nodded and two of the Fae courtiers, a man and a woman dressed alike in embroidered tunics almost as gaudy as the King's, approached her. She looked at Clive, not knowing what she was supposed to do. He kept his attention on Oberon. Some help he was. He was supposed to be her guide here.

The Fae woman took her right hand and pulled her to standing. "Your King welcomes you home," she said, her voice honey-smooth, but without any real warmth. Lydia gritted her teeth at the obvious cheerleader equivalent. "Lord Oberon wishes to offer you refreshment and raiment as befits your station," she said, looking her up and down and frowning at what she saw.

Lydia struggled to keep her body from trembling. This woman was going to take her somewhere. Beside her, Clive was standing now, anger in the set of his shoulders. Something was happening here. Something was stirring just below the surface of all this stilted courtesy. Something dangerous.

"Lord Oberon," Clive began. Lydia held her breath, knowing he was going to say something about her.

Oberon stared only at Lydia and she felt the heat rise to her cheeks.

"Your King thanks you for your service, Clive Barrow." A small Fae man stepped forward, out of the King's shadow. The two Fae courtiers stepped to either side of her. Lydia glanced at Clive for guidance, but he kept his gaze on Oberon, his hands fisting at his sides.

The Fae woman swept her away from the scene in front of Oberon's throne toward a smaller covered pavilion. Her companion fell in behind them. She couldn't pull away without making a scene and though Lydia didn't know much about Fae politics, she knew that wouldn't be good.

She risked a glance back. Clive stood before the throne, his back rigid, his shoulders tense. Oberon's attention followed her, his smug expression turning her uncertainty to anger.

After all the trouble Oberon went to keeping her safe outside of Faerie, she didn't think they were going to hurt her, but that didn't mean they had her best interests at heart. So far, Oberon hadn't inspired her trust. As far as she could see, they needed her a lot more than she needed them. She had to find a way to make that work for her.

Lydia was going to have to pay attention. She studied her escort. The woman had wildly curled dark hair and deep brown eyes set in copper-colored skin. Her face was completely unlined without even the hint of crow's feet or forehead creases, but Lydia was certain she was a lot older than she looked. Even her twenty-something cousins didn't move with this much self-assurance and grace. The woman paid little attention to the man following them. Perhaps he was some kind of guard, though he didn't carry any obvious weapon.

Lydia knew next to nothing about the Fae other than what was in Faerie tales. She read them to Taylor often enough to know some things: be careful what you wish for, and hospitality always comes with a price. But did any of that apply to this?

The woman dropped Lydia's arm and held the fabric of the tent open for her. Lydia stepped through. The inside was the size of her family's living room. Brightly colored rugs overlapped along the floor. She stopped, looking down at her muddy sneakers. Her companions moved past her. Maybe there was some Faerie magic that kept their slippers clean and dry. She slipped out of her sneakers, leaving them by the entrance.

"My Lady Lydia, be welcome here," the woman said.

Lydia rolled her eyes. Lady Lydia. Right.

The two Fae bowed. Could they be mocking her? Their expressions gave nothing away, but she felt their scrutiny. They were waiting for something. For her to do something. The weight of her bag was familiar. Her blue jeans, torn and bleached with use, were ugly and awkward against the exquisite embroidery of the Fae's clothing. She frowned and squared her shoulders. This was who she was. Lydia Hawthorne. And her mother taught her good manners when she was Taylor's age.

"Thank you for your hospitality," Lydia said, nodding toward them. It was never the wrong thing to mirror your host.

They stood with the same neutral expressions on their too-perfect faces, but she didn't think she'd screwed up. It was like visiting a foreign country. She'd have to be careful. There was no knowing what would be a grave insult here. She didn't even know the rules. Or maybe it was the stakes.

The two Fae glided around the large room readying the table. It was set for two, which meant the man probably wasn't going to sit with them. He offered her a bowl full of scented water and a soft white towel. A quick glance around the room confirmed that there was no convenient indoor plumbing. It was going to be embarrassing when she had to ask about bathroom arrangements.

Lydia washed her face and hands and thanked him.

"Will you dine with me, Lady?" The woman was utterly polite and utterly sure of her place at court. She was like the popular kids who had never looked twice at her. Not even to crib her homework. Now they needed something from her and suddenly the game had changed.

They still hadn't told her their names. She glanced back at the tent entrance hoping to see Clive, but there was only the sound of flapping pennants. Where had he gone? Lydia turned and joined them at the table.

The man held her seat before retreating to the tent flap. The courtesy was starting to get on her nerves. Lydia slipped off her bag, placed it beside the chair and sat stiffly, her hands folded in her lap. The table was set with gilded plates and cutlery. The woman poured a deep red wine in each goblet. She reached for her glass and waited.

Lydia shook her head. Her folks were pretty strict about some things and only let her sip some of their wine on special occasions. "I'm sorry. Back home, high school kids aren't supposed to . . . I don't really drink. Wine, I mean." She knew she was stammering. "Do you have any water or something?" Inwardly she cringed. God, she sounded like a teenager.

"You will not join me in a toast to your health?" The woman drew her eyebrows together.

As much as she didn't get the Fae, it was clear they didn't get her, either. "I appreciate your kindness, but I'm not even sure what I'm doing here. I mean, I don't even know who you are."

"Ah," the woman said, putting her glass down. "Your mother was my kin," she said, staring directly at her. "King Oberon thought I would be a more," she paused for a moment, "familiar presence."

"You've got to be kidding," Lydia said.

The woman cocked her head and frowned.

Lydia sighed. "Okay. Look, nothing about this is familiar and none of it makes sense. Until yesterday, Faerie meant the stories I read to my little sister at bedtime." She took a deep breath and kept going. "I'm sure you mean well and all, but I don't know what the hell is going on." She hadn't meant to be so blunt, but the ever so polite speech of her host was infuriating. It was like the Fae had a thousand ways to say nothing. "Who are you?"

The Fae woman frowned before smoothing her expression back to its neutral blandness. If Lydia hadn't been staring at her, she would have missed it. Maybe she wasn't used to someone not recognizing her. Lydia guessed she'd just snubbed her.

"I am Deirdre," the woman said.

Lydia glanced over her shoulder. "And him?"

Deirdre blinked, a slight frown creasing her forehead. "That is . . . my brother Galvin."

Lydia noticed her odd hesitation over the word, "brother." Well, they looked alike enough to be siblings, but they didn't act anywhere near how she and Marco did. "Well, you already know me." Or at least they knew her name. Even Clive didn't really know her and he'd spent weeks studying her. She would have to use that to her advantage. Lydia lifted her chin and looked directly at the Fae across the table. "Why isn't Clive here?"

"Please, refresh yourself," Deirdre said.

So, she wasn't going to answer any more of her questions. Great. Just great. Now what?

"Oberon insists that you feel welcome," Deirdre said as she uncovered the waiting platters.

Insists. Lydia swallowed a snarky reply. Could Oberon force her to stay? She had thought coming here was the lesser of two evils, but now she wasn't so sure. In this sun-drenched place, it was hard to remember the threat of the darklings or what it was about Aileen that pushed her to choose Bright. Lydia gripped the edge of the table with suddenly cold hands. She could grab her bag and run.

The scent of fresh bread made her mouth water and she glanced at the food spread in front of them. Deirdre slid a bowl of fruit over to her. An open pomegranate spilled its red seeds in the center of a mound of apples and grapes. A chill ran through her. All the stories warned about the dangers of taking Faerie food. The pomegranate reminded Lydia of something.

She looked up into the Fae's watchful eyes.

It was a Greek myth she'd studied in English class. Persephone had eaten several pomegranate seeds in the underworld and it trapped her there for half of every year.

Suddenly, Lydia wasn't very hungry.

Chapter 9

Clive watched them take Lydia away and turned to Oberon, his hands tingling. He let the power and his rising anger drain into the ground. Oberon raised an eyebrow. Clive took a deep breath.

"My Lord, she is bound to give offense. She is ignorant—"

Oberon cut him off, speaking directly to him without using his Seneschal for the first time. "I'm certain the Lady will find her way."

Oberon wanted to keep her isolated and off-balance. He looked toward the pavilion where they had taken Lydia. She would think he had betrayed her.

"Is there something more?" Oberon asked, his eyes glittering even in the bright sunlight.

Clive stepped back and bowed his head. "No, my Lord." The words tasted like ash on his tongue, but it was the truth. There was nothing to be gained now in open confrontation. And much to be lost. If he had any hope of keeping his tangled oaths, he would have to tread carefully.

The Seneschal leaned in to whisper something in Oberon's ear. The King glowered at him, but eventually nodded. Clive took a breath. Regardless of Oberon's game, niceties had to be observed. The King owed him a boon and Clive would need to choose it wisely.

He couldn't risk asking for direct access to Lydia. No. Oberon had made that quite clear. Setting Deirdre as Lydia's keeper was telling. She was the highest ranking Fae at court right now. That made Lydia important. Very important.

Well, she complained about not being noticed. Little chance of that here.

"We wish to reward your faithful service," the Seneschal said.

Oberon's eyes were like banked coals. If this was how Oberon treated success, Clive didn't want to know how he would have reacted to his failure. But Lydia had chosen Bright. And he had been responsible for her choice. The boon was his to claim.

The rest of court had returned to their amusements. A small chamber orchestra picked up their instruments and began to play music written by a Mortal composer long dead. It was beautiful, but stale, like the Fae themselves, unchanging. They nibbled on the crumbs left over from when the doorways between the worlds were open. Before Oberon and Titania divided the Fae and took their tithe in magic, leaving the rest of them squabbling over the remains.

Oberon was watching him, waiting. Clive could ask for a gift, or a favor, and Oberon would have to grant it. The delicate compact between the Fae and their ruler demanded it. That's what made an undeclared boon so dangerous.

He even had the power choose a personal conduit between the worlds at the time of his preference. It was a gift beyond price. It would allow Clive to choose a Mortal lover and bring their child back to Faerie. He could finally claim the status so long denied him.

Oberon's mouth curved into a slight smile as if he knew just what Clive was thinking. Then again, how hard was it to figure out? Without an heir, Clive could not rise in court. And given his family history, he would not likely get this chance again.

He glanced back at the pavilion. It wasn't as if he could help Lydia overtly now, despite his oath. His skin tingled with restrained magic, but even if he had enough power, Clive didn't dare directly oppose Oberon.

The Seneschal frowned at him. "We await your word, Clive," the Seneschal said, using Oberon's inflections. The King's gaze flicked to Lydia's tent and back to him so fast Clive wasn't sure he saw it. It was unusual to see Oberon impatient. That was interesting.

He thought of Lydia standing up to Aileen and smiled. Oberon had no idea what he had taken under his protection. Protection. Clive needed to give her some protection from Oberon. He gave the King a formal bow. "The honor of serving my King is the only boon I require," Clive said.

Oberon stiffened on his throne and Clive heard several of the Fae around him mutter.

Clive made sure his voice would carry through the assembly. "So I grant this boon to our guest and kinswoman, Lydia Hawthorne."

The music stilled. Clouds boiled overhead, shading the court. Magic rippled across the surface of the King's pavilion, revealing the stone at the heart of the gilt throne and the drab cloth underneath the skillful glamour. The dusky skin on Oberon's cheeks burned red with anger and his eyes narrowed, fixing Clive in their stare. He forced himself to hold his ground.

"You would deny your King's gift?" the Seneschal said.

Power, fueled by rogue emotion, swirled in the space between them. A stiffening breeze plucked at Clive's hair and clothing. He was still dressed in jeans and a t-shirt. He could have easily clothed himself and Lydia in glamour to match the court, but he hadn't. It was a choice that Oberon could not have failed to notice.

"I honor the gift and the gift giver," Clive said, keeping his head level and his eyes fixed on the King. "I honor our guest in Oberon's name." There was little Oberon could do. To deny Clive's request would bring dishonor to the Bright Court and give Titania an advantage in their endless skirmishes of words and power.

The clouds steamed and boiled away, leaving them in the sun's direct glare. Oberon cloaked himself and the court in its usual beauty and bid the musicians to pick up their bows. "So be it," Oberon said.

The anger was still there, churning beneath the surface of Oberon's perfect courtesy. But that was nothing new to Clive. He had been dealing with Bright's veiled hostility for a life-time.

Lydia would have her measure of protection and his oath

would be fulfilled. Clive should have been relieved, but a deep tremor of unease moved through him. What would it have been like to take his place beside Deirdre or even someone like Galvin as a full courtier of Bright?

His time in the Mortal realm had turned that path into an impossible tangle.

Someone was going to have to tell Lydia about her boon. And as with all Fae gifts, it came with a price.

Clive felt eyes staring at him and he looked up to see the Seneschal, fury in his gaze. Oberon's throne was vacant and the rest of the Fae had dispersed when the King left.

He had a feeling Lydia was going to have a lot more to worry about than just Oberon and Titania.

*

DEIRDRE ROSE FROM HER SEAT so quickly, Lydia was certain she'd given some terrible offense. She wasn't sure she could risk eating anything, but she also remembered reading that to reject Faerie hospitality led to terrible things. It was crazy, trying to piece together bits from all the tales she had ever heard. A hot breeze blew through the tent, rustling the gauzy material. She blinked and Oberon was there, his presence filling the room. Her Fae keepers bowed. She scrambled to her feet, the chair tipping backwards. The breath caught in her chest and she was suddenly furious with Clive.

The Fae King stared at her and Lydia backed away, her feet tangling with the downed chair. She tripped and fell, striking her elbow on the chair back. Oberon raised one eyebrow and moved toward her.

Great. Just great, she thought, wincing as a bright line of pain traveled up her arm. She scrambled to her feet before Oberon could touch her.

He bent to pick up the fallen chair. "This must feel quite disorienting," he said.

In the tent, he seemed merely larger than life rather than utterly overwhelming. He wanted her here. That had to count for something. She bowed her head, looking down as much to collect her thoughts as to show what she figured would be the proper respect. Not much call for dealing with royalty in the good old U.S. of A. She struggled to remember what they had read about Oberon and the Fae in her Shakespeare unit in English class, but iambic pentameter wasn't going to be a whole lot of help.

"There is too much I don't understand." She risked peeking at his face. In a dozen summers at the beach, she would never look that bronzed. "I appreciate all this hospitality and stuff." The memory of baking cookies with Taylor hit her with the force of a punch in the gut. "I'm sorry. I really don't belong here."

Deirdre drew in her breath. Oberon's expression didn't change. He was watching her like someone might watch an interesting specimen in science lab.

"I'm really sorry, Lord Oberon," Lydia added, "I mean no disrespect. This isn't my home." The silence stretched out. Lydia had no idea what he was thinking, but she didn't suppose he was too happy with her.

"Child, if anyone has cause to apologize, I do." The voice was warm and smooth and if Lydia had kept her eyes closed, she would have been relieved. But Oberon's gaze was almost painful in its intensity. She noticed he didn't actually offer her an apology. "I left you overlong in the Mortal world."

She shivered, despite the warmth in the room. "Please. I want to go back."

Deirdre gripped the table edge.

Lydia's face flushed hot under the glare of Oberon's total attention.

"That door is closed," he said.

She opened her mouth to protest, but didn't know what to say. Tears gathered in the corner of her eyes. She squeezed them shut. The squeal of Marco's clarinet replayed in her memory, a sound of painful and flawed beauty. "Why have you done this to me?" she asked.

"Lord Oberon honors you," Deirdre said. Lydia felt as if she'd been slapped in the face. "You will take your place in his court and offer him your tithe."

Lydia stared at the woman. "This is crazy." Back home, she struggled to assert her independence from her parents, fought to make her own decisions, but this was another league altogether. Here, she was powerless again. She looked down at her ratty jeans. The knees were faded nearly to white. What could Oberon possibly want that she had?

"Deirdre, the child has offered no willful offense." Oberon rested his hand on Lydia's shoulder and she had to brace herself beneath its weight. "Do we not owe her our patience?"

Deirdre frowned, but bowed her head toward Oberon. "Of course, my Lord. I spoke with haste."

Snagged. Lydia hid her smirk.

"There is much you will come to value in Faerie, child." Oberon gripped her shoulder and his casual regard became something almost painful. "I see you have already tasted the allure of glamour."

Lydia looked up at him as he glanced first at Deirdre and then at Galvin and then back to her.

"Tell me, was this Clive Barrow's doing?" The words were soft, measured, but the heat from his hand was searing.

Lydia forced herself not to cry out or pull away. "No. I don't . . . I don't understand." A memory of leaves rustling in the breeze rose to the surface of her mind. "It was the woods." Her voice faded to a whisper. "Clive told me to keep my eyes shut. The woods." Clive had tried to tell her it was her own power that created the glamour, but she couldn't wrap her thoughts around it. "The trees. They did something to me."

Oberon's grip softened and the breath surged out of her in a rush.

"It is well that you are here now, Lydia." Oberon's courtesy was like a mask he pulled on. "Power ungoverned is a danger," he said. "Deirdre and Galvin will safeguard you."

"And Clive?" The words were out of her mouth before she thought about what she was saying.

Oberon's face stilled and the careful blank expression chilled her more than any outburst would have. "Clive Barrow has fulfilled his task and has received our gratitude."

Lydia clasped her hands to keep them steady. It was clear she was on her own now.

"We will speak again, child."

She blinked and he was gone.

"Come, Lord Oberon wishes to formally present you to your people," Deirdre said, "but first you will need to harness the simplest of glamours." She looked Lydia up and down again, not bothering to hide her distaste.

Lydia grabbed her bag and hugged it to her chest. "I don't. I can't . . . " She took a step away from her, shaking her head.

"You are Fae," Deirdre said, piercing her with a pitiless gaze. "You will learn."

Chapter 10

CLIVE STARED AT THE WOMAN who had given birth to him. Myra Barrow stood almost as tall as Clive himself. Her black hair was untouched by the gray that marked Lydia's Mortal mother, her face unlined. She could have passed for twenty or thirty by looks alone, but the expression in her eyes showed decades of contempt. It had been a mistake to come back here.

"You are a fool," she said. "Did you think you would earn anything with this senseless sacrifice? Whatever you had thought to gain is an illusion."

Illusion. He almost choked on the irony. How could he explain? Myra had always disdained Clive's fascination with the Mortal world. He thought she had relented when Oberon sent him to retrieve Lydia. But her approval started and ended with how his actions would affect her standing at court and with Oberon.

"I had no other path," he said.

"The taint of the ephemeral hangs on you," she said. "You are more Mortal than Fae."

Clive gathered a spark of his will and set it to his words. "I will not speak again of this," he said. He was tired of taking the brunt of her anger over his grandmother's shame and choices made long before he was born.

Myra's eyes widened and Clive suppressed a smile. He would not be bullied by her any longer.

"Why have you returned?" she asked.

Clive stared off into the distance. Why had he come? There was little for him here than the physical reminder of his childhood, but by law, he had a claim. And Oberon had made it as clear as he ever did that Clive was not welcome at court.

"I will reside here for a time."

A flash of anger passed over Myra's face before her icy control exerted itself again. There was little she could do, unless Oberon banished him from Bright altogether. Only then could she claim his holdings, much good as that would do her. But he didn't think he had crossed that line. At least not yet.

"I will not interfere with your bindings, only restore those that are mine by right," Clive said.

Myra nodded, satisfied by his concession. Having him here would not rest easily with her, no matter how little he exerted his power. He would be a splinter in her finger, a constant irritant, his magic abrading against hers. It had been like this for as long as Clive could remember—his mother resenting him, his magic, and his affinity for the Mortal world. Perhaps she had simply hated his Mortal father, or the fact that having a child had still not given her the status she craved in Bright Court.

"Do not worry, Mother," he said, deliberately using the Mortal word. Myra looked as if she had tasted something sour. "I will not be here long." No matter his right, he could not stand to stay in the place longer than absolutely necessary.

He left her sputtering with unexpressed anger as he followed a familiar thread of old magic back to his boyhood rooms. She had walled them off from the rest of the house, but she didn't have the ability to destroy them completely. Clive strode through the corridors decorated with her personal colors. The muted purples and greens were the shades of bruises. Peeling away the edges of her glamour, he found the door to his apartment. He rested one hand on the rich paneling, savoring the clarity of his own name and will unsullied by Myra's magic.

It took only a small nudge to open the wards he had set. He stepped over the threshold. His rooms were just as he had left them years ago. Stark white walls framed a space that was all grays and blacks, an antidote to his mother's gaudy style. The air tasted stale, as if time had settled over everything like Mortal dust. He whispered the word for breeze and opened a window to the boundary forest, bringing the scents of fresh pine and rich loam to the room. Clive took a deep breath. The tension he carried with him from Oberon's court and into his mother's house dissipated with the exhale.

"Interesting choice in decor."

Clive whirled around. Aileen stood across the room, leaning against the window sill.

"How did you get in?" There was no stirring from his bindings. She should never have been able to get anywhere near here.

She glanced around, a tight smile on her face. "This looks

more like something of Titania's than your Oberon's heraldry."

Bright magic filled his chest and flowed down to his fingertips.

Aileen put her hands up in mock surrender. "I have no will to harm you, Clive Barrow. I am here only as an emissary from the Shadow Court. Will you hear me?"

Clive let his gathered power drain back into the ground. It was true. She retained only enough magic to cloak herself in a personal glamour. She was as powerless before him as a Mortal. And she knew it. Beneath Aileen's arrogance, fear nibbled at the edges of her discipline.

"So Titania punishes you for your failure," Clive said.

"My Lady Titania trusts me with her own words," Aileen said, glaring at Clive, her throat and jaw tight.

"Then speak them and leave."

Aileen studied his face for a moment. Clive wasn't sure what she was searching for, but he kept his expression neutral, schooling himself to patience. If Aileen would let herself be used like this, there had to be a good reason.

"So be it," she said.

A pulse of raw magic poured into her, turning Aileen into something with enough power to extinguish his. She stood taller, her blue eyes so dark they were almost black. Raven hair spilled over one bare shoulder and down her back nearly to her waist. A cloak the color of midnight wine shimmered over her other shoulder.

"It has not gone unnoticed how Oberon has honored your service." Aileen's words were clipped, precise. Clive shivered. He had never been in Titania's presence before, but he had no doubt it was she who spoke now, a powerful glamour turning Aileen into the Shadow Queen.

"My Lady." Clive bowed, furiously thinking of any precedent to guide him.

She laughed and it was the music of icicles breaking. "How polite you are, Clive Barrow."

He swallowed.

"I have surprised you," she said, the hint of a smile warming her face. "Did you expect some twisted, vengeful thing? An ugly crone? Your King would see me so. "

"No, Milady," Clive said, though in truth, he had imagined Titania to be an old spider, spinning intrigues like sticky webs.

She smiled and Clive's heart sped up. The Shadow Queen was painfully beautiful, seemingly sculpted from marble and ice. A fine net of diamonds woven in her hair glittered like the night sky sprinkled with stars.

"Oberon speaks of your power, but I was not prepared for your beauty."

"Aileen didn't tell me how well-spoken you were." Titania clapped her hands together in girlish delight. "They say you are like your grandmother. I see it is true."

Clive held himself motionless, betraying none of his shock. Titania laughed again.

"I have surprised you again. It was I who gave her permission to leave Faerie. I opened the door when Oberon refused his own kinswoman. Do you know why?"

"No, Milady." Clive couldn't decide what words might be safe to say.

"I remembered love," she said, shrugging. Bells sewn into

her cloak sang. "Oberon wasn't amused." Titania reached forward and placed one finger beneath his chin and tipped his head up.

Clive froze, holding his indrawn breath.

"There is still her debt to be paid," she said, her voice barely a whisper. "What say you?"

He thought of his mother and realized she had been right in her own way. If he had kept Oberon's boon, he could have used it to fulfill this obligation. Now he had nothing.

"What will you have me do, my Lady?" Clive was as bound to her as Aileen was.

The room filled with the sound of laughter and bells and she was gone, leaving Clive a hand's breadth from Aileen.

*

DEIRDRE LED HER AWAY FROM the table and behind a screen that partitioned off what looked like a small bedroom. A thick sleeping pad took up the space against the far side of the pavilion. It was heaped with embroidered pillows in what Lydia assumed were Oberon's colors—reds, oranges, and golds. It was exquisite, like everything she'd seen in Faerie, but Lydia missed her own room, with the rainbow wallpaper she'd chosen as a child and the mound of well-loved stuffed animals on her pillow. Compared to this room, it was garish and infantile, but it was hers. Lydia tossed her bag down on the bed.

"Now what?" she asked.

Deirdre stared at her for a few long seconds before handing

her a bundle of tan cloth from an ornate storage chest. Lydia shook out the plain fabric and found a long tunic and leggings made from a scratchy fabric.

"No offense, but my jeans look better than this."

Deirdre smiled. "Consider these a blank canvas."

Lydia looked between Deirdre and the clothes. Was the Fae woman making fun of her? She let the silence stretch out, but Deirdre didn't explain. "Okay. I give up. What are you talking about?"

A brief smile flitted across Deirdre's face. "You have power," she said. "You bear the mark of one who has already trans-formed through glamour. This is far simpler."

"Right." Lydia dropped the clothes on the floor and crossed her arms. "I don't think so."

Deirdre's jaw clenched briefly, her dark eyes narrowing as she stared at Lydia. "Watch," she said and pointed to the pile of clothes. Lydia held Deirdre's gaze for several seconds, ignoring the woman's outstretched finger. Deirdre blinked and looked away.

Lydia's smirk faded as a heat shimmer rose in the room, smearing all the bright colors and leaving her momentarily dizzy. "What was that?" she asked, leaning on a chair for support.

Deirdre nodded to the floor.

A red tunic and gold leggings lay where simple cloth had been. Lydia blinked her eyes as the distortion faded. "How did you do that?"

Deirdre glanced at the clothes again. They were colorless once more. "The stronger the will, the simpler and more subtle the glamour."

"What's that supposed to mean?"

"It means what it means. Now you try."

Right. Irritation made her teeth clench. "Where I come from, we buy our clothes. In stores."

"Do you refuse?"

The question was simple and Lydia wanted to answer it directly by walking out. She'd found her way through the maze once, she should be able to find it again. What would happen if she refused? Oberon didn't seem like the kind of person who would take that well. Lydia picked at the cuticles of her thumb. And if she did get past the maze, then what? Clive had been the one to open the door between the worlds. And he was conspicuously absent.

"Lydia Hawthorne, do you refuse?" Deirdre asked again. There was a curious formality to the question, along with an eagerness that Lydia sensed even if she couldn't explain how. She glared up at Deirdre's perfectly even features. She wanted her to refuse. Well, Lydia wasn't going to let one stuck-up Fae chick win that easily.

"No," Lydia said. "But you have to teach me."

"If you cannot see, then you do not deserve your claim on the Bright court."

"I have never claimed a damned thing from you," Lydia said, heat spreading through her chest. Oberon had her snatched from her life and dumped here. She closed her eyes. It was too much to hope that this was all some weird hallucination. She opened her eyes and Deirdre was still standing in front of her, graceful and dressed in Oberon's finest. "I'm sure Oberon will not appreciate your failure here," Lydia said, matching Deirdre's mocking tone.

For a moment, silence filled the small room before Deirdre burst into laughter as eerie as it was unexpected. "You are as arrogant as any Bright courtier, I'll give you that."

Lydia held her tongue and waited.

"There was a time when Mortals understood magic," Deirdre said. "Oh, they feared it, but they didn't try to systematically deny it the way they do now. And here you are, fairly dripping with Fae magic, without the knowledge to harness even a drop." She shook her head. "What was Oberon thinking?"

For all that she looked like Oberon, Deirdre's sarcasm and her smugness reminded her of Aileen. Something teased her memory. Aileen, talking about magic. About persuasion. She thought of one of Taylor's bedtime stories. The Little Engine that Could. "I think I can, I think I can." Could it be that simple? Lydia was aware of Deirdre's quiet waiting. She expected Lydia to fail.

Well, she was over living up to someone else's expectations. Especially someone like Deirdre. Lydia bit her lower lip as she studied the embroidery on the Fae woman's tunic. "That is so not my style," she said.

So, the game was she had to show she could change something into something else. A breeze fluttered the walls of the pavilion. Lydia lifted her face to the air and wanted to run. Not run away, not run to anything in particular, but to run and let her body slice through the wind. It was something she was good at. An ordinary thing. A Mortal thing.

"I think I can, I think I can," played over and over in her head. Heat raced through her body, her leg muscles warm, her face blazing as if she'd already run miles. She pulled more warmth from the ground and felt the hair lift from the back of her neck. Deirdre's mouth was set in a thin line and Lydia wanted to laugh. She didn't need to look at the clothes at her feet. She knew they were there. Mesh shorts and a tank top, both in red and gold tie-dye.

"Tell Oberon I'm going for a run," she said, smiling at the look of fury on Deirdre's face.

Chapter 11

Clive's ears rang with the sudden clearing of magic from the room. He looked up and Aileen was watching him, her expression perfectly neutral. There was nothing neutral about the emotion seething just below the surface of her control.

"My Lady has granted me a doorway for us both," she said, disgust coloring her voice.

He wondered how many such crossings she had the power to create.

"We must go now," she said.

Clive frowned at the urgency and saw fatigue in the stiffness across Aileen's shoulders, the set of her jaw. He shuddered, knowing where Titania had found her reserve of power, enough to slip through Oberon's wards.

"I do not need your pity," Aileen said. "I serve My Lady. Do you do any less for Lord Oberon?"

Clive turned away. At the heart of the compact between the Fae and their ruler was the tithe. But this went beyond any normal price. If Oberon commanded such, he doubted he would have the power to refuse. Such was the service of the Fae, he thought, and turned from Aileen. Sympathy was a Mortal thing. She would scoff were he to offer it.

"And what is our task?" Clive asked, painfully aware of the obligations he had bound himself to already. He could not refuse the onus Titania placed on him, not even if it set him against Oberon's wishes. And what of the promises he had made to Lydia? Bright magic swirled through his heart in a confused tangle. There was no possible future he could imagine that would allow him to tread all three paths.

"Once upon a time, a Fae daughter was hidden," Aileen said. "We seek the story that was hidden along with the child."

"I don't understand," Clive said.

"You will," Aileen answered. "Take my hand."

Clive put his hand in hers. Her fingers were long and graceful, with red lacquer like wet blood shining on oval fingernails, so different from Lydia's calloused hands and bitten cuticles. At her touch, his room vanished to a distant pinprick of light and then darkness. A winter wind bit through him. Frost stiffened his fingers. He couldn't feel Aileen's hand. Shuddering, he gathered a memory of summer and focused his will. The Bright magic was sluggish. Clive struggled to create a glamour of heat and light, but the air absorbed all the warmth from his body.

When he thought he had turned to ice, a dim light cracked open the blackness. They were no longer in Faerie. Clive's hands burned. Aileen drew a sharp breath. Her body was outlined in moonlight. Frost limned her eyebrows and glistened on her black hair like silver cobwebs. She was shivering. Clive pulled a warm cloak around his shoulders and eased his hands into fur-lined gloves.

"Does your Lady smooth the path like that for all her faithful servants?" Titania had just about turned his blood to slush. Aileen stared at him silently, her exhaled breath visible in the night air, her clothes too thin for the chill evening. Clive clenched his jaw, regretting his harshness. Titania had left her almost nothing.

Clive warmed the air around them both until she was dry. He glamoured her a matching cloak and gloves. She pulled the deep hood over her head with shaking hands and turned away. If she had been Mortal, she would have expressed her thanks, but the Fae had no words for gratitude. This was a debt. No more, no less. Through the bare trees of what was hardly a forest, Clive saw the outline of a swing set against the night sky. This was Lydia's childhood park.

"Why are we here?" Clive asked.

"I told you. My Lady bids us to discover what Oberon conceals." A sliver of moonlight struck Aileen's eyes and they glowed in the dark recess of her hood. She paused, staring at him for several long moments. "You will need to keep us hidden." Clive could hear the shame and irritation beneath Aileen's imperious tone. This was just another debt to be repaid when she had already given everything she owned to Titania.

Under other circumstances, Clive might have enjoyed having someone from Shadow beholden to him. There was power and status to be gained in obligation. But seeing Aileen so vulnerable shamed him on her behalf.

Weeks had passed on this side of the barrier and most of the leaf litter had been swept away. The ground was damp beneath their feet. It looked like it had been a wet, miserable autumn here.

"Come," Aileen said as she started walking across the park. Her boot heels struck the concrete sidewalk with a sharp snick. Clive fell into step beside her as they walked the short distance to Lydia's house.

"Why there?" Clive asked.

"Why did Oberon choose this family?"

Keeping what he knew of Lydia's history secret any longer was pointless now that she had chosen Bright. "They had a dying child. She needed a place to be concealed." It was less mercy than expediency. He knew nothing beyond that. Why she was hidden in the first place was a question only Oberon could answer.

"And you are so certain of your facts?" Aileen said, stopping abruptly outside the halo of a street lamp.

"That is the truth from our Seneschal's own lips," he said.

She stared at him for a moment and nodded her head. "Then we shall see," she said.

Clive looked out into the night. "And you are certain there is a quarry we seek?"

"You ask for certainty here? Mortal lives have only one certainty. Come."

They reached Lydia's house. There were lights blazing from the downstairs rooms, but the second floor was dark and quiet.

"We need to go inside. Are you sure you can shield us both?"

Aileen asked.

Clive nodded and created a pocket of disinterest around them. Mortals would simply glance past. It was like and unlike the glamour Oberon had used to cloak Lydia. It had not rendered her invisible, only less noticeable, easier to overlook.

They entered through the screen porch door. It swung silently behind them. Making no move to conceal themselves, they strode through the house. Clive followed Aileen through the dark laundry room and into the empty kitchen. A clock in the shape of a cat ticked loudly, the tail swishing from right to left, counting off the seconds. Music and voices rose from the living room. The glow of the television cast its blue penumbra over the kitchen doorway. Lydia's Mortal brother was watching something loud with images that flicked and whirled too fast for Clive to follow.

The boy didn't stir. Sitting across the room from him was an older woman Clive did not recognize. "Not here," Aileen said. "Upstairs."

He followed her to the threshold of Lydia's room, wondering what she had thought she'd find here. "Now what?"

She turned to him, a flash of triumph in her eyes. "Behold the lie of Oberon." Aileen flung the door open and pointed to the bed. A sleeping form mounded the blankets. Clive reached out and pulled the edge of the covers away from the girl.

Taylor murmured a protest and grabbed for the blanket with a chubby hand.

Aileen's breath hissed through her teeth.

"That is Lydia's little sister," Clive said.

"Yes, I know," Aileen said, glaring at him. "What has he

done with her?"

"Who? What are you talking about?" Clive asked. Taylor stirred in her sleep.

"The Mortal child. What has he done with her?" Aileen said.

Clive knew she wasn't talking about Taylor. He turned to Aileen, confused.

"You're Lyddie's friend." He whirled to see Taylor sitting up, her legs dangling off the side of Lydia's bed. There was no way she should have been able to push through the glamour. But this was twice now that the little girl saw true. Aileen shot him a sharp look. He shook his head, hoping she'd keep her silence, and knelt by Taylor's side.

"Yes," he said. "I am Lydia's friend." He said it plainly and he knew it was true. "This is Aileen. She is," he paused, trying to find a word for their relationship that would be true and that the girl would understand, "like my cousin."

Taylor nodded, her brown eyes large in an oval face. In the moonlight, she looked almost Fae herself. "I want to see Lydia," she said.

Clive felt a pang of something he suspected was guilt. "It cannot be."

"I'm not scared of the hospital," Taylor said. "Not like Meggie. She cried and cried when she had to visit her granny. I promised not to cry, but they still won't take me."

"Who? Take you where?"

"To see Lyddie. At the hospital. You could take me. You're almost a grown-up," Taylor said.

"Did your parents tell you Lydia was sick?" Clive asked. Perhaps that was easiest on the child. Though she would find the truth of her sister's disappearance soon enough.

The child reached beneath her pillow and pulled out a glossy brochure. "This is where she is. If you won't take me, I'll find someone who can." She thrust out her chin and for a moment, he recognized something of Lydia's stubbornness in the girl's face.

Clive reached for the brochure and studied it. Riverton Rehabilitation Hospital. There were photographs of smiling patients in wheelchairs on a rolling green meadow fringed by willow trees. A small creek meandered through the trees. Scrawled in marker was Lydia Hawthorne, Room 717.

Taylor's lower lip quivered. "She wanted me to tell her if I saw you. But you're here and I can't tell her." Tears splashed down her cheeks.

Clive glanced at Aileen, but her face was closed. This made little sense. Lydia was at Bright.

"We can't take you anywhere without your parents' consent," Clive said. Least of all into Faerie, he thought. Taylor's tears flowed more freely. "But we can give her a message from you."

The little girl nodded her head. "I drew this after dinner, but Mommy and Daddy already left." She hiccuped twice and handed Clive a card. Two smiling stick figures, one taller than the other, stood holding cookies in their hands.

"How long has Lydia been sick, Taylor?" Aileen broke her silence with a voice more gentle than Clive had thought possible.

"Since she fell down in the park." The little girl's face crumpled and her thin shoulders shook with the strength of her sobs.

"Fell down?" Clive hated to press her, but he didn't under-stand what was going on.

"She fell down. Mommy and Daddy were angry. Lyddie didn't come home to babysit. They found her sleeping. She . . . she won't wake up."

A look of triumph flitted across Aileen's face. She knew something. He stood up, holding Taylor's drawing. "I promise I will give this to your sister." There. Another pledge to entangle him.

Taylor frowned, looking between the two of them. "You're not going to take me."

"No," Clive said. "We need to leave now, Taylor. It's time for you to go back to sleep." He dropped the temperature in the room by several degrees and patted the pillow. "Here, I'll tuck you in."

She shivered and slid her bare feet back into the nest of blankets on Lydia's bed. "Tell Lyddie that I'm going to sleep here until she comes home."

"I shall tell her," Clive said, but it would be a long time be-fore the girl she knew as her big sister would be back again.

He held his tongue until he and Aileen were safely out of the house and in the peace of the sleeping park. Dropping the concealing glamour was a relief. "Tell me what we are doing here," Clive said.

"Showing you Oberon's lie," Aileen said.

"What lie?" Lydia was at court. The only lie here was one told to protect a little girl. Clive couldn't figure out what the Shadow court gained with this charade. Certainly he was not so important that Titania needed to mortgage her court to entice him away from Faerie.

"You are a fool. The Mortal babe did not die. Oberon secreted the child in Faerie and now that he has the trueborn, he sent her back."

"What is your proof?"

Aileen met his stare with her own. "You need more than the testimony of the little girl?" Aileen pointed at the brochure still in Clive's hand. "There is your proof."

"I don't understand."

"It took my Lady many years to discover the deception. That the Mortal was taken and raised at Bright until Oberon tired of her. And now that he has what he wishes, he has closed Lydia's path back to the ephemeral life she so desperately desires."

Clive wanted to say it didn't make sense, but Oberon rarely did anything without a purpose. He must have glamoured the Mortal child well. There had been no hint of her at court. He rubbed his eyes, fatigue tangling his thoughts. He stared into the distance, seeing the door to Faerie in his mind's eye. What would Lydia do when she found out? She would see this as another betrayal. Clive looked into Aileen's eyes and found triumph there again.

"And my part in all of this?" Surely Aileen hadn't needed him here.

"You will tell the Trueborn what Oberon would conceal," she said. "That is my Lady's price."

Clive winced. No wonder Titania risked trespassing in Bright to speak with him. Why she stripped so much magic from Aileen and who knows how many others of Shadow to create the doorway here. Titania had played him well, indeed. He would fulfill his oath and in doing so, drive Lydia right into the arms of the Shadow court.

Chapter 12

LYDIA WALKED AWAY FROM THE pavilion and Deirdre made no move to stop her. It wasn't as if her babysitter was likely to suddenly take up running, but the Fae surely had different ways to keep tabs on her. It didn't matter. Lydia had to at least pretend she had some space. Bouncing up and down on her toes a few times, she felt the ground spring beneath her. It would be like running on the dirt track at school.

Looking up, she saw the statues flanking the entrance to Oberon's maze. A wildness, like the first breath of spring after a long, harsh winter, moved through her. She smiled and jogged through the twin guardians. The hedges reached taller than her head and after a few random turns, Lydia could no longer see the entrance or remember the way out. It didn't matter. She had mastered Oberon's maze once and either it was a fluke and he would have to rescue her, or she would find her way again. But for now, she was free.

The air stirred, filling the maze with the scent of lilacs and roses. Her feet made no sound on the soft earth. The deeper she ran, the calmer she felt, her thoughts settling into the rhythm of her steady stride and even breaths.

She wanted to run right out of the weirdness. Clive, Aileen, Oberon, and Deirdre all insisted she was Fae. But what did that really mean? She glanced down at her shorts. Magic. She could do magic. That was pretty cool. But that couldn't make up for everything she had to give up to come to this side of the looking glass—her life, her choices, her family. Her folks must be going crazy. Lydia stumbled to a stop, a stitch burning in her side.

If they even knew she was gone.

She crouched down, dropping her head to her knees.

How hard was it to convince reality? Changing the blank cloth to her running clothes had been effortless. She wasn't even sure how she'd done it. But erasing someone's whole life? Could Oberon do that? Thinking of the Bright King, she realized that wasn't the right question. There was no doubt in her mind he had the raw strength. She could feel it, just standing in the same room as him.

Tears rolled down her hot cheeks. If by some miracle she could open a door back home, would they even know her? The enormity of loss came sweeping over her like an icy wind, leaving her shaking with more than cold.

"Who am I?" she whispered.

"That is an excellent question."

Lydia jumped up from her crouch and whirled around, looking for the source of the low, raspy voice. The hedges seemed to loom in, the interweave of nettles creating the Fae equivalent of razor wire. There was nothing but green and silence. She stared into the gloom created by the overgrowth. Someone was here.

Hands on her hips, she turned around in a full circle one more time. "I've had just about enough," she said. She wanted straight information. And she wasn't going to play Oberon's little games until she got it.

"Oh, good. Me too."

The voice came out of the maze walls. Lydia swore she was looking right at whoever was speaking, but she still couldn't see anything. "Who are you?"

"Now, that is a question I can answer." A smudge of fog obscured the hedge right in front of her and out of the fog drifted the strangest little man Lydia had ever seen. His skin was the color of old parchment and sagged with more wrinkles than a sharpei puppy. Brown eyes gleamed like oiled mahogany in his round face. He was maybe five feet tall and deeply stooped. A shock of white hair sprang away from his head as if he'd touched a live wire. He swept off an imaginary hat and bowed deeply. "Aeon, at your service."

"Did Oberon send you to find me?"

He cocked his head and stared off into the distance, considering. "Why?" he said, finally, after she was sure he wouldn't answer. "Are you lost?"

Lydia looked around at the impenetrable maze walls. "I don't know. Maybe."

"Many travelers get lost in my maze. Some get found, too. Which do you think you are?"

"Your maze? I thought it was Oberon's maze."

His eyes darkened and the hedges stirred in an absent

breeze. She saw a tremor of movement out of the corner of her eye. A vine was snaking its way across the path opening.

"So you're a friend of our King, yes?" he asked, his voice pleasant, but his face set in stern lines.

She took a step away from him, but there wasn't far to go. "I don't think Oberon's anybody's friend," Lydia said, as the creeper twined with a dozen more vines to form a lattice that the hedge crawled up. It was like watching some set of invisible hands weave green on an imaginary loom. Clouds rolled overhead and Lydia shivered as the maze closed in on them. "And especially not mine."

Aeon laughed and the clouds shredded, letting the sun stream through. Where it touched the fresh hedge, the green retreated, leaving the path clear again.

She stared at him and at the opening in the maze. "Did you? How?"

"I told you. The maze belongs to me." He looked down, frowning. Lydia followed his gaze. Where his feet should have been, gnarled tree roots disappeared into the loam. She shuddered, remembering what it felt like to be a tree. "Or maybe," he said, "I belong to the maze. 'Tis hard to remember."

"Are you stuck here?"

"Stuck? Why, where else would a gardener be, child?"

He laughed harshly and it echoed the mocking of crows. Lydia looked down at the ground. "You really can't leave, can you?"

Smiling, he waggled a bony finger at her. "But you can," he said, his voice sing-song. "You waltzed through my maze once before." He stared up at her and under other circumstances, she would have laughed at his wizened face scrunched up in concentration. "You saw past all my dead ends and switch-backs." He paused. "How did you manage that, I wonder?"

Lydia shrugged. "Oberon wanted me."

"Ah, but even Lord Oberon gets lost in my maze some-times." He beckoned her closer. "It's my only revenge, you know. And sometimes I just let him find his way through. Do you know why that is?"

Lydia shook her head, her heart beating faster as he leaned in even closer.

"So he thinks he can." Aeon slapped his thigh and let loose peals of wheezing laughter that startled birds from hedges all around them. For a moment, wings obliterated the sky and Ly-dia swallowed, thinking of the darklings.

As suddenly as he started laughing, Aeon stopped, the mad-ness slipping from his expression as if was a kind of mask. "Oberon's lapdogs are looking for you."

Lydia folded her arms across her chest. "Let them look."

Aeon winked at her. "Do you want to see where they are?"

"No."

"Even if they cannot see you?"

"Oh," Lydia said. "You can spy on them?"

"More like Hide and Go Seek," he said. A jack-o-lantern grin spread across his face. "A game."

"I don't like games."

"This is a different kind of game," he said. "Like it or not, one you are already playing."

"Why are you helping me?"

"You are interesting. My trees like you. You have shaped

one, yes?"

Lydia felt the heat rise to her cheeks, but she nodded. How could he have known?

"Besides, Oberon is vexed with you," Aeon said, shrugging. "Is that not reason enough? Here."

He handed her a flawless ripe peach. It smelled like summer sun and light rain. She would have sworn it hadn't been in his hand a moment ago.

"Go on, take a bite. It grew in the heart of the maze."

Lydia hesitated, her mouth watering. "What will it do to me?"

Aeon laughed again, but this time there was only amusement in it. "Wrong question, Lydia Hawthorne."

She shivered, despite the warm sunshine. "What's the right question?"

"The right question? Why, that is simple, child." He clapped his hands in delight. "The right question is what will you do to us?"

He was a strange little man, but he seemed to have no particular love for Oberon or her Fae babysitters. That would have to be good enough for her. She took a bite of the peach. Her eyes widened as the sweetness exploded in her mouth. It made every other peach she had ever eaten taste dull and distant. Aeon was watching her, his eyes bright and his face flushed.

This was the first she'd eaten or drunk in Faerie. Did that mean she was trapped here now? The juice trickled down her throat and a hunger that was not only for food drove her to nibble the flesh down to its pit. Aeon held out his hand. She gave him the peach stone. He closed his brown fingers around it and the whisper of a summer breeze warmed her. He opened his hand again and the stone lay shining on his palm, clean and smooth, sheathed in gold and strung on a piece of green vine.

"A gift," he said. "Take it."

Lydia hesitated.

Aeon laughed again. "Oh, child, you have nothing to fear from old Aeon or his garden."

"Thank you." She lifted the pendant from his leathery hand and without giving herself a chance to think about it, leaned in to kiss him on the cheek.

Leaves rustled all around as Aeon blushed the color of holly berries. "You are a surprise, Lydia Hawthorne. Go ahead, put it on," he said. "It is my sigil. The maze will always open itself to you now."

"Oh," Lydia said, "but I have nothing to offer you in return." Wasn't that what she was supposed to do? It probably was a bad thing to be in debt to the Fae.

"Ah, but you do," he said. His dark eyes stared at her, full of curiosity and amusement.

"What do you want from me?" She had to remind herself that this kind, old man was still Fae. And from what she'd seen so far in Faerie, everyone was self-centered, manipulative, and vain. Not so much different from high school, she thought, except for the magic part.

"Not to worry, child. Something quite easy to grant." He paused, smiling, and Lydia thought of Rumpelstiltskin.

She glanced down at the pendant. It was gold. Maybe she could give it back. "I'm not going to promise you my firstborn child or anything." She meant it as a joke, but that's not how it sounded in her ears.

Aeon giggled until tears rolled down his craggy cheeks. "Are they still telling that tale in Mortal lands?" He shook his head. "No, dear Lydia. What I want from you is far simpler still." He reached out his hand. "Just your friendship."

Lydia took a deep breath and clasped his calloused hand.

Aeon winked at her. "Hold on tight," he warned, and the maze whirled around them in a kaleidoscopic blur of green on green.

Shock nearly shook her free of his hold, but he tightened his grip, drawing her deeper into the heart of the maze. She slowed down her panicked breathing. If Aeon had wanted to harm her, he could have just trapped her in the maze.

"Ah," he said, "here we are."

The blurred colors resolved into an orchard on a compact green meadow. Looking around in delight, Lydia counted peach, apple, pear, and cherry trees, all laden with fruit, all ripe. Not a single rotten piece littered the ground.

"Welcome to my home," Aeon said.

"It's beautiful."

He blushed. "Thank you." Frowning, he cocked his head, listening for something Lydia couldn't hear. "We have to hurry. Your minders are starting to get annoyed with my pets. I don't want them to get hurt."

"Who? Deirdre and Galvin?" Lydia wouldn't mind seeing them on the receiving end.

"No," Aeon said, "my plants. Come with me. Use your magic and the hedges will hide you."

"How?" Lydia asked.

Aeon laughed once more. "You only need to ask," he said. "Ready?"

"Ready," Lydia said. This time she was prepared for the disorienting spin.

"Remember, ask the hedges to hide you," he said, winking at her. "I'll seek out your friends." He smiled and glided back into the maze.

The sound of voices carried through the thick greenery. Deirdre and Galvin weren't close enough for her to make out their words, but the tone was clear enough. They were annoyed and they were coming nearer. Aeon was nowhere to be seen. Lydia looked around, but there was nothing but the unbroken living walls of the maze. Taking a deep breath, she curled her hand around the gilded amulet. She hoped Aeon wasn't making fun of her. "Okay," she said, "can you keep them from seeing me?" The leaves rustled. She looked down at herself, but didn't feel any different. "Please?"

She could make out Aeon's voice greeting the two Fae. It was hard to tell, but she thought they were just a few turns away in the maze.

"Look. I don't know how to do this. They keep telling me I'm Fae and that I belong here. That I have this magic. And yeah, I've done a few cool things." She didn't quite believe she had been a tree, even if only for a little while. "But I need your help."

A strange hush settled around her, not erasing sound, but muffling it. A light wind peppered her face with rose petals. Aeon's high-pitched laughter rang out. They were here.

Lydia stiffened, her spine pressed up into the maze wall. The hedge softened at her back and tendrils of green twined around her, more hug than stranglehold. It was still weird, but not threatening. "Thank you," she whispered.

"Welcome, travelers," Aeon said, bowing with a flourish. "Can I offer you refreshment to ease the dust of your long road?"

"Oberon has you on too long a leash, gardener," Deirdre said. Lydia winced at the mockery in her voice.

"My leash is as long as my maze, and my maze as long as my leash," Aeon said. A vine trailed from his arm into the hedge.

"Where is the girl?" Pieces of torn leaves were stuck in her hair. Her face was flushed with anger or effort. "She is called for at court."

Aeon looked right at her and winked. Lydia shivered as Deirdre followed his gaze, but her cool eyes slid right past her. "Ask the trees, my dear," Aeon said. "They know." He beamed a wide smile and his eyes were full of mischief.

"Beware, Aeon. You mock your King," Deirdre said.

"I am what my King has commanded me to be," Aeon said, shrugging. There was a sadness in his voice that no one but Lydia seemed to catch. It was gone in a blink, replaced by the merry smile. "What revels has Oberon planned for our guest? A dance? A masque perhaps? Then I would ask leave to attend as a tree. As upstanding a citizen as can be found in all of Faerie." He straightened his bent frame to its full height and lifted his arms above his head, striking a dramatic pose. His outstretched arms barely reached the top of the maze walls.

Deirdre scowled. Even lined by anger, her face was too perfect, too beautiful. Lydia wondered if the woman looked like that, or if she was truly old and wrinkled like Aeon. "Lord Oberon commands your assistance in finding the child," Deirdre said. "He did not limit how we might compel your co-operation." She nodded to her silent companion.

Galvin drifted over to the hedge near where Lydia was hidden. He was so close, his breath warmed her face. She closed her eyes. "Don't let him see me, don't let him see," she thought.

"Open the maze, Aeon," Deirdre said.

"You did not say please," Aeon said, frowning.

"This is no joke," Deirdre said.

Galvin reached out and snared a branch in his hand. Where he touched, frost withered the green. Lydia shivered, feeling the hedge cry out in her mind.

"Lost and found, lost and found," Aeon sang, distracting the two Fae. A pulse of reassurance flowed from him to the greenery. "I know," he said. "If you get lost, then she shall be found!" He raised his arms again, but in a way that seemed at odds with his jovial buffoon image.

A green haze swam before her eyes and the walls shimmered. Lydia blinked and she and Aeon were alone in an open clearing. The long line of a tall hedge formed a border she could not see past.

Aeon clapped his hands. "We have sent them on a merry chase. The angrier they are, the more deeply they will lose themselves."

"I can't let them hurt you," Lydia said, stepping toward him.

He cocked his head and studied her. "You are worried for old Aeon and his plants? I have no standing at Oberon's court," he said, "not even as a tree."

"I don't like bullies," Lydia said.

A smile lit up his face. "Ah, child, whatever shall we do with you?"

Chapter 13

Clive paced the confines of his room. Aileen had brought them back to Faerie and slipped away before he could find the right words to ask all the questions whirling in his mind. It all came down to Lydia. Who was she, really? He tried to put the pieces of her story together, but there were too many gaps. He needed to find out about her parents, but it wasn't like he could just confront Oberon and ask him why he had them killed.

Had Oberon lied? Clive thought back to how all this had begun. "Bring back our lost kin and you will be rewarded," the Bright King had promised him. The rest had come from Oberon's mouthpiece. The Seneschal. Once, he must have had his own name, but it was lost even to the long memory of the Fae court. Oberon had sprawled on his throne, drenched in sunshine while the Seneschal gave Clive orders and deigned to answer his questions. Oberon had never directly said the Mortal girl was dead. What exactly had the Seneschal told him?

Lord Oberon found a Mortal family in pain and gifted them

with a child to love. The time has come for that gift to be repaid.

There was no lie. Only the ordinary deceit of the Fae. Clive should have known better, but his own desire had turned the questions he should have asked from his mind.

He had to speak with Lydia.

*

BY THE TIME DEIRDRE AND Galvin had fought free of the maze, Lydia was sitting in her rooms, sipping watered-down wine. She tucked Aeon's pendant under her shirt and forced a smile of welcome on her face.

The two Fae had cloaked themselves in their flawless glamour, but Lydia knew they were a little worse for the wear. She feared for the trees and hedges. If it came down to the Fae or the maze, she knew whose side she was on.

She stood as they approached her and waited for them to bow before inclining her own head. The run had done her a world of good and so had Aeon. This was a game of status and appearances. She could play that game. She'd been studying it all her life from the outside.

"I did not mean for my actions to worry you," Lydia said, keeping her voice level. It wasn't an apology exactly, and it was strictly true. She hadn't thought of them at all, only the need for space.

"We are pleased at your safe return, my Lady," Deirdre said.

Of course she was. Oberon would have the woman's head if Lydia were otherwise. Deirdre stood silently, fighting to hold onto an outward seeming of calm, but Lydia was sure that was just an illusion covering over a seething anger.

"Oberon would present you to the full court this evening at a masque in your honor," Deirdre continued.

Lydia's knuckles tightened around the wine goblet. Deirdre's mouth tipped into a brief smile. So her Fae nanny was watching Lydia as closely as Lydia was watching her. That would make tonight interesting. It would also be exhausting if she had to be this careful and this controlled with a whole party full of Fae.

"And what am I expected to do at this masque?" Lydia asked. She was beginning to understand getting anything out of the Fae was a cross between tug of war and twenty questions.

"You are Oberon's guest of honor," Deirdre said.

Lydia unclenched her jaw. "Yes, that's lovely. What must the guest of honor do?"

Deirdre laughed and there was anything but amusement in it. "Do? Why, Lydia, you shall dance and be celebrated by the entire Bright court."

So they would all be watching for her to make some stupid mistake. But why would that matter? She had no standing here to speak of. Who would care if she screwed up some old Fae protocol? The breath caught in her throat. This wasn't really about her. What had Clive told her? The Fae were about power and status. Deirdre was playing her own game. But who were the other players?

"And what would Lord Oberon have me do?" Lydia asked.

Deirdre's nostrils flared. It was like Aeon said. She had to ask the right question.

"You must glamour yourself in costume and dance with whomever asks," Deirdre said, her voice tight. "You must not give your name or seek your partner's name. At moonrise, the glamours will fall and Oberon will formally accept you in his court."

Great. A costume party. Lydia hated costume parties. And the last thing she wanted was to have to go to some Fae version of the high school dance. As if she didn't feel enough like an outsider to begin with. "What will you be going as?"

Deirdre smile broadly. "That I cannot say."

Lydia had a feeling there was something they weren't telling her, but she didn't know what else to ask.

"Until this evening," Deirdre said, offering a shallow bow before leaving the tent, Galvin following her silently.

Lydia drained the goblet and put it down with trembling hands. The wine's warmth burned a path down to her stomach. How the hell was she going to manage tonight? Looking down at her running clothes, she frowned. She had to glamour herself some sort of costume. The only Faerie she could think of was Tinkerbell. "Do you believe in Fairies?" she muttered and shook her head. Somehow, Lydia didn't think that was going to work.

This was worse than falling out of the sky and ending up in Oz.

Oz. A blue gingham dress and ruby slippers might be just the thing. And it wouldn't be simply the clothes. If Clive was right and she had turned herself into a tree, then changing herself into a young Judy Garland as Dorothy should be a snap.

She'd seen the movie enough times.

They'd just watched it a few months ago, Taylor snuggled in her lap. Lydia blinked back a flood of tears. "Focus, damn it," she muttered, swiping at her eyes. She had to get through tonight if she had any hope of getting back home. That meant figuring out how to use glamour, not just to change her clothes, but to change.

It wasn't so hard to accept she had magicked some running clothes. Especially after she watched Deirdre work the simple glamour. But it was another thing to admit she had altered reality so completely in the boundary forest. Pushing away the fear, Lydia forced herself to remember how it felt to actually be a tree. Her mind kept trying to shy away from the contradiction. If she was Lydia, she couldn't be a tree. If she had been a tree, then there was no Lydia.

And yet, the memory also brought a deep sense of peace. For a little while, at least, there was no pain and no loss. She had been part of the fabric of Faerie. Complete and connected. It was a kind of belonging she didn't have outside of her family.

It scared her to admit how much she craved it. And the power itself.

Lydia ran her hands through her hair. Time was running out and she couldn't afford to let Deirdre make her look like a fool.

Closing her eyes, she focused on picturing Dorothy, standing surrounded by munchkins, in full Technicolor. There was the capped-sleeved white shirt, the gingham jumper, the thick braids with blue ribbons, the wicker basket. Lydia tried to capture the same feeling she had when Deirdre stood over her looking distant and smug. A memory of warmth teased her like a summer breeze. She turned her head back and forth, searching for its source. It was the same warmth she sensed in Aeon's maze, when she followed its thread all the way to Oberon's court. Bright magic. It was all around her, floating in the air, shining in the light that filtered through the cloth of her pavilion, pressing against her closed eyes, and pulsing in the ground beneath her feet.

She only had to tap it, take it into body and let it transform her into an image of Dorothy.

Only.

The more she reached for Fae magic, the more natural it seemed. It was no part of the life she'd left behind. Aeon was wrong. It was Faerie that was changing her and she wasn't sure she could fight it. Or even how much she wanted to.

Goose bumps prickled the bare skin of her arms. Her sense of herself as Dorothy lost in Oz faded and she was only Lydia again, alone in a billowing tent.

If she couldn't do this, then Deirdre would win. She hugged herself tighter. Aeon had called Deirdre Oberon's lapdog, but if that were truly who she was, then she should do everything in her power to help Lydia, not leave her alone here to fend for herself with a magic she barely understood. The Fae woman's beauty couldn't mask her disdain. Why could Deirdre possibly hope to gain by having Lydia crash and burn?

If Fae glamour was difficult, then Fae politics were impossible. Lydia paced the room from one soft wall to the other. The sun angle was a lot lower than the last time she'd noticed. Nightfall was approaching and even if she didn't understand everything swirling around Oberon's court, Lydia did know she couldn't show up at the masque in her running shorts.

She wrenched her thoughts back to *The Wizard of Oz*. There's no place like home, she thought, smiling grimly before methodically rebuilding the image of Dorothy in her mind again. Dress, braids, basket. Lydia repeated them to herself like some sort of mantra. Dress. Braids. Basket.

Like water wicking from the ground through roots and into the capillaries that nourished a tree, Fae magic fed her. Her cheeks warmed and her skin shifted and pulled, molding her into something else. Something other. Something her imagination had created. Her heart beat faster, both from success and fear. The sense of herself as Dorothy wavered, threatening to collapse.

Lydia gritted her teeth and held on. She might not be as stubborn as Taylor, but Lydia was a Hawthorne. And Hawthornes didn't give up.

Before she opened her eyes, she knew.

She didn't think she could pull off Toto. But the red shoes? Lydia looked down at her feet. Dorothy's ruby slippers gleamed where her muddy sneakers had been.

She clutched the basket to her side and tapped her heels together once.

"Show time."

She stepped outside her small tent. The open area where Clive had brought her to meet Oberon earlier this morning was utterly transformed. Where there had been garlands of flowers, paper lanterns now draped along the gauzy fabric of Oberon's pavilion. Candles floated on the surface of a narrow river that snaked around a large, open dance floor. The golden throne was still there at one end. A band played on the far side of the dance floor. Classical music drifted through the warm night air.

Like everything else she had seen so far in Faerie, it was flawless; flawless and cold. Lydia never thought she would be nostalgic for the sound of Marco practicing his clarinet. She shook her head, pushing images of her family from her mind. This was not the time to be distracted.

Small groups of glamoured Fae stood talking and laughing on the edges of the dance floor. They glittered in the soft lantern glow. She looked for Clive, but even if he was there, how would she recognize him? The Fae around her wore elaborate gowns and formal wear from the past. Between the towering hair constructions and the layers of fabric and bustles, Lydia felt like she was in some weird Marie Antoinette look-alike contest. Some of the men were dressed in ancient military uniforms. Well, the uniforms weren't ancient, but the wars definitely were. Hose and breeches were common themes, but she even saw some kilts and a Roman toga or two. She shook her head. There were even a few Fae costumed as children from various centuries, but nothing from anything like Lydia's time.

She wondered how they would have reacted if she came in emo-black or even basic jeans and a hoodie, the uniform of high school students everywhere, but then it would be easy to guess who she was beneath the glamour. The only Fae who revealed himself was Oberon. He was dressed in a gold brocade tunic that would have looked at home in the court of Louis the Fourteenth. The sunburst design across his chest was repeated in the banners flying from the pavilion and the carpet leading to his throne.

Completely in character for him, she thought, and turned away from the Bright Court king and to the party. The Fae were twirling and sweeping across the dance floor in perfect time to the perfect music, their steps even. If anyone asked her to dance, she was a goner. It wasn't like she was clumsy or anything, but no one alive for centuries had danced like this. And even when they had, it wasn't with this almost-robotic precision.

Who would have thought—the Fae were all OCD.

Lydia hid a nervous giggle behind her hand and turned to the tables heaped with food and drink. The basket in one arm and a goblet in the other should have been a signal she wasn't here to dance.

"Milady?"

A Roman soldier was standing in front of her. He looked just like the toy soldiers Marco used to play with obsessively in elementary school. She'd suffered through his lectures enough times to be able to figure out who this Fae was supposed to be. He was wearing what looked like a silver skirt crisscrossed with a sword belt. She looked down at her jumper. He was showing more leg than she was. A flexible armored top clinked softly as he moved. The costume was literally topped off with a silver helmet that made him look like a peacock, a crest of what seemed to be an inch thick red broom stretched across the helmet from ear to ear. It was more than a little goofy-looking and she knew from the helmet and the sword at his left hip that he was dressed as a Roman Centurion. Having a war games geek as a little brother had never been a useful skill, until now.

"A dance, Milady?"

Lydia hated offers she couldn't refuse. Well, here goes nothing, she thought, setting down the basket and her drink. The music drifted to a stop to polite applause. The Centurion took her arm and led her to the center of the dance floor.

Great, she thought, I can't even disappear in the crowd.

The strains of violin and what sounded like a cross between a harp and a piano started up as the Fae took their places, couples lining up in an imaginary square. She tried to mimic the arm position of the Fae woman next to her. Just her luck, not only was it a dance no one alive had ever done, it was the equivalent of a line dance. So much for her disguise.

The dancers waited through a short musical introduction and at a signal Lydia hadn't picked up, her partner placed his right hand on her left shoulder and took her right hand in his left. Here goes nothing, she thought, as he swept her into a series of intricate steps mirrored by all the couples on the dance floor.

It was as if her feet had a direct line to the music, completely bypassing her brain. Her red shoes winked in the lantern light as they stepped and skipped along with her Centurion partner leading. After the first few weird moments, Lydia started to relax and let the dance unfold. As they whirled around, she caught a glimpse of Oberon watching her, his eyes glittering, a self-satisfied smile lingering on his face.

All the joy in the movement drained out of her. She was a freaking marionette and Oberon was pulling the strings.

Chapter 14

CLIVE TOOK HIS HAND FROM the wine goblet with regret. He could not risk the allure of drink tonight. He took a glass of peach nectar instead and sipped it as he walked around the party. Lydia could be anywhere or anyone. He scanned the crowd, but without too much hope of spotting her.

It had been a risk coming here. None of the court Fae would be able to see through his glamour, but Oberon was another matter. It was just an issue of whether the Bright King would care to notice or not.

Clive was betting on not. Tensions drifted through the night air in currents he could almost taste. Part of it was the effort each of the Fae was exerting to mask his or her identity. He could end up dancing with his mother and neither of them would know it. That was a thought guaranteed to sour his mood and his stomach.

He studied the dancers, getting lost in the blur of motion and color. Where was she? What would Lydia choose as her glamour? Certainly not what most of the Fae would clothe themselves in. He ignored all the golden gowns swirling around him. No, she would never pick anything as flashy as those. He knew Lydia. At least better than anyone in Faerie did. He had studied her for weeks even before he entered her school as her classmate.

A slim girl glamoured as a tree sprite glided past him, laughing. He watched her, wondering, before dismissing her. Clive doubted Lydia had come to terms with her adventure as a tree earlier. He was sure she wouldn't choose anything so directly connected with the Fae or Faerie mythology. A flash of color snagged his attention. A young girl in a blue dress was dancing with a Fae dressed as a Roman soldier, her red shoes sparkling as she moved.

He couldn't ask her who she was and risk Oberon's ire, but he could spend the time of a dance or two with her. Perhaps something in what she said would reveal her identity. And if it was Lydia beneath the young girl's glamour, he had little choice but to tell her Titania's truth.

The music ended and the couples drifted off the dance floor to the refreshments. The girl with the red shoes walked away from the Centurion, a polite smile on her face. Clive snagged a fresh goblet of nectar and handed it to her.

"Thank you," she said.

"My pleasure," he said. "May I have the honor of this dance?" It was a formality. Oberon enjoyed watching the dancers, so they would dance.

She nodded, finishing the drink. He took her arm and they began to glide to the formal strains of a waltz. Clive struggled to think of something to say that Lydia might know, would react to, but any of the Fae would see only as polite conversation.

"You look lovely tonight, Milady," Clive said. It was never wrong to compliment a woman of the Fae.

"There are many in more elaborate glamours, sir," she said.

"Yours is unique," he said, guiding her around the dance floor in the precise three-step movements of the waltz. The Fae had long memories and were ruled by the habits of their long lifetimes. If the choice were hers alone, Lydia might choose something like this. Something different. But what if Oberon or Deirdre had dictated her glamour?

"Is that a compliment or a criticism?"

Lydia might say that, but so might any of the court. "Oh, a compliment, lady, most definitely a compliment. Though not everyone here would see it as such."

"So you set yourself apart from court?" she said.

"Not so," Clive said, though in truth, he had never felt very much part of court life. They edged closer to Oberon. If Clive could have glamoured himself invisible without bringing more attention to them, he would have. He turned her in the dance, so his back was toward the throne. She frowned, and Clive wasn't sure if she was reacting to Oberon or to their conversation. The waltz was coming to a close and he still didn't know if this was Lydia. He fought the urge to grip her arms and call her name, uncomfortably aware of time sliding away from him.

*

HER PARTNER LED HER WITH the effortless grace of the Fae. He was clothed as a nobleman of some sort in a costume that would have been at home in a Shakespeare play. High boots ended well above his knee and his upper legs were wrapped in tights. Velvet pantaloons ballooned out over his thighs. It should have looked silly, but didn't. He seemed as if he always glided through life dressed as one of the Gentlemen of Verona or maybe a tragic hero out of Romeo and Juliet. Lydia forced a smile on her face. To anyone watching, she had to look like she was enjoying herself.

It would be simpler if he didn't keep trying to talk to her. What if she blurted out something that none of the Faerie court would every say? He was speaking again and she had to force her attention back to him.

"Would you care for refreshment?"

It would be a relief to get out of the line of Oberon's direct gaze. "Thank you."

She let 'Shakespeare' guide her to the tables laden with fruits, cheeses, and elaborate pastries. Groups of glamoured Fae stood flirting, goblets of wine in their hands. There was an edge of desperation to their laughter. Lydia knew she didn't want to be there. Could it be that they didn't, either? She wanted to ask her companion if he, too, wished to be elsewhere, but feared that anything except the Fae equivalent of talking about the weather would mark her as an outsider.

She had never felt more like an outsider before. High school was a group hug and warm fuzzies compared to Faerie. Lydia wished Clive, at least, were here.

Her basket was where she had left it and she hugged it to her side, comforted in a strange way by being Dorothy. At least at the end of her story, she woke up back in Kansas. Gazing at the dance floor at the Fae, hidden from one another and celebrating at Oberon's command, she shivered. As beautiful as Faerie could be, there was a coldness here, even in the midst of the Bright court and its revels. "There's no place like home," she whispered to herself.

*

HER WORDS ECHOED IN CLIVE'S mind. There's no place like home. He stiffened, his gaze darting around them, but no one else had heard her. It was Lydia. It had to be. It was what she had said in the Between, before bringing them through to the Mortal side. Five small words, but Clive was willing to stake his life on it. Home meant little to his Fae kin, but it meant everything to Lydia.

She was already drifting away from him. Clive lengthened his stride to catch up with her without seeming to rush. It was all about appearances. They had to seem to be immersed in the celebration, to enjoy the casual flirting the glamours encouraged. If he confronted her now, she would betray his presence to the court. He could risk nothing Oberon might notice.

"Milady, a moment," Clive said, letting his voice be merry.

She turned, annoyance flitting across her face before her polite expression returned.

"Surely, I can beg another moment before losing your beauty to another," he said, pitching his voice loud enough that others would hear. Many couples were pairing off, drifting to the edges of the large pavilion.

Lydia glanced into the shadows, frowning.

"Only a quiet moment, nothing more." He bowed as if she were royalty, sweeping off his hat and letting its feather brush along the ground. Time crawled by. If she refused his offer, she would have to push past him to rejoin the main festivities. If it came to that, he would have to confront her and hope she would not betray him.

"Of course," she said, but her body vibrated with unease.

He led her away from the lights and music and toward the stream that ringed the clearing. Oberon had glamoured benches at discreet intervals along its length. The bright gurgle of water over stones was artfully designed to cover the sound of soft conversation and private laughter.

"Please, sit. Be at ease." He took a deep breath as she perched on the edge of the bench. There was no way to avoid this. "Lydia," he said. Her eyes widened and her body stiffened. "Regardless of what you believe, I keep my promises."

*

SHE SCRAMBLED TO HER FEET, her basket dropping to the ground. "Clive?"

"At your service," he said.

"Where the hell were you all day? I thought you were sup-posed to be my guide. You weren't there when Oberon's babysitters were playing games with me."

He stared at the ground and she had to suppress a surge of pity. "I had no choice, Lydia. I cannot act directly against the Bright King."

"Then what do you want?" she said, and it came out far

more hostile than she intended. It was hard not to take out her frustration on Clive. Maybe he deserved it and maybe he didn't, but he was the only one of the Fae aside from Aeon who seemed to want to help her. She had been sure he was her friend, but now it was hard to know anything for certain when it came to the Fae.

He glanced around them. "Please, sit down."

"Why?"

"Think, Lydia. The only thing that protects us is illusion. That we are two glamoured Fae enjoying the anonymity of the Bright King's hospitality. I risk far more than you do here."

Even more than the pleading in his voice was the fear in his eyes. It was weird knowing this stranger with brown eyes and light hair was Clive, but then again, as far as anyone could tell, she was Judy Garland. She sat down, but the tension didn't ease. It was clear in the set of his shoulders and the lines across his forehead.

"Risk? When you're basically Oberon's darling for dragging me here?" she said, fighting another surge of sympathy for him.

Clive flinched, but didn't break eye contact. "There are things I must tell you, Lydia. But I also have a gift for you. A boon."

"What do you mean?" She felt the invisible weight of Aeon's pendant against her skin.

"It's complicated. And it's part of the reason I could not be here to fulfill my oath in person."

"Spit it out, Clive," she said.

He frowned again.

"It's an expression. Never mind. Just tell me." She gripped her hands together, hating how snippy she sounded.

"Nobody told you, but you may ask anything of the Bright King and he is oath-bound not to refuse."

"Anything?" She thought of her parents and her home with a longing that pulled her like a riptide.

"Anything that is within his power."

"I could go home," she said, hardly daring to believe it. She tensed to stand, ready to run back to court and demand it of Oberon.

"Wait, Lydia. It's not that simple."

"What do you mean?" she repeated, fear a cold lump in her belly.

"Have you not learned? Nothing is straightforward in Faerie. If you demand it, he will open the door, but Lydia—"

"So I can just leave? Really? And Oberon will just let me go?" She tried to lace her words with sarcasm, but even she could hear the yearning behind them.

"No." Clive turned away from her, but not before she saw the torment in his expression.

"What aren't you telling me?" she said, her mouth suddenly dry.

"You are already home."

"You've got to be kidding. This place will never be home."

"Lydia," he turned to face her and grabbed her arms. She was too surprised to jerk out of his hold. "That's not what I mean. You cannot return home because you're already there."

"You're not making any sense," she said.

"Listen to me," Clive said. "The mortal Lydia. The babe you

replaced. She is home in your stead."

"What?" Lydia felt the blood drain from her face. She was suddenly freezing cold. Clive was receding into the distance. Haze obscured the stream and the trees around them. It wasn't possible. The baby had died. Clive said so.

She stood up, shaking.

Oberon lied.

Fury and frustration spilled over her like a wave. She let it build, carrying her on a surge of pure emotion until she stood in front of the gold throne with no memory of how she got there. Silence rang in the place music had filled. The musicians and dancers stood stiffly, their faces devoid of any expression.

Oberon met her gaze with his. Her cheeks blazed. She refused to look away.

"You have troubled my revels," he said. If she hadn't been fixed by the fire in his eyes, she would have believed him only annoyed or even amused. He waved to the musicians. "Take up your instruments. Play." He nodded to his subjects. "Dance, enjoy."

She took a step forward, closer to Oberon. The corner of his mouth twitched.

"No," Lydia said. The stillness was so profound, she thought she could hear her own heartbeat. "This ends here." For all of Clive's assurance, everything in Faerie was a lie. The glamours and the false celebration. And now this betrayal. "I will never be one of you."

The fabric of fancy gowns rustled behind her. Oberon's face twisted into a rictus of rage.

"Through your own choice does the Bright Court claim you and its rightful tithe." He raised his hand toward her.

Clive gasped beside her.

"Don't touch me," she said, her voice a low growl. In place of fear was a choking anger. How dare he? She reached inside for the truth of who she was and ripped apart the glamour. It was simple, far easier than constructing the glamour had been. Warmth spread across her skin as her body stretched and settled into its familiar shape. "This is me. You can't take that away." Her muddy sneakers were more precious to her than any ruby slippers could be.

"You think not?" Oberon's eyes widened and two bright spots of red highlighted his bronze cheeks. He stood and walked toward her, his face utterly still. The rigid expression shook her more than his visible anger had. She stepped back as he advanced.

Lydia jerked to a stop as she backed into someone.

"Lydia," Clive whispered.

She whirled around. Clive stood as she had seen him that morning, dressed in jeans and a t-shirt like any normal high school kid. His eyes were open too wide.

Fae stood in groups of ones and twos, looking everywhere except at her. Their glamours were broken, too. A chill breeze pushed inside the silent pavilion.

"Run," he said.

Lydia turned and ran.

Chapter 15

LYDIA'S LEGS POUNDED AGAINST THE hard earth. The back of her neck prickled with warnings. She plunged into the darkness of the maze, praying that it would remember Aeon's promise of protection. Paths opened before her and she turned blindly, following wherever they led, losing all sense of time and distance. Her body felt awkward and unfamiliar. Stumbling with exhaustion, she fell to the ground sobbing, her lungs burning. If Oberon had followed her here, there was no use in bothering to get up.

She hugged her legs to her chest and rocked forward and back. Aeon's pendant swung free of her shirt and glittered in the moonlight.

"Not quite the party anyone expected."

She blinked up at Aeon's smiling face, his eyes almost lost in the deep wrinkles. He held out an arm, twig-thin, and helped her to her feet.

"How did you know?" she asked.

"All the trees in Faerie whisper their secrets to old Aeon." He looked away, listening for something in the distance. "You have caused quite a stir in the Bright Court."

"I'm sorry," she said, "I didn't mean to—"

Aeon interrupted her with a deep laugh. "When has that ever stopped anyone?"

Lydia shivered, her bare arms rippling with gooseflesh. "Can you help me?" She swallowed, shook her head and started again. "Will you help me?"

He cocked his head and smiled. "You are learning, child." He laughed again. "Now, which question shall I answer first?"

Lydia hugged her arms across her chest. Kind and jovial Aeon might be, but he was still Fae and still a member of Oberon's court. Resisting the urge to look over her shoulder, she listened carefully instead, but the only sounds were the soft chirrups of night insects and the rustle of leaves. Where was the Bright King?

Aeon leaned close to her. "Oh, he is out there, but he cannot come in this night unless I will it." His bark-colored eyes watched her with the patience of an old tree. "And," he said with a shrug, "I do not will it."

Lydia shook with cold and relief.

"There is no need for you to be uncomfortable, Lydia."

She was through with glamours. "This is who I am," she said.

Aeon studied her for a few moments. "Yes, there is much of you who is Lydia Hawthorne. But child, is not that just a glamour, too?"

She didn't know what to think. Part of what Aeon said was true. She was Lydia in the first place because of Oberon and

Fae magic. "I don't know," she said, close to tears again. "I won't go back to Bright." And then the tears did fall. "I can't go back home, either."

"My trees can only shield you for a little while," Aeon said.

"I can't stay here?"

"And garden with old Aeon?" He shook his head. "Nay, child." His face lost all of its wry humor. "If Oberon chooses, he can unmake the maze."

Lydia pulled away from him. "I'm sorry. I thought . . . It was stupid to come here." If Oberon blasted his way through the hedge walls, it would be her fault.

"Stay a moment. We are safe a little while yet. He does not know about our friendship and he'll not be eager to spend power against my tangled garden even for such a prize as you."

How strong was Aeon? And what did he mean by prize?

He smiled, but it had none of the innocent joy of his earlier greeting. "He believes you lost and cowering amongst my green pets. When the sun rises and his strength is renewed, he will deign to rescue you." Throwing his head back, he giggled. Distant owls answered him. "Do you not see the ending of his Faerie tale?"

Lydia shook her head, confused and uneasy.

"Oh, it is so perfect. And so perfectly wrong." Aeon took several deep breaths, quieting his laughter. He glided closer to her, leaning in to whisper. "At the end of Oberon's version of the story, you are helpless and grateful. Begging forgiveness, you will offer him your tithe and he lives happily ever after."

Tithe. Oberon had used that word before. In the Mortal world, she knew some people gave ten percent of their money to a church or charity. They called that a tithe. "What does he want from me?" She didn't have any money and besides, what would he need her money for? "I don't have anything to give him."

"Oh, but you have much for him to take."

There was hunger in Aeon's face. Lydia balanced on the balls of her feet, poised to run again, but where could she go? Forcing herself to take a deep breath, Lydia relaxed her knotted up muscles and gripped the necklace Aeon had given her.

He looked away, but not before Lydia saw the look of shame that flitted across his face. "Will you spend a little time in my garden, child?" he asked, his voice light and amused once more. "I have been a negligent host."

Lydia hesitated, trapped between threats she didn't fully understand. "What do you want from me?"

Aeon turned to lock her eyes with his. He stood still, waiting. Pressure mounted against her ears, like a silent thunderclap. The smile and the wrinkled face thinned and she saw through what she knew was glamour to another kind of truth beneath. He was still small and wizened, eyes a soft brown, but vines thick with black thorns wound around his throat and down his body. Blood dripped where they pierced his skin. When a drop touched the ground, a new green shoot reached up to him, twining around his legs. She barely had time to take in his torment when the image faded and the laughing gardener stood before her again.

Only the eyes had no mirth in them.

"My freedom," he said, answering the question that lay between them.

Her hands fluttered in the air in front of her. She wanted to reach out to him, but the image of the thorns burned in her mind. "Why?" she asked, her voice shaking.

Aeon's eyes glittered with unshed tears. "I am sorry. I have repaid kindness with obligation." He shook his head. "You owe me nothing."

"He did this to you," she said.

Aeon didn't answer. He didn't have to. Lydia knelt beside him and finally touched the side of his face. His eyes widened, but he didn't pull away from her.

"I swear I will find a way to help you."

"It is dangerous to make promises to the Fae," he said, his voice barely a breath of wind.

"I swear it," Lydia repeated.

Aeon shook his head, but Lydia ignored his unspoken warning.

"A third time, I swear it. By my name."

He winced. "Go, now. I will hold the maze against him."

"What will happen if he finds out you helped me?" She imagined the thorns slowly tightening around Aeon's throat and shuddered. "I can't let him hurt you."

Aeon laughed and his slender body shook with the force of it. "Oh, my dear child, he has no idea."

A flush of anger crept up her face. "Now you're making fun of me."

He laughed harder, until he was gasping for breath. Lydia fumed as he gained control of himself. "Go," he urged, "before the sun rises."

His changing moods made her dizzy. Now her heart raced

with the echo of his urgency. "What do you want me to do?" she cried.

"Shh," he whispered. "I have a secret even Oberon doesn't know."

She shook off her frustration and leaned in to listen.

"There are trees all over Faerie," he said, his voice solemn.

"How does that help me?" she said. He made her want to pull her hair out. Or maybe his.

He smiled. "My maze touches them all."

"Oh," she said, seeing a glimmer of his influence.

"Find the place Oberon has no power," Aeon said.

She rubbed her tired eyes. "And where is that?" she asked.

The silence of the maze answered her.

Aeon was gone.

"Great. Just great," Lydia muttered. "Crazy, old tree."

The full moon was directly overhead, shining into the maze with daylight's intensity. Too restless to stay put, she paced the narrow lane between the hedgerows. At one end, the path split into two possibilities, right and left. She looked down both green corridors, but there was no helpful neon sign. Nothing. Nada. Her pockets were empty, not even a coin to flip.

"Okay, then," she said. "Eenie meenie, minie, mo," she whispered, pointing from one direction to the other with each nonsense word. A game Taylor played. Her lip quivered and she bit it to keep from crying again. She was done with crying. ". . . and if he hollers, let him go . . . " She finished the rhyme pointing to the left and pushed herself into an easy jog. At each turn, she chose the opposite way. Better to keep moving. Find the place where Oberon had no power. Right. Well, that ruled out anywhere in the whole Bright court.

Lydia stopped so quickly, she nearly fell over.

What was the expression? The enemy of my enemy . . . She held to an image of icy perfection. Pale blue eyes. Night black hair. She had no idea where Aileen was, but if Aeon was right, it didn't matter. The maze would take her there.

She stood at a turning in the path and touched the pendant she wore. "The Shadow Court. Show me the way."

There was no wind, but the leaves and the hedges rustled. Green blurred her vision and she felt a familiar dizziness as the walls changed and spun around her.

A path opened up. At each turn, there was only one choice and she took it without hesitation. The moon followed over her shoulder as she spilled out of the maze and into a tangle of tall trees, their canopies spreading deep shadows against the night.

*

CLIVE SLIPPED FROM COURT, RETURNING to his mother's house in the aftermath of the party's dissolution. It was certain Oberon had seen him. What was less certain was what the Bright King would do in the face of Clive's trespass. He had not been formally banished, but it had been fairly clear he was not welcome to have free access to Lydia. Had they actually been seen together?

Beyond the confines of his rooms, his mother held her own kind of court. She would already be looking for a way to turn Oberon's humiliation to her advantage. Perhaps if her hatred of Oberon had been less overt, Clive's presence at court would have been more easily tolerated. But between his grand-mother's shame and his mother's constant sedition, he hadn't stood a chance. Deep into the night, Fae had arrived in ones and twos, not even bothering to mask their presence. The irony was not lost on Clive. He would only need to whisper a list of names into the ear of Oberon's Seneschal to gain status with the Bright King.

Clive paced the room. Its peace failed to soothe him. The trail of all his thoughts led back to Lydia. How had she broken Oberon's control? The look on the King's face was enough to raise gooseflesh along his arms even in memory. No one had openly defied the Bright King in more than Clive's lifetime. Not since Titania and the start of the war that had sundered the court and the peace of Faerie in two.

Fear washed through his body in a cold wave. Lydia was alone with all that hurt and all that power. In Faerie, like drew to like. There was only one place she could go, one place where her rage would be welcomed and nurtured.

Lydia was a weapon, ready to be aimed at Bright Court.

And he had been the trigger.

"What have I done?" he whispered.

"What, indeed, Clive Barrow."

Clive whirled around, his hands shaping themselves into claws. The Seneschal stood, the picture of calm and courtesy that was itself an impenetrable glamour. Clive forced himself to stand down. If Oberon had intended him dead, he would have already been feeding Faerie with his blood and power. "To what do I owe the honor, oh mouthpiece of Oberon?" Clive said, not bothering to mask the sarcasm.

"You are called," the Seneschal said, turning without looking back.

Clive suppressed a shiver. He followed, swept in the wake of Oberon's magic like driftwood in the tide. There was a bright spike of his mother's terror as the Seneschal tore through her bindings as if they were gossamer. The Fae attending her scattered and Clive sensed the Seneschal's amusement.

Outside, the moon had set. They were hours away from dawn and the power of the Bright Court was at its wane. The Seneschal outlined a doorway in the blackness. Oberon was spending his power even now. Spending it on him. Either Oberon wanted him awed or terrified. Clive wasn't sure which was worse. He followed the Seneschal into the Bright King's private quarters. The door sealed itself and became a gilded wall panel. There were no other exits.

Clive took in the rest of the sitting room with a single glance. Oberon lounged on one overstuffed chaise. A single table, carved from the heart of an ancient walnut tree held one goblet of wine. Clive stood, waiting for Oberon to attend to him, as the Seneschal took his place by the King's side, smirking.

"Bright has need of you, Clive Barrow," the Seneschal said.

Clive forced himself not to react. He kept his eyes on Oberon. The Bright King stared at Clive, his face unreadable.

"How can I serve, Lord Oberon?" Clive said.

The Seneschal started to speak, but Oberon cut him off with a single gesture. The Seneschal's look of fury was the only overt emotion in the room. Clive kept himself perfectly still.

Oberon spoke slowly, spacing out each word, his eyes glittering like a banked fire. "Bring her back."

"I know not where she has gone," Clive said, falling into the utterly careful, formal speech of court.

"Is that so?" Oberon said. Clive forced himself not to step back as the Bright King stood and walked forward. "You seem less than content in my court. Maybe living amongst the Banished would be more to your liking."

At this point, it might be a blessing to live apart from either court, but he held still and silent, certain only that Oberon had his own rules and his own game.

"You are an interesting one, Clive Barrow. But why should I be surprised? Your history is unique."

Clive pressed his lips into a thin line. It was no secret Oberon loathed his family. He could understand why his grandmother's betrayal would rankle, but Clive couldn't figure out why Oberon hated his mother so and she him. She was no more or less ambitious than any other Bright Courtier.

"If I cannot threaten you, then I must find another way to ensure your cooperation."

The room felt overly hot and close.

"Leave us," Oberon ordered. The Seneschal bowed and vanished.

Clive kept his eyes on the Bright King, watching him pace the room. He had been very, very careful. There was no way Oberon could have known what he'd told Lydia.

"She trusts you," Oberon said. "And I find I must put up with your insolence in order to get back what is mine."

Clive thought Lydia might take exception to that. On both

counts.

"There seems little enough I can offer you." Oberon's smile sent chills down Clive's spine. "And it appears banishment would provide me no particular leverage. Nor would punishing your mother cause you any great concern." He tapped his long, elegant fingers on the side of his face. Clive felt like a mouse being toyed with by a very large, very hungry cat. "Yet, perhaps I have a way to persuade you, after all."

Clive willed his body to remain motionless under the regard of dark predator's eyes.

"The Mortals place a large value on their families, do they not?"

Clive shifted his gaze around the room. The mirrored walls seemed to reflect an infinity of Oberons, but only one Clive. There was nowhere he could go and no way to challenge the Bright King. Oberon leaned close to him, fixing him with the power of his stare.

"Bring Lydia back to me and I will have no reason to seek out her Mortal family once more. I understand she is quite attached to her younger sister."

A rush of Bright magic brought heat to Clive's face.

Oberon smiled, lifting an eyebrow. "Have I discovered your motivation? How interesting," he said. "I shall have to tell the Seneschal that he has lost our wager."

"If you harm Taylor, you will make Lydia your enemy," Clive said, the memory of the sisters baking cookies vivid in his mind.

"I have no intention of harming the child." Oberon's laugh filled the room. "Is it not a high honor to be offered a place in the Bright Court?"

Oberon could bring the little girl here and in a very short time, any memory of her Mortal life would disappear. That, more than anything, would destroy Lydia.

Oberon shrugged. "If this concerns you, find my kin and return her to court." He did not need to add any further threat. The outline of a door shimmered in the air between them. "Can we count on your assistance?"

Clive bowed his head.

Oberon touched the door with his will. It solidified and swung open.

"Lydia will not be controlled so easily as I," Clive said as he stepped over the threshold. It was a small act of defiance, and likely a stupid one. He saw Oberon's eyes flash with anger before bright magic whirled him from the court.

Chapter 16

LYDIA WALKED OUT FROM BENEATH the canopy of trees. There was no flash or throne here in Shadow Court. A roofed gazebo, its sides made up of an open lattice woven with greenery reminded her of Aeon's garden. A quiet gathering of Fae sat beneath its shelter. She recognized Aileen and forced herself to edge closer, despite the flutters in her stomach. Ready or not, she thought.

Aileen stepped forward to meet her. "Welcome to the Shadow court, Lydia Hawthorne." Either her arrogance was gone, or else it was hidden beneath perfect Fae courtesy. At her nod, her companions faded into the trees at the edge of the clearing until only Aileen and one other Fae remained.

"Leave us, Aileen." A woman's voice, soft, but without any touch of gentleness, drifted through the cool night air. Here was someone used to being obeyed.

"As you wish, Lady," Aileen said. She bowed and vanished, leaving Lydia facing a statuesque woman covered head to foot by a night-dark hooded cloak.

Lydia dropped down to one knee. "Queen Titania." The Fae woman needed neither throne nor gaudy ornament to identify her. The power swirling around her was more than enough.

"Lydia Hawthorne," the Queen said. "An unexpected delight. Be welcome in my Court."

She rose, wiping her sweaty hands on the legs of her jeans. There wasn't a trace of irony in Titania's voice and that surprised her. Lydia wasn't sure what she had expected after her time in Bright, but this wasn't it.

"You must be weary. Come; let me offer you a place to rest."

The benches beneath the cover of the gazebo looked as comfortable to her as a soft bed, but she needed to stay focused. "I want answers, not courtesy," Lydia said. Fatigue and confusion left her punch-drunk. She pushed through caution and into recklessness, wincing at her harsh tone even as she kept speaking. "And I am not promising you my allegiance or anything. I'm not anyone's property."

Laughter rang out in the still night. Lydia was prepared for Titania's anger or mockery, even the threat of darklings if she didn't cooperate, but not this.

"Aileen was right. You are a bold one," the Queen said. "You must have driven Oberon quite mad. How refreshing."

The woman giggled, sounding more like a child than the ruler of half of Faerie. Lydia took a small step backward before she realized what she was doing. She stopped and straightened her spine. It wasn't as if there were many other places she could go right now. She needed a place to hide from Oberon long enough to figure out what to do next and this was it. If she had to bite her tongue, she would.

Titania slipped off her hood and shook out a river of long, dark hair. Even in the fading star glow and the dim light of paper lanterns ringing the gazebo, Lydia could see how beautiful the Queen was. She glanced down at her worn, grubby clothes. Titania had stepped forward so quietly that Lydia didn't realize she was there.

Tipping Lydia's chin up, the Shadow Fae ruler smiled down at her. "You have a loveliness that does not dim, regardless of the outer seeming you wear."

Despite herself, she warmed to the Shadow Queen's approval. Titania's expression sobered suddenly and Lydia wondered if she had done something wrong. There was something unnerving about Titania's rapidly shifting moods.

"I am sorry you had to hear the truth of Oberon's deception from another's lips," Titania said.

Lydia thought of Clive. She had left him to face Oberon's anger when she fled Bright.

"Please do not blame my messenger."

Her messenger? "I don't understand," Lydia said. "Clive answers to Bright." Was there such a thing as a Fae double-agent? Had he been manipulating her all along?

"He owes his tithe to Bright, but Clive Barrow had an older debt to repay Shadow. I chose the manner of his repayment." Titania laughed. "I suspect he is as caught between the courts as you are, my dear."

Lydia shook her chin out of Titania's hold. Despite the Queen's apparent courtesy and candor, she wasn't about to trust anything or anyone here. "Everyone seems to want something from me," she said. "What's your game?"

Titania laughed again, and again Lydia was startled. It was as if the Shadow Queen changed shape with every shift of the light. "You have much of Shadow's touch in you. But, then again, knowing your father, that is not surprising."

"You knew my father? My Fae father?" An image of her dad was so clear in her mind, she felt like she could reach out and touch him. Lydia closed her eyes briefly, knowing she had to let him go and find out as much about her Fae history as she could. So far, all she had done in Faerie was react to everyone else's choices—Clive, Aileen, Oberon, Deirdre, and even Aeon. Each of them had set her on a path. And now that path led her here. She could continue to be a pinball bouncing around in someone else's arcade or she could start making the game work for her.

"Will you sit and take your ease with me, Lydia?"

The annoyed part of her wanted to refuse and make Titania stand there all night, but Lydia was shaking with fatigue and the after effects of her emotional storm at the masque. Sitting would be a good thing. She nodded and followed Titania to the benches inside the gazebo. Starlight filtered through the lattice roof. The little lanterns winked like trapped fireflies.

"Can I offer you refreshment?"

She would kill for a cup of coffee, but she doubted they served lattes in Faerie. Titania seemed to be in a chummy mood and Lydia was going to take advantage of it. "Tell me about my father," she said.

"He was the brother of Aileen's mother."

"Oh." That made them first cousins, if the Fae counted family the same way. Aileen's sculpted features rose in Lydia's mind. They looked nothing alike.

"You may not favor him in looks, but I see his caution in you." Titania leaned forward. "But he was also reckless." She paused, meeting Lydia's eyes with her own, bright blue and glittering in the low light. "Perhaps that is why he was so vulnerable to Bright's temptation." Titania looked as if she'd tasted something sour. "And your mother stole enough from Shadow to hide her own intentions from both Oberon and your father."

"What do you mean?" Lydia asked. According to what Clive had told her, it sounded more like both of them had ulterior motives.

Titania's features softened. "Donal Burdock was a fool. He was foolish enough to defy me and then foolish enough to believe allying with your mother would ensure his safety."

Lydia turned the name over and over in her mind. Donal Burdock. She fought a wave of homesickness. Her father was Joe Hawthorne. He had nearsighted hazel eyes and graying blond hair and was more of a father than any flawless Fae courtier could ever be. Family was who loved you. She'd tried to tell that to her friend Emily once upon a time. Emily had blown up at her. "You can't possibly understand," she had said. Well, now Lydia could say she did, much good as that would do either of them now.

Titania's gaze and her curiosity held Lydia motionless. "You make it sound like Donal loved her." He would be Donal to her, not her father.

"Love? No, child. At least not the way Mortals understand it."

Lydia studied Titania's face. It was strange—the Shadow Queen seemed sad. She wasn't anything like Lydia had expected. And nothing like Oberon. "Can I ask you a question?"

"Of course. You are my guest here."

Taking a deep breath, Lydia struggled to figure out how to word it so she wouldn't cause some kind of international incident. "You and Oberon." She paused and Titania frowned. Lydia pressed on, afraid if she backed off now, she'd never get the answers she needed. "You were once . . . there was only one court. What happened?"

Titania looked past her into the darkness of the surrounding trees. "It was a long time ago."

Lydia waited as the silence took on weight around them.

"There was a time when Mortals were free to come and go at court and magic more easily moved between the barriers." Titania looked into Lydia's eyes with her piercing blue gaze. "We inspired generations of poets and artists, musicians." Titania trailed off, her eyes turning glassy and distant.

"Then what happened?"

Titania's expression turned cold. "We had a child. Oberon and I. He was what the Mortal physicians call stillborn."

She held her breath, not wanting to risk distracting the Fae Queen from finishing her story.

"All of Faerie mourned with me, but Oberon wouldn't speak of the babe." Titania searched Lydia's face. "You are but a child. You cannot understand my loss. Even then, there were so few born of the ancient Fae bloodlines."

An image of Taylor rose in her mind and Lydia had to blink back tears. Taylor wasn't her baby, but yes, Lydia knew about loss. Far better than the Fae seemed to, despite what Titania said.

"I mourned my lost child for many seasons and finally Oberon decided he had had enough."

Lydia was fascinated, despite her wariness. "What did he do?" she asked.

"He took a baby boy from a Mortal family and gave him to me."

Another family torn apart by Oberon's lies. Her stomach clenched. "What happened?"

"Thinking me distracted, he took one of my attendants for his lover. I left the child with her and never returned."

"The baby. What happened to the baby?" Her voice was low, insistent.

Anger danced in Titania's eyes. "I neither know, nor care to know. My child was gone and Oberon thought to placate me with a Changeling. As if one equaled the other."

A hot surge of answering rage pushed Lydia to her feet. It was hardly different than what Oberon had done to her family or the Fae had done with their half-Mortal offspring—change one child for another. As if. As if. Tears burned their way down her cheeks and it only made her madder. Now a stranger was living in her life, being the big sister, the daughter, and the friend. It was Oberon's fault. He had no right.

A breeze rustled the night dark leaves, tugging on Lydia's loose hair, and sweeping dust around her in a small whirlwind. The bottom of her feet tingled. The skin along her arms buzzed as if she were charged with static electricity. Thunder rumbled close enough for her chest to vibrate with the thrum of it. Heat lightning flickered around the clearing.

"I can show you how to aim your anger like a weapon," Titania said, her voice so close to Lydia's ear, she could feel the heat of the Queen's breath. The lost little girl was gone, replaced by something eager and brutal, her beauty only a thin mask. "I will take nothing from you that you do not freely offer. Neither true tithe nor allegiance. I only ask for your vengeance."

Lydia staggered as if she'd been hit. Raising her hands in unconscious defense, she stood and took a step away from the Shadow Queen.

Titania's face gleamed. "Do not deny your desire, Lydia. You have been grievously wronged. I feel you cry out for justice."

It wasn't justice she wanted, or at least not the kind the Fae seemed to offer. "I want my life back," she said, barely breathing the words. "I want to wake up in my room with its stupid rainbow wallpaper. I want to argue with my brother and complain about too much homework and not having a car." Lydia shoved a knuckle in her mouth to keep from crying out. The wind died. The trees stilled.

"You cannot unmake what Oberon has designed," Titania said, her words like the slap of sleet across bare skin. "But he can pay like for like. His pain for yours. For mine." The Shadow Queen smiled and Lydia swallowed, her body urging her to escape. Behind the elegance of Titania's features, the jeweled brilliance of her bright eyes, and the sculpted cheekbones, there was a madness eroding her perfect control. If Titania was a smoldering fuse, then Lydia was the spark.

She fought the urge to flee Shadow court and take refuge

with Aeon in his maze for however long she would be safe there. But that would mean placing the gardener in danger and punishing him for sheltering her. If both courts pursued her there, he wouldn't stand a chance.

And neither would she.

Titania studied her, trapping Lydia in her gaze for several long minutes as her heart galloped in a panicked rhythm. The Queen nodded, satisfied, and Lydia feared what she had seen in her.

"Then we are sisters in this," Titania said.

Lydia turned away so the Queen wouldn't see the answering fury in her eyes. She already had a sister. And she was going to find a way to get back to her. Even if she had to destroy Faerie to do it.

"We will speak again tomorrow," Titania said. "Lady Aileen will see to your comforts."

Aileen appeared silently at the mention of her name. Lydia searched her cousin's face, looking for anything familiar and seeing only the sharp planes and angles of the Fae. She touched her own face and wondered if they saw her as Fae or other now.

Lydia bowed, knowing the Queen expected it. Besides, she would gain nothing by being deliberately provocative here. When Lydia lifted her head, she was alone with Aileen.

"You burden us, cousin."

"Excuse me?"

"You will not offer your tithe to our Queen, yet you will take her protection and her hospitality, leaving others to pay the cost."

There was no emotion in Aileen's voice. No anger or hurt. That chilled her more than the words themselves. "Look, I don't want anything from you people."

"That is not true. You fled here from Bright. At the very least, you seek safe harbor, food, and shelter."

"I didn't ask for any of this," Lydia said.

Aileen met her gaze without blinking. "It was your decision. You chose Bright," she said. "When you realized you had chosen poorly, you came to us of your own free will."

Lydia felt her cheeks flush and she turned away. In a way, Aileen was right. She was using the Shadow Queen. But then again, wasn't Titania using her?

"Come. My Queen bids me to attend to your needs."

Lydia followed her from the clearing and through a pergola formed by a row of curved saplings. Aileen had been perfectly polite. And perfectly obnoxious. As they walked in silence, Lydia's mind churned, looking for just the right comeback. Something that would cut through Aileen's composure. But fatigue made it hard to think straight. She stumbled and would have fallen, but for Aileen's firm hand on her arm.

"Thank you," Lydia said. Automatic courtesy asserted itself almost before she was aware of the words in her mouth. Her parents were easygoing about most things, but pretty strict when it came down to what they called "the niceties." Please. Thank you. Excuse me. By the time Lydia had been Taylor's age, she had been well-drilled in how to be polite.

"You are not what I expected," Aileen said.

It almost felt like an apology.

Lydia paused at the walkway of what looked like any of the

houses in her neighborhood. For a confused moment, she thought they must have left Faerie. "Where have you taken me?"

"We thought it would be more comfortable for you to rest in familiar surroundings."

She frowned at Aileen, unable to figure out if the Fae was patronizing her. Lydia walked inside and had to bite her tongue not to call out her usual, "Mom, I'm home." It seemed so terribly normal that she wanted to collapse in the hallway and weep.

Aileen opened the door at the top of the stairs into the image of Lydia's own bedroom at home. Her knees buckled and she grabbed the door frame for support. It had been less than one full day since she'd walked out of this room and into Faerie. One day ago, the thought of turning herself into a tree, or learning to create a glamour would have been something out of the fantasy books she used to read as a kid. Oberon and Titania had just been characters in a Shakespeare play. She was once simply Lydia Hawthorne, hoping to finish her senior year relatively unscathed.

The pulse pounded in her ears. "I can't. I can't do this." Lydia heard her own voice from far away. Strong hands gripped her and wouldn't let her leave. She struggled against their hold in a blind panic, struggled to breath, as if all the air had been sucked from the room. Small animal sounds escaped from her throat as she thrashed her head back and forth.

"Lydia!"

The sound of her name was like a slap. She took a shuddering breath and forced her body to stop fighting. Aileen's hands fell away.

"No. This is not my home," Lydia said. As the adrenaline washed out of her system, a wave of cold raised goose bumps along her arms. She reached out and tore through the Shadow court glamour with a thought, leaving them standing in a small, elegant room with a carved wooden bed and a small hearth.

Aileen took a step back, her eyes wide. She took a deep breath. "I will return in the morning with refreshment," she said, backing out of the room, her voice low and shaky.

Lydia stumbled to the bed and collapsed, her hands trembling.

Chapter 17

THE WHISPER OF TREES BROKE the pre-dawn silence as Clive paused to catch his breath. Hedge walls cast their long shadows through the maze. He would either have to fight through its tangle or hope that Oberon had smoothed the way for him. Given the Bright King's fury, it would probably be the former. That anger masked the real truth: Oberon was afraid.

That alone gave Clive pause. He thought back to the girl he had first seen: mouse-quiet, hidden behind plain features, and utterly ignorant of what lay beneath and between the life she understood. She was worlds away from that girl, and growing in power. Power that Oberon wanted to control, but the Bright King's mistake was in confusing Lydia with the meek disguise he had created. Now she was loosed upon Faerie and no one, not even Clive, who knew her best, could predict what she might do.

But not where she would go. There was only one place Lydia would turn after leaving the Bright Court. Now all Clive had to do was to figure out how to get into Shadow to find her. Aileen had managed to slip inside the boundaries of Bright Court without raising the alarm, but she had been shielded by Titania. Oberon had offered him no such protection and Clive would rather not have to face the Shadow Queen again.

"Clive Barrow, do you do our King's bidding, or your own?"

He whirled and stood face to face with Oberon's mad gardener. Clive exhaled his relief. Unlike most of the Fae, Clive liked Aeon, despite the number of times he had gotten lost in this maze. He looked down at the trail of vines tying the ancient Fae to his garden. His own ties to Bright were less overt, but no less constricting.

"For the moment, both my desires and my King's run together." It was best to answer Aeon carefully. His help could be the difference between finding Lydia quickly and not finding her at all.

"Often the safest course," Aeon said, nodding. "Have you come to pluck my secrets from me?"

"No," Clive said. He smiled, remembering. Fae children dared one another to slip into the maze and return with the fruit of one of Aeon's trees. It was the rare child who escaped with such a prize. When Clive had braved the garden, he had gotten all the way into the orchard Aeon maintained at its heart. What he had never told another Fae was that he held one perfect plum in hand before deciding to leave it on the branch. Clive had trailed vines and the sound of Aeon's mocking laughter halfway home. "I would ask your help," Clive said, "but I will not compel it."

"Aren't you an interesting one." Aeon cocked his head and winked. "I knew your grandmother," he said, his eyes nearly disappearing in smile wrinkles.

Clive had never met her, but it seemed just about everyone else in Faerie had. Certainly she had cast a long shadow over his life that he hadn't ever been able to shake. "Please. Don't tell me how like her I am." His mother had never spoken of her. All he knew was that she crossed into Mortal lands to quicken with child. She returned to stay amongst the Fae just long enough to wean her daughter before leaving Faerie for good.

"But you are, you know."

Clive shook his head. Aeon delighted in riddles, but this was not the time or place for traveling the twists of the gardener's mind.

"But you are nothing like your mother."

Clive took a deep breath, quelling the urge to strangle Aeon in one of his own vines. His mother wasn't the issue here. "I need to find Lydia," Clive said slowly. "Will you show me the way?"

"Poor Myra, always supping on the Royal crumbs. Not the future Oberon had promised her when she was saddled with a babe to suckle." Aeon tapped Clive on the chest three times before trailing his fingertip along the edges of a nearby branch. New green shoots sprang from the ends and leafed out as he watched, his heart tingling from Aeon's touch.

Now Aeon was simply baiting him. It was no secret that he and Myra shared little good will. He had gotten barely more than nourishment and a room to sleep in from her. Poor mothering, even by Fae standards. Perhaps this was some test of Clive's patience, but he had neither the time nor inclination to play Aeon's game. "I'm certain my family is of endless fascination, but I must follow Lydia."

There would come a moment when Oberon's hunger would overwhelm his caution and he would send others to find her. If representatives of Bright pushed into Shadow, the covert war between the courts would erupt into an overt one. If he could remove Lydia from both courts, he would remove the source of so much temptation. One step at a time. First, she had to actually agree to speak to him.

"I have given you something," Aeon said, shaking a finger at him and laughing. "A puzzle to solve. Now you must go and seek Lydia Hawthorne."

Clive wanted to shake the mad little Fae. He forced his hands to unclench. "Yes, that is my intent."

"Lydia left the shelter of my trees some time ago, but I see that doesn't surprise you."

"I know she has gone to Titania. I must find her," Clive said, though that was not really the biggest issue. Whether or not she would hear him out was the real problem.

"And what would you do then?"

Clive closed his eyes briefly, seeing Taylor's bright, pleading eyes. "I have a message from her sister," he said. The card was tucked into his pocket. "And a warning."

"And what of Oberon?"

"What of him?" Clive said. He hadn't actually agreed to do the Bright King's bidding; he only took the door offered. "I am oath-sworn to Lydia Hawthorne. Beyond that, if my path takes me where Oberon wishes me to go, well . . . " He shrugged, spreading out his hands. "I will not force her to return to

Bright."

"My trees whisper their secrets to me. Lydia knows something," Aeon said.

"Lydia knows many things," Clive said. "But she doesn't know what I am bound to tell her."

Aeon touched a finger to the side of his nose. "She knows something you don't know," he said in a child's sing-song. "Something about a Changeling."

"She is the Changeling," Clive said. And so was the Mortal Lydia. Oberon's deceptions had bound them all.

"But not the only one," Aeon said, staring at him.

Aeon had been trapped here alone far too long with only his trees to talk to. It wasn't his fault if his thoughts wandered as twisted a path as his maze. Time was running out. Clive ran his fingers through tangled hair. "Show me where she crossed into Shadow. Before our King loses patience and tramples through your garden." He had no idea how he was going to safeguard Lydia and prevent Oberon from taking her sister. The stars above the maze were fading in the approach of dawn.

"Ahh, you and your Lydia, both worried for old Aeon." He beamed and although he staggered under the weight of Oberon's task, it was hard not to smile back at the gardener. "Follow the turns and do not stray from the path." Aeon leaned closer, squinting his eyes in concentration. "You have a touch of Shadow about you. The passage should not be overly difficult."

Titania must have marked him, somehow, when he agreed to her task. "Your aid is well met and most welcome, milord," Clive said, using the formal language usually reserved for court. Aeon's eyes widened, but he quickly masked his surprise with an equally formal bow. The little, twisted man faded into the greenery and Clive was alone. As he watched, the walls of the maze blurred and reformed. He followed, leaving the tangle of Aeon's riddle for another time.

It was as the gardener had promised. The way eased open for Clive at each turn and as the sun rose, he stood at the threshold of Shadow. It was at least auspicious timing. Bright magic would be waxing as Shadow's waned. Perhaps he would be able to slip into Titania's court unremarked.

So often in Bright, Clive was beneath notice. He used the painful memories of disdain not to make himself invisible, but simply unimportant. Letting Bright magic sink into Faerie's thirsty ground, he kept only a trickle of it to feed the illusion. It would render him defenseless, but being overlooked would be his only true security. To enter Shadow otherwise would be folly—Bright magic would only betray his presence.

Clive shivered as Faerie eagerly drank in what he offered. It would only be for a short time. One more step and Clive would be in Shadow. He moved away from the shelter of the maze. Even with his power damped down, he felt a jolt spread through his body from feet to crown as the wards of Shadow recognized him as belonging to Bright. The static charge dissipated quickly, leaving Clive lightheaded, but unscathed. Aeon must have been correct about Titania's touch.

With the sun rising in front of him, Clive was light-dazzled, as well. He shook his head to clear it. Now that he was here, how would he find Lydia?

He caught a flicker of shadow on shadow out of the corner

of his vision. Blinking, he tried to clear his eyes and turned to see what had followed him through the maze. It was doubtful it was Oberon, but he would believe the Bright King had sent his Seneschal after him. Oberon didn't trust him, after all. No surprise there.

A dull buzzing was his only warning before a living shadow completely blocked out the sun and filled Clive's mind with a familiar stifling blackness. Darklings.

They wove a dark net tighter and tighter around him while Clive struggled to break free of their stranglehold.

He toppled to the ground like a felled tree.

A steady pounding in his head competed with nearby shouting, forcing Clive to full wakefulness. Titania had turned her darklings on him and he was the fool who had divested himself of most of his power at Shadow's threshold. He had been far too clever for his own good.

Clive opened his eyes, blinking in unexpected bright light. He was outside, lying on hard ground at the base of a weeping willow tree. Closing his eyes against the aggressively cheerful sun, he tried to focus on the raised voices.

". . . risk using them again." The Fae speaking was unfamiliar, his voice hoarse, the words clipped.

"Who are you do decide what we dare risk?" a woman answered. It was neither Aileen nor Titania. Other voices called out, some supporting the first speaker, others agreeing with the second.

The man raised his voice, cutting off the argument. "It is not my fault that the darklings captured the wrong prey."

Clive had to force his body not to jerk in his surprise.

"We don't have enough power to send them out again today," the woman said. "Unless you have reserves the rest of us do not know about." Her voice was thick with suspicion.

What was going on?

"I think our guest is awake," she said.

Feigning sleep wouldn't get his questions answered. Clive rolled to sitting. "To whom do I owe this debt of hospitality?" He imbued his words with as much sarcasm as he could, given his position. He looked up into green eyes set in a haughty face framed by shoulder-length blond hair.

She smiled, deliberately ignoring his question.

"What is a Bright Court lordling doing sneaking into Shadow, I wonder," she said.

"I have a debt to the Shadow Queen that must be repaid," Clive said, not wanting to say more than he had to. Derisive laughter surprised him.

"And you expect us to be impressed?" The man said, pushing the woman aside and stepping forward. She gave him a sharp look.

"I expect you to honor your Queen's wishes," Clive said.

That provoked a fresh round of laughter. The man crouched by Clive's side, staring him down. He had pale gray eyes and hair the color of silver, tied at the nape of his neck.

"You think you are in Shadow?" he said. "Look around you, Bright Lord. Does this look like a Fae court?"

Clive looked past the knot of Fae surrounding him into a wide clearing ringed by scraggly pine trees. Simple wood frame cottages were partly hidden in the greenery. Both the houses and the Fae seemed drab and worn. He pushed outward, searching for signs of glamour, for evidence of other hidden structures, but either there was none, or else his brush with the darklings left him too weak to tell.

"Who are you?" he asked, studying his captors. They were an odd assortment of Fae—young and old, dressed in raiment from different places and times. Some were clearly from Bright court, others wore clothing from Mortal lands, but nothing Clive recognized as current from his last visit across the realms.

"Bind his eyes and send him back to Bright," an old woman said. Her face was deeply lined and she looked as ancient as Aeon. Clive didn't think she would share the gardener's wry humor.

"But why was he in Shadow?" the silver-haired Fae said. "I would sooner believe I could wield iron than believe the King and Queen reconciled."

The rest of the gathered Fae laughed. Clive frowned, thinking of Lydia.

"Tangle his thoughts and send him on his way, Isidore," the blond Fae said. She looked as if she were used to scowling. "This ends badly for us."

There was a murmur of agreement, though not as loud as the earlier laughter.

Isidore shook his head. "You let your fear talk, Callie. I think our guest offers us an opportunity."

"And when he recovers from the darklings' touch? No, he is no outcast. This is one of Oberon's."

"Callie speaks true," the old woman said, glaring down at Clive. He resisted the urge to wink at her. "We risk too much keeping him here. Send him back now, before he learns enough to pose a threat."

Others in the group nodded their heads. Clive sat still, thinking harmless thoughts.

"You worry too much," Isidore said. "I simply wish to speak with our guest. If you are so concerned, stay, though I am certain most of you have better things to do." The assembled Fae left the clearing in ones and twos until only the two leaders were left. Callie glared at Isidore. He looked back at her, his face calm. "He poses no threat to us now and later when we are restored . . . "

Isidore shrugged and Clive stared at him, wondering what he meant. He pressed his back against the willow's trunk. Wherever he was, it was still Faerie and he could replenish his magic. The darklings had drained him, but only of the little power he had let himself retain. When he needed to, he could return to strength. Clive let Faerie continue to drink his magic for now. Better to let them think him powerless.

"So, you have our names. Give us the courtesy of yours, Bright Lord," Isidore said, the model of Fae civility.

"Clive Barrow," he said, though he thought it unwise to tell them his true status in Oberon's eyes. "Am I a prisoner here?" Clive kept his focus on Isidore and Callie.

Isidore frowned. "I prefer to say guest."

"Yes, I am sure you would," Clive said. Certainly, they could have bound his hands and feet as he slept. Either they thought him harmless or themselves firmly in control. Perhaps it was a little of both. He studied the two of them more closely. They were not of the same bloodline, and he couldn't tell if they carried Bright or Shadow magic.

"Have you figured out where you are?" Isidore said, smiling as he stood up, looking down at him.

"You are the Banished," Clive said. They were the outcasts of the Fae. Those with little power and less standing with either monarch. Where Oberon had threatened to send him. The irony almost made him howl with laughter.

Anger flashed in Callie's green eyes and her light hair fanned outward as if touched by lightning's static. "We prefer to call ourselves Unbound," she said. "We bow to no Fae and you do not threaten us, Clive Barrow of Bright Court."

"I mean no disrespect, milady," Clive said, raising his hands before him, palms out, empty.

"None taken, none taken," Isidore hastened to say. Callie glared at them both and Clive knew that while Isidore thought himself the leader here, Callie was the one he had to be most wary of.

Clive's thoughts whirled like leaves caught up in a dust devil. "The darklings. You sent them." It hadn't been Titania at all. The attack on the bus—that wasn't Shadow court's doing, either. It was them. The Unbound. What were they playing at?

"You haven't said why you were in Shadow, Clive," Isidore said.

"That is true," Clive agreed, adding nothing more.

"You are not as clever as you believe," Callie said. "There is no way back for you unless we will it."

"Callie," Isidore warned. She shot him a smoldering look and he took a step away from her.

Clive felt for the living pulse of the tree at his back. If he closed off the siphon, they would certainly sense the stirring of his Bright magic. But if he kept himself vulnerable, he might not survive should they act against him now. And then there were the darklings.

Callie and Isidore were both watching him. Reluctantly, Clive pushed away from the tree trunk's support. Any show of strength here would be a risk. All the reasons he masked his magic at the threshold of Shadow remained even more valid here. The less of a threat he posed, the more he could discover.

He again spread out his empty hands and stood slowly. "I am only a messenger. My own place in the court is less than certain." The bitterness in his voice was sharper even than he had intended. "If I cannot deliver my message, then I make an enemy of both courts." And for different reasons. For a moment, he envied these Unbound Fae.

Callie raised an eyebrow. "No spoiled court favorite here," she said. "You interest me. Perhaps you are one of us, though you do not yet know it."

Clive closed his eyes. She didn't know how close she was to the truth of it. How easy would it be to turn his back on Bright forever? "And if I align myself to you? What then?"

"Then you can help us bring the Changeling here," Isidore said.

Lydia. They were seeking Lydia. Clive forced himself not to react. Of course. They must have been searching for her when they snared him instead. "Oberon has sent me to bring her back to Bright."

"Then we must oppose you," Callie said.

If it came to that, they would be obliterated. None of the

Fae here could possibly withstand Oberon if the Bright King chose to turn his power against them.

"I see that you doubt us." Isidore smiled. "Dross of the Fae courts we may be, but we are not completely powerless."

"Isidore," Callie warned, shaking her head.

They had commanded the darklings. Clive knew the amount of magic that required. It was why he had assumed Titania had sent them against Lydia. Neither Isidore nor Callie alone could have that kind of power or control. He looked from one to the other, his mind drifting back to the snippets of conversation he had overheard as he was waking from the Darkling's touch. "You tithe power." They had formed a court of sorts.

"No, no tithe," the old woman said, her eyes flashing. "We do not suck the life from one another."

No. They saved that for strangers, he thought, biting back the sarcastic reply.

"The courts have nothing but disdain for us, but we have learned to pool our small magics," Isidore said. "Together, we are able to hold the wards that keep us hidden and command the darklings at need."

Clive hadn't thought that was possible. "You sent them after Lydia."

Callie's eyebrows lifted. "The Changeling?"

He stared directly at her. She was the one he had to convince. The irony of representing a court that treated him only with contempt filled him with frustration and bitterness. "Oberon may command my tithe, but I am oath-sworn to her. To Lydia."

Isidore and Callie looked at one another and shared a moment of silence. "We have more in common than you know," she said.

"I don't understand."

"There was another with that name," Callie said. "She took refuge with the Unbound for a time after Oberon tired of her."

The Mortal girl. So this is where she had been. No wonder Titania hadn't been able to find her in Faerie.

Callie shook her head. "Oberon lured her back to Bright and she ran to him like a starving cur."

"She is no longer in Faerie," Clive said.

"As we surmised."

"Lydia—the Fae Lydia. Why do you seek her?"

"Is it not obvious?" Callie crossed her arms over her chest. "What happens to us if she allies herself with either of the courts?"

There would be war and the Unbound's wards would never hold against the massed will of both rulers. Trapped in the conflict between Bright and Shadow, Faerie itself would be drained dry. An image of felled trees and soil crumbling into dust shook him. This was his doing. In convincing Lydia to choose Bright, he had brought this to be.

Callie gripped his shoulders with both of her hands. "Something disturbs you."

The warmth of her touch helped the fear retreat. "I cannot let it happen." Another promise leapt to his lips. Another oath to tangle with the myriad of oaths he had already sworn. He was bound as helplessly as Aeon. "I will help you."

She let her hands fall away. "And how can we trust your

word?"

If he was the Bright Court emissary Callie saw him as, he wouldn't trust himself, either. "I have no way to convince you. Only let me go to her. I swear on my name, I will bring her to you." He had promised Lydia safety. Perhaps now, he could fulfill that promise.

Callie studied him with unblinking eyes. He met her gaze with his own, not challenging her, but with an openness that frightened him almost as much as the war he hoped to prevent.

"Isidore, this is not for you or me to decide alone."

"We will meet in the council house." He touched Callie lightly on her arm. "Come, we must gather all the Unbound."

She nodded, but shook off his hold, waiting until he left before pinning Clive with her gaze once more. "He believes it is our wards that keep us safe. I know better." Her scrutiny didn't waver. "We survive only because we are beneath the courts' notice."

Clive nodded. "I understand."

"Do you?" Callie asked. "Truly? If you bring her here, then war will come to us, anyway."

"You are willing to risk this for her?"

Callie laughed a crow's mocking laugh. "No. I risk this for us."

"You would use her just as they would."

Color flushed her cheeks before she turned away. "Do you know why we are here?"

"Tell me."

"I was only a small child when I followed a swarm of

dragonflies out of my yard and into Faerie. I cannot remember my mother's face, but I remember her hands braiding my hair. Oberon made me a darling of the court, until I came of age."

Clive stared at her, the hatred and longing in her voice painful to hear.

"I could not command enough magic to offer sufficient tithe to remain at court and by then, I was more Fae than Mortal." She laughed again. "Besides, even if Oberon had opened the way back for me, my Mortal family was long dead and turned to dust."

Until he had met Lydia, Clive had never questioned how the Fae survived. "You must hate him."

Callie's eyes flew open. "I hate myself," she whispered.

He wanted to reach out to her, but he had no guide for this kind of comfort. "Why do you seek the Changeling, then?" he asked, filling the silence with something.

"We are trapped here, neither Fae nor Mortal. It must end."

Clive felt as if he were corralled in one of Aeon's blind turns. Any direction he chose was wrong. Bright, Shadow, and even here, in the twilight that was no court and only half a life, Lydia would be someone's weapon.

Perhaps it was time for her to choose.

Chapter 18

LYDIA WOKE FROM TANGLED DREAMS where she was trapped in Aeon's maze, unable to find her way home. Right. No hidden symbolism there. The room was as she left it late last night. At least Aileen hadn't tried to reinstate the glamour Lydia had broken.

A soft knock startled her and she had to force herself not to grip the edge of the blanket. "Come in," she called, pushing herself to sitting.

Aileen walked inside carrying a small basin of water. "Milady bids you a good morning and wishes to provide for your comforts."

"Thank you." Titania may have been a few food groups short of a balanced meal, but she didn't freak her out as much as Oberon did. When she thought of what Titania had gone through, she felt sorry for her. Just not sorry enough to take her side against Oberon. Lydia didn't want anyone's side. She just wanted to get her life back.

"Milady provided some fresh clothes for you as well." Aileen gestured at the stack of clothes neatly folded at the foot of the bed. More glamour. It was hard to tell what was real and what was illusion. It didn't seem to matter to the Fae.

"When you are ready, I will be waiting outside to escort you to the Queen."

Lydia reached for the basin and set it down. The warm water was lightly scented with lavender. A door she hadn't noticed last night led to a dressing room with a chamber pot. She sighed. Indoor plumbing would be a lot more enticing than any Fae glamour. After washing up as best as she could, Lydia looked at the clothes Aileen had left. An ankle-length silk shift in alternating panels of black and midnight blue. The Queen's colors, but certainly not hers. Lydia wondered how much of an insult it would be not to wear it. Frowning in concentration, she looked down at her jeans.

This was what she had worn to meet Oberon. It would have to do for Shadow court, as well. Dirt from Aeon's garden stained the knees. Brushing at it only ground it in further. Holding on to her own sense of herself was one thing, but showing up filthy was another. It wasn't like there were any convenient washing machines in Faerie. She glanced at the basin of mostly clean water, but even if she scrubbed them, there wouldn't be enough time for her jeans to dry before Aileen brought her back to Titania.

She would have to use glamour to clean them up. Trying to ignore the unavoidable irony, she smoothed her hands down the faded material, watching the denim brighten. A crease edged itself along the front of her pant legs. The frayed cuffs and thin knees knitted themselves whole again. Closing her eyes briefly, she refused to think about how effortless that had been. She folded up the formal clothes and left them on the bed. Insult or not, glamoured or not, she would wear what she was comfortable in. A small rebellion, but it helped soothe the unease.

Aileen frowned as Lydia walked out to meet her. She was probably annoyed about the delay and the clothes, but there wasn't a thing she could do about it. It wasn't like Faerie had a dress code or anything.

They walked in silence along the dirt path that meandered around a grove of hemlock trees and back beneath the living pergola. Now that it was daylight, Lydia could see the severe simplicity of Shadow court. Where Oberon dazzled, Titania was understated, her subtle magic reinforcing the message that there was more here than could be easily seen. Lydia felt the hidden buzz and thrum of the Queen's power in every stone and leaf. She couldn't let the apparent peacefulness blindside her.

Their footfalls made little sound on the carpet of pine needles. "Why have you come here?" Aileen asked.

"What do you mean?" Aileen was the one who had tried to get her to choose Shadow in the first place.

"You have no love for my Queen. You offer her nothing but reminders of pain and vengeance denied."

"I have nowhere else to go," Lydia said, looking down. She scuffed at the dirt with her sneakers. "Oberon made sure of that."

"You are Fae. Trueborn." Lydia looked up into Aileen's narrowed eyes. "This is your place. You have the chance to add your power to the court of your choosing and change the balance in Faerie forever. Instead you whine and mewl about your precious Mortal life."

A surge of anger tightened Lydia's throat. "You don't know anything about me," she said, her words clipped.

"I know you give Titania only false hope."

"I am not the bad guy here!" Lydia shouted. Her body vibrated with the need to strike out at someone, anyone. A rising breeze swirled around her, lifting her hair and setting hemlock branches swaying. She stared Aileen down until the Fae woman turned her face away. The wind died. Lydia didn't feel any sense of triumph. "I just want to go home. This isn't my fight."

"How can you say that? The Bright Court has wronged you as it has wronged our Queen. Shadow suffers under Bright's yoke. How can you not ally yourself with us?"

"You look at me and see Fae. But no matter what you think, I'm just Lydia. I don't belong here."

Aileen laughed. "In the face of all evidence, you cling to your ephemeral life. I cannot understand you. You have magic like none have seen in generations and you persist in turning your back on your true heritage."

"Yeah. I'm so powerful, I had to run from Oberon."

"You, who use glamour as easily as taking breath?" Her voice was laced with scorn. "You ran because you fear your own power more than you fear the Bright King."

"That's not true." Lydia clenched her hands into fists, willing a surge of Faerie magic away. "I don't understand."

"Oh, I think you do. You defy both courts; you destroy glamours with a thought. My Queen fears you and still you persist in playing the poor, helpless child."

"Right. Why would Titania be afraid of me?" The Fae Queen had practically vibrated with power. Power tinged with hurt and madness. If anyone should be afraid, it was Lydia.

Aileen held Lydia's gaze for a long, uncomfortable moment. "We were fools to have sought you out. We should have left you in the Mortal world to live and die ignorant of your heritage."

"Why didn't you?" Lydia whispered. Then she would be home, worrying about college and arguing with her parents about buying a car. The concerns of that girl seemed distant and dull.

"Because we are dying." She turned her back on Lydia, but not before she saw color flood Aileen's cheeks. "This is all Oberon's doing and yet you punish Shadow for it."

"I'm sorry. I . . . I don't know what to believe anymore." Lydia rocked back and forth, hating this pang of sympathy and hating herself for standing there stammering like an idiot.

"Just go," Aileen said. "Leave us. Leave our Queen to her mourning. We will dwindle and soon enough, there will only be one court in Faerie again."

Lydia hugged her arms across her chest, fighting the urge to apologize. "Go? Where can I go? I won't return to Bright. I like Oberon even less than I like your Queen." At least Titania hadn't tried to control her. She wasn't the one who had killed her Fae parents, though part of Lydia suspected that was only because Oberon held more power, not because Titania could claim any moral high ground.

"You really don't know, do you?" Aileen said.

"Know what?"

"You have the power to open the way between the worlds, Lydia Hawthorne."

"What?" Heat made her cheeks blaze. She could go home. Home.

"It is just another kind of glamour. And with your inborn affinity for Bright and Shadow magic, you have no need of anyone's tithe."

Gooseflesh tightened the skin along Lydia's arms. It was her way out. "Why are you telling me this?"

Aileen stared at her for so long, Lydia was sure she wasn't going to answer.

"Since Titania discovered that you lived, she has thought of nothing else but her revenge. She has demanded more than her rightful tithe and we are all diminished. And now you are here, but you will not add your strength to ours."

Lydia looked away, embarrassed by the raw need in Aileen's eyes.

"Leave us. Seal the doors behind you. Then neither court will have the advantage."

Without access to Mortal fertility, all the Fae would die out. Not right away, but eventually. As hateful as stealing Mortal children was, could she condemn a whole people to oblivion? And what about the child she replaced? Lydia could send her back to Faerie, but then she would be as guilty as Oberon. She dropped her head into her hands. "Why are you doing this to me?"

There was no pity in Aileen's voice. "You are a trueborn Fae. This is your path. One way or another, you must end this stalemate between Bright and Shadow."

Aileen's words hammered into Lydia like a punch to the gut. She couldn't catch her breath. A loud buzzing filled her ears. Her heart squeezed out a panicked rhythm. She turned to confront Aileen, to tell her to fight her own damned war, but Lydia couldn't force the words through her tight throat. Something was unraveling her from the inside out, pulling at the center of her chest.

Aileen stood still, her jaw clamped shut, her eyes wide in surprise or fear.

Time slowed. Lydia's thoughts were sluggish. But she knew this was familiar. This was wrong. She pressed her hand to her chest, wincing with the ache.

A buzzing filled the clearing and darkness smothered the sky.

Her body was rooted to the spot even as her mind screamed at her to run. It was like what happened on the bus all over again.

Darklings.

Her head was spinning even as her body crumpled into the ground.

*

THE UNBOUND'S DARKLINGS HAD TRAILED behind Clive, as much his tool as a threat against his cooperation. They led him directly to Lydia. Aileen was a complication he hadn't counted on. The hungry cloud swirled. He forced himself to wait until the darklings coalesced around them and Lydia and Aileen were both still. Were he more like Oberon, he would simply abandon Aileen to them and leave with Lydia. But if that was so, he wouldn't be in this situation.

He plunged into the cloud, interrupting its feeding. The darklings buzzed around him like a swarm of gnats. If he reached for Bright magic, the darklings would attack him. It would also announce his presence in Shadow. But it wasn't like he had much of a choice.

Clive let power bubble up from the ground to fill him. The buzzing rose to a high-pitched shriek. The darklings pulled away from Lydia and Aileen, arrowing toward him instead. He counted ten heartbeats, until the entire swarm was oriented on him before creating a shield around himself and the two prone Fae. With nothing to draw power from, the darklings should return to Isidore and Callie. At least that's what Clive hoped.

They flattened out against the front of his shield, clinging to it and turning it black. He was plunged into an eerie twilight. The longer he used Bright magic, the greater the chance Titania would find them here or Aileen would wake. He turned to Lydia, hesitating for a moment before calling her name. When she realized he had turned the darklings on her, she was going to be furious.

His head pounded with the effort to hold the shield solid while keeping watch on Lydia and Aileen. Even if he could see through the massed darklings, there was no way he could attend to what might be happening outside this small bubble of safety. Crouching down, Clive placed his hand lightly on Lydia's shoulder. "Lydia?" he whispered, struggling to wake her while watching the shield. It was still thick with the swarming trackers.

"Thorn prick me," he muttered. Isidore and Callie should have called them off by now.

Something struck him in the side, overbalancing him. A weight flattened him to the ground, his forehead rebounding off the hard earth. The breath whooshed out of his chest. His ears rang. The shield buckled. Darklings streamed through.

"Clive, I'm sorry." Lydia scrambled off of him and his breathing eased. "What's happening?" Her eyes were bright and her cheeks flushed. A thick black funnel swirled around her as if she were the eye of a tornado. They were too close for him to shield her and she didn't know how to shield herself. She was swatting at them, but for every one she hit, two more filled the breach.

"Lydia, stay calm!"

The more chaotic her use of magic, the more the darklings would feed. And she was fairly thrumming with power. She would be irresistible to them.

Clive had to draw them off her somehow. But he couldn't match her magic. Not unless she could let it bleed off the way he had earlier. "Don't attack them, Lydia. You have to make yourself invisible."

"Get them off me!" she cried. "I can't breathe!"

"Lydia, listen to me!" Clive shouted over the buzzing of the swarm. "You drank power from Faerie when you turned into a tree. You have to let it drain back into the ground." Where were Callie and Isidore? Surely they didn't want Lydia hurt. "You can do this," he said, willing it to be true with every ounce of power he had left.

They were moving faster, vibrating as they fed. The more Lydia fought, the stronger they would get, until she had nothing left to offer. All her power drained into the darklings. Back to the Unbound. To Callie and Isidore. Sweat turned cold and clammy on his body. They wanted her power. He hadn't thought they would take it like this.

He glanced at Aileen, hoping she could help him, but she lay still and silent. The attack must have blindsided her and with as little power as she had access to, the darklings had drained her reserves easily.

There was nothing he could do.

It was up to Lydia now.

Chapter 19

LYDIA SWATTED AT THE DARKLINGS. They had been the size of gnats. Now they were as big as bumblebees. They swirled around her so fast, she couldn't see Clive anymore. Her pulse surged. Adrenaline dried her mouth and made her body shake. They plucked at her, pulling something from the center of her soul. If she had felt like a spool being unwound before, now it was the gush from an open fire hydrant. She tore at them and still they swarmed her. The vibration bored into her bones.

Clive's voice was like a lifeline, but he wanted her to let her magic go. That couldn't be right. Sweat dripped down her forehead and into her eyes, the salt burning, hazing her vision. "I can't. They'll get inside me!"

They were hungry.

"Lydia, you have to calm yourself."

Her palms were slick.

"Taylor needs you," Clive shouted. "She's worried about you, Lydia."

She trembled on legs that felt like jelly. "Tails," Lydia

whispered. She had sworn she would get back home. To her family. To Taylor. She blinked through tears and sweat.

"I saw her. Talked to her. She misses you."

The incessant buzzing made her dizzy. Lydia closed her eyes on the danger in front of her and struggled to picture her baby sister. It was like trying to wrestle smoke. The images shredded as fast as she could create them. Taylor, swinging her chubby legs at the tall kitchen stool. Taylor, her face smeared with chocolate. The smell of baking cookies. "No!" she shouted and reached out to claw through the dark mass.

"Lydia, the more you fight them with power, the stronger the darklings become."

"They're taking her away from me!" Lydia cried. Wait. Wait. That wasn't right. That's what Clive had tried to do before she even set foot in Faerie. It had been an illusion then. It was an illusion now. Her heart steadied its rhythm. Her breathing eased. The darklings still pulled and tugged at her, but she was able to observe the attack from a kind of distance. She recognized the feeling. It was the same calm that came over her after she struggled to find her stride on a long run.

Clive was wrong.

She could use magic against the darklings. They weren't really bugs or bees. They were just power and directed will. Another kind of glamour. And whoever controlled them was standing between Lydia and going home. No matter how strong they were, Lydia knew she had the advantage here—whatever the Fae believed, Faerie magic wasn't her only source of power.

Lydia drew on memories. Her scrapbook was somewhere

left behind in Bright court, but her family lived inside her. Taking a deep breath, she pulled comfort and strength from the love they had given her. It was a kind of magic the darklings couldn't touch. That the Fae didn't understand. She wove it into the essence of Faerie itself, both the brash power of Bright and the subtle whisper of Shadow, to create a tight fabric that she wrapped around both her and the darklings like a blanket, cutting them off from their sender.

For a long minute nothing happened. Lydia held her breath. What if she was wrong? What if whoever sent the darklings were stronger than she was? The seconds seemed to stretch out like taffy as she held on with all the stubborn insistence that drove her mother crazy. "You can't have them, do you hear me?" She forced the words through gritted teeth.

The darklings milled around her, the swarm losing coherency and purpose. The buzzing quieted as the insect-like constructs slowed, flying into one another in a jerky rhythm until they fell, one by one, at Lydia's feet. As they hit the ground, they vanished with a hiss. Her ears rang in the sudden silence. Lydia shivered, looking up to meet Clive's wide-eyed gaze.

"What . . . How?" he stammered.

He seemed very far away, his voice tinny. Saliva flooded her mouth and she swallowed, hard. Her legs buckled. Clive caught her before she hit the ground.

"Lydia—come on. We have to go. Now."

"Go? Go where? How did you get here?" She shook her head, trying to clear it. The last thing she remembered was Aileen's anger. Just before the darklings came. Lydia looked for her. The Shadow Fae was lying on the ground just a few feet away, her face deathly pale. She pulled out of Clive's hold and knelt by her still form. Her own fingers were so cold, she could barely feel the flicker of a pulse in Aileen's slender wrist. "What's wrong with her?"

"We can't stay here, Lydia." The quiet urgency in his voice sent a shiver through her.

"We can't leave her like this."

"She will recover. See? She stirs." The Fae woman's eyes shifted beneath closed lids. "Let's go." He reached for Lydia's arm and pulled her to standing.

"Where?" She wasn't going back to Bright. Not now. Not ever.

"A place of safety." He wouldn't meet her gaze.

She let him pull her to her feet and away from Aileen. "Wait. I don't understand. Why would Titania attack one of her own with darklings? We were on our way to see her." It didn't make any sense.

Clive's face flushed. "She didn't. It wasn't her."

"Then who sent them? Oberon?"

"I swear, I'll explain it all to you if you'll only come with me." He shifted back and forth, his gaze darting all around them, but never quite meeting her own.

What was he hiding?

His hand tightened around her arm. "If we stay here, we will be captured." He did meet her eyes this time. "Both of us."

"You're hurting me." He didn't let go. The muscles in her shoulders and jaw tensed. Magic flared through her body, her hands tingling as she gathered more power from the air around her. "I won't let Oberon touch me," she said, directing the flow up her arm, where Clive held her. "Let go of me. Now."

"Please, Lydia."

She ignored the fear in his voice and loosed the waiting magic. His eyes widened in shock as heat seared his palm. The scent of ozone bloomed in the air. He stumbled away from her, cradling his hand.

"Lydia," he whispered, pleading for something, but she didn't know what. His face was ashen, lined with pain.

Shame brought heat to her face. She forced herself to stand still when her instincts fought between the urge to flee and the need to help Clive. "Isn't this what you wanted? You've made me as Fae as you are." Power drained out of her in a rush that almost brought her to her knees. Hot tears gathered in her eyes. How could she explain this to her mom?

"Clive Barrow, you dare attack one under Shadow's protection?"

Lydia whirled as Aileen struggled to her feet, her cheeks flushed. Aileen and Clive stared at one another, as if Lydia wasn't standing between them.

"That was not my intent," Clive said. Lydia stared at him, her mouth falling open. He sent the darklings? Against her?

"My Lady Titania comes," Aileen said, smiling tightly.

Lydia rocked back and forth on the balls of her feet. Her pulse hammered against her ears. Aileen and Clive looked like the statues flanking the entrance to Aeon's maze.

"I thought you were my friend," Lydia said.

"I am," he whispered. "I swear it."

Aileen laughed.

Lydia shook her head, but she couldn't shake the confusion.

The Fae didn't lie. They didn't always tell the truth, but they didn't lie. Clive was her friend and he had set the darklings on her. The seconds crawled by. He couldn't be here when Titania came.

"Lydia . . . " He stretched out his injured hand, palm up. Blisters splayed across reddened skin. She had done this. A light breeze set the leaves sighing. Shadow magic rippled in the air around them. There was no more time.

She clasped his injured hand in hers. Clive gasped. She took his pain like thirsty ground drank water. Shock turned her legs rubbery and she stumbled, her hand on fire, throbbing in time with every heartbeat. He yanked her after him, just as he had on the bus, a lifetime ago.

In the distance, she heard Titania's anguished cry.

Then there was only cool darkness.

*

"SO THIS IS THE CHANGELING," a woman's voice said.

Every muscle in Lydia's body ached. She was in another ubiquitous Faerie grove. "What is it with all the trees?" she said. No Fae cities and towns, just the cliched forests and knolls. The ground was hard and she felt as if she'd been run over by a truck. Nope. No trucks in Faerie, either. Barking laughter, mixed with sobs shook loose from her chest. She couldn't stop. Her breath came in huge, wracking gasps. She balled her hands into fists and the pain finally shocked her to silence.

"Lydia!"

It took her a few minutes to realize Clive had been calling

her name over and over. She looked up into his tear-stained face. Why was he crying? She didn't think the Fae could cry.

"Lydia, I'm sorry. I'm so sorry."

"Why did you send the darklings?" she asked. An odd assortment of Fae stood in a knot all around them, but right now, only Clive mattered. Her hand screamed and she healed it with a memory of cool water.

"She uses power without a thought, without cost," the woman said. Lydia didn't look up.

"I didn't . . . I didn't mean for it to happen like this," Clive stammered. He hung his head. "I'm sorry. It was the only way."

"He did not send them. We did." The woman's voice intruded again and this time Lydia looked for her. A tall Fae, with piercing green eyes, and hair so blond it was nearly white, stood staring down at her.

Lydia turned back to Clive, her eyebrows furrowed. The hand he offered her was trembling. He was afraid of her and that was her doing. "I'm sorry," Lydia whispered, half expecting him to withdraw. He kept his gaze locked on her, his hand waiting. She reached out and let him help her to standing.

"How touching, but will she help us?" A man's voice this time. Silver hair framed an angular face with sharp gray eyes.

"Leave her be," Clive snapped. "Your darklings nearly drained her."

She turned back to him, confused. "Where are we?"

"Where neither court can claim you. You're safe now," he said, glaring at the two Fae as if daring them to contradict him.

Safe. Right. She wasn't sure there was any place in Faerie that was safe. The man and woman stepped forward. Lydia held herself still, staring them down until they both stopped a few feet away. Clive moved a step closer to her, keeping his gaze on their two hosts. That was interesting. But why would he bring her here if he didn't trust them?

"We are the Unbound and no court claims our tithe," the woman said. "I am Callie. Isidore and I loosed the darklings. We needed to track you in Shadow. Clive requested our assistance." Her smile accentuated the hunger in her eyes. "It was effective. You are here and unharmed." Callie paused, frowning. "That's more than I can say for the darklings."

Lydia looked around again, studying the quiet group of Fae beyond Callie and Isidore. It was odd to see gray hair and lined faces. Other than Aeon, these were the first Fae who seemed like real people. Both Bright and Shadow courts were Disney World meets Faerie world. But not here. Some of the Unbound looked the same ages as her parents or grandparents. It was strange and familiar all at the same time. The odd part was the clothes from all different eras. A man in civil war homespun stood next to a woman in a flapper dress, complete with fringes and sequins. They all looked weary and beaten.

Either she was on the back lot of some Hollywood movie studio or she had fallen into the island of Misfit Fae. Lydia closed her eyes, not wanting to feel too much sympathy for them. "What do you want?" She would be damned if she was going to be grateful for being kidnapped.

"Lydia, at least listen to them. Please," Clive said.

"Whose side are you on, anyway?"

"I am trying to help you."

"You let the darklings attack me."

Clive looked down at his hands and Lydia fell silent. Yeah. About that. That was twice she'd hurt him without meaning to. "All right. I'm listening."

"Callie and Isidore speak for the Unbound."

Callie nodded to the rest of the Fae gathered around them and they dispersed. "Walk with us," she said.

Lydia looked back at Clive. He nodded and fell into step with her. The four of them slipped beneath the canopy of oak and elm trees. They walked past cabins that seemed part of the trees themselves. So it wasn't just clearings and woods. She smiled briefly, wondering if Aeon could see her here. The power trapped in Faerie called to her, buzzing beneath her feet as they walked a meandering path, but there was no sign of glamours. Callie and Isidore were as worn down as the rest of the Unbound.

"What am I doing here?" Lydia asked.

"We asked you here to petition for your help," Isidore said.

"You have a funny way of asking."

"We did what we had to do," Isidore said. "Titania wasn't going to let us waltz into the Shadow Court and invite you for a visit."

Callie placed a hand on her arm. "Like it or not, you are part of this. I would think you of all people would have sympathy for the plight of the Unbound."

The Fae woman had all of Aileen's arrogance. "Why should it matter to me which court ends up on top?" Lydia was tired of everyone wanting something from her.

"If you will not help us, then we have no future."

The Fae were starting to sound like a broken record. "I

didn't ask to be brought here." Not here with the Unbound, not in any of the courts. Not in Faerie. "And I don't owe you anything." Why did they all expect her to be some kind of Fae superhero?

"You are as self-centered and entitled as any Fae courtier," Callie said. "But why should I be surprised. You are trueborn." She turned her back on Lydia and walked away.

"How dare you?" Lydia shouted, storming over to where Callie stood. Clive tried to slip between the two women, but Lydia glared at him and he moved back. "You don't know me. You have no idea what I've lost." Power swirled under her feet. It would be so simple to aim it as a weapon. She didn't know if she wanted to hit the woman or take off running. Maybe both.

Isidore stood quietly next to Callie, one hand on her arm.

"Yes. Yes I do." Callie shook Isidore off and glared at Lydia. "Do you think you are the only one with a grievance against the courts? Open your eyes. We are the dregs of the Fae. The castoffs. There is not one amongst us who hasn't been harmed by Oberon or Titania."

Lydia met Callie's stare with her own, holding on to her anger. "Why should I care?"

"Lydia . . . " Clive frowned and she realized how callous her words sounded. How like the Fae.

"Trueborn," Isidore said, spitting out the word as if it was a curse.

"You are not the only one torn from a life you loved," Callie said.

"I don't understand." Lydia folded her arms across her chest.

"Are you sure you wish to?"

Lydia took a breath, trying not to respond to Callie's biting tone. There was real pain in the Fae's voice. Pain that matched her own. She nodded.

"I was taken as a child," Callie said. "From your world."

The color drained from Lydia's face, and with it the anger she'd clung to like a lifeline. "You're not Fae?"

"By blood, Callie and I are Mortal," Isidore said. "But it is not blood alone that makes the Fae. The land of Faerie itself calls to those who live in her."

Clive had said that the Fae breed true, that children of mixed Fae and Mortal blood would always be Fae. She had felt the call of Faerie magic from the moment she'd set foot here, but she was trueborn. Fae by blood. Callie and Isidore were fully Mortal. If they could use Fae power, too, it had to be some of both, then. Nature and nurture, just like she'd studied in science class. Faerie genetics, 101.

Silence stretched out between them all. Isidore put his arm around Callie's shoulders. The Fae woman looked into the distance, her face set in a frown. Lydia turned away before Callie could see the sympathy in her own eyes. "How long have you been here?" she asked, afraid of the answer.

"A long time. Longer than Mortals measure even a long lifespan. I was a small child when I was taken."

Taylor was only six. What would happen if she stumbled through a door into Faerie? Lydia didn't want to think about it. "How are you able to use magic?" she asked. It seemed like a safer question to ask. A less personal question. One that wouldn't make Lydia want to help Callie and the rest of the unbound.

"We are not so different as you believe," Isidore said. "Most Mortals can use magic on this side of the divide. The younger they are when they come here the better."

Lydia couldn't help herself. "And you?"

"I have been in Fae since before the courts were split. Unlike Callie, there is little of your adopted world that I remember." Isidore shrugged. "It is a blessing."

"I'm so sorry," Lydia whispered.

"Don't be, child. I crossed into Faerie during a time when Fae and Mortals moved easily back and forth between the worlds. This is where I chose to stay."

"Then why are you here?" Lydia swept her arms around the small settlement of the Unbound.

"I sided with Titania during the dissolution. In time, she banished me. She said I reminded her overmuch of Oberon."

"Now do you understand?" Callie asked. "We had little choice but to bring you here."

Lydia looked closely at her, looked past the haughty expression and the arrogant formality to the woman beneath. She could all too easily imagine her at Taylor's age, following a thread of magic into Faerie. And not being able to find her way home again. Her poor family. They must have gone crazy. So many kids went missing every year. Lydia wondered how many of them ended up here.

"I can open a door. I can send you back," Lydia said. She could get them both back home.

Callie shook her head. "You are almost a century too late."

What would it be like if everyone she knew were dead? "I'm sorry."

"We need your help, not your pity," Isidore said. "Add your strength to ours and both courts will fall."

"And then what?" Lydia asked. "Will you rule Faerie?" She met Isidore's gaze, half afraid to ask the question, but forcing herself to push on. "Steal children to raise as your own?"

"That's not fair, Lydia," Clive said.

"No. She asks a valid question," Callie answered. She sent Isidore a hard look before turning back to Lydia. "We do not have magic enough to rule. But you do."

Lydia backed up into a tree trunk, her mouth falling open.

"Help us," Callie said. "We know the Fae and hidden ways into both Bright and Shadow. We can show you how to command the darklings."

"I don't . . . I can't . . . " This was crazy. She never even wanted to run for student council back home. The last thing Lydia needed was to take over in some sort of Faerie coup.

Isidore moved so close, his breath stirred her hair. "Take the power held in tithe by both Oberon and Titania and they cannot threaten you."

"What about you?" she asked.

Isidore laughed. "How can we threaten you? Look what you did to our darklings."

Everyone wanted something from her. They looked at her and saw raw power they could use. Clive was watching her, worry in his eyes. What did he think she was going to do?

Lydia looked away. She had no answer for him.

Chapter 20

CLIVE WAS UNCOMFORTABLY AWARE OF Taylor's card in the back pocket of his jeans. How could a folded piece of paper weigh so heavily on him? Giving it to Lydia would only add to the pressure she was already feeling. But what choice did he have?

If she believed Oberon was threatening her sister, she would act. But what would she do?

Isidore and Callie brought them to a clearing where a table was set for two with fruit, bread, cheese, and wine. So they were expecting them both. Maybe Clive had been wrong about their attack on Lydia with the darklings. Or maybe they had just been hedging their bets. Regardless, Clive had been complicit in getting her here. He was certain he would have to answer for that.

"Will you think on what we have said?" Callie asked.

Lydia nodded, scowling as they left.

Clive poured them both glasses of wine. Lydia played with hers, twirling the goblet and staring at the ruby liquid.

"Did you know?" she asked.

"Know what?"

"This. Them." She pointed her glass in the direction of Callie and Isidore. "Me?"

Clive shook his head. Would he have chosen otherwise if he had known?

"I didn't ask for any of it," she said.

"I know." His heart ached for her.

She set the glass down and wine sloshed over the rim to the table. "Everyone wants a piece of me. What do you want?"

They were long past the luxury of friendship, he feared. "There's something I have to tell you." Clive gulped down half his wine in one swallow. She would likely hate him for this.

"Your little sister. She wanted me to give this to you." Clive pulled the creased paper from his pocket and smoothed it out on the table between them. She reached for it with shaking hands, her eyes bright. There was so much Clive wanted to say, but he had no idea how to make this easier for her.

He waited as she opened the card and studied it.

"When? When did you get this?" Her body was completely still.

It was going to be hard to explain his debt to Shadow. "I was sent to find proof. Proof that the Mortal child yet lived. That Oberon lied."

"And?" Her hands were flat on the table, her fingers rigid.

Clive dropped his gaze to the floor, not wanting to meet Lydia's eyes. "She is there. But she is ill. I don't understand what Oberon has done, but she is in a hospital." He took a deep breath, not wanting to go on, but he owed her it all. "Taylor believes it is you. That you are very sick."

"Then it's true. I have no place to go."

He had no comfort for her. There was only the onus of his obligations. "There's more."

"Tell me," she said, her hands fisted in a white-knuckled grip.

Clive would rather have faced the Bright King himself than the fear and pain in Lydia's eyes. "Oberon believes I have come to collect you, bring you back to Bright."

She narrowed her eyes. "And?"

"If I do not, he will lure Taylor here."

*

SHE DIDN'T REMEMBER GETTING TO her feet. Her cup toppled over. The wine soaked into the table linens and her chair crashed to the floor. "No," she said.

Clive gripped the table's edge.

Wind buffeted her hair and plucked at her clothes. She ripped warmth from the sun and coolness from a deep underground spring, feeding her will with their elemental magic. The patience of trees and the moodiness of a summer thunderstorm mingled with the sweetness of roses, the fisted bud of a peony. Potential energy surged through her bloodstream with every beat of her heart.

"Lydia . . . " Clive's voice was far away.

She clutched her sister's hand in a memory and looked down, expecting to find Taylor looking up at her.

Clive pushed back from the table and stood, calling her

name. Lydia ignored him. She closed her eyes, and reached out her hands, searching for the edge of a door she knew was there. There was only the emptiness. She poured swirling currents of power through her arms and into her fingertips. The space in front of her thickened, taking on weight and texture. Fatigue burned in her shoulders and she gritted her teeth against the pain. The door was here. It had to be.

Something sharp caught the pad of her little finger. She opened her eyes to a bead of blood welling from a pin-prick-sized wound. A brick red smear hung in the air in front of her, coloring the edge of a door.

She laid her hand flat on the door's surface. The wood grain was smooth beneath her touch, but her eyes saw nothing. Her eyes were wrong. She closed them again and traced the boundary of the opening, looking for the latch or the knob without success. "Taylor!" she called, pounding on the door with a fist.

"Lydia," Clive whispered. His breath was warm against her ear. "Lydia, the door is just a kind of glamour. You can do this."

She stepped closer to it, building an image of home. The scent of burning leaves and pumpkin pie filled her mind. Before she had left, they were planning for Halloween. Marco was old enough that their folks were going to let him go trick-or-treat with his friends, but Taylor had been excited to go with her. Mom probably had the decorations up already. Dragging the Halloween box from the attic was usually Lydia's job. So was carving the jack-o-lantern.

Holding to thoughts of family, she reached for her Fae magic. She looked at Clive through the heat shimmer of her rising power. His eyes were open wide, staring at her without blinking. Magic spilled from her fingertips. The door warmed at her touch and swung open.

Effortlessly, Lydia stepped from one world to the other. Fallen leaves crunched beneath her feet. She was back where she had started—her old elementary school playground. For a moment, she let herself believe it was all a daydream. That it was still Saturday and her parents were waiting for her to come home from Emily's house to babysit.

The park was empty, lit by the last red rays of the setting sun. Her ears popped with a sudden change of air pressure as the door slammed shut behind her. A damp wind lifted her hair. Goosebumps prickled her bare arms. It was the same park, but everything else had changed. She reached for her magic. Currents flowed beneath her feet and through the air, but they felt as stiff and clumsy as her cold hands. She clenched her teeth to stop them chattering.

An image of Aeon's garden brought a memory of summer to chase away the chill. Lydia wondered if the gardener could even hear the trees this far from Faerie. Grasping at the distant, sluggish magic, she glamoured a thick hoodie and a pair of gloves. That was better.

In the scant light, she found the hollow stump where she'd hidden her phone and keys what was only days ago for her. Their weight felt both familiar and strange in her hand. She wasn't sure how much time had passed here. The phone wouldn't turn on. Its battery must have died. She slipped both into her pocket.

The swings creaked in a light breeze. The moon was rising. It was time to go home. What she would find when she got there was a question she couldn't answer.

The evening was uncomfortably silent. Lydia walked a path home she had traveled hundreds of times, but it was different somehow. Sound fell flatter here, the sky loomed closer, the trees sullen and sulking. Streetlights flickered on and off as she walked past them, their yellow bulbs casting a jaundiced light over the houses and lawns. A dog barked once.

She stopped in front of her house, blinking hard. From the curb, she whispered, "Mom, Dad, I'm home." Pulling invisibility around her like a cloak, she walked up to the back door and through it to the laundry room. The slight lemon of her mom's laundry detergent brought back a thousand memories of normal. She steadied herself against the washer. "I can do this."

On any typical night, her mom would be arguing with Marco about practicing, Taylor would be singing in the bathtub, and Lydia would be in her room finishing up homework with headphones on and music turned up loud. Tonight, the house was too still. The indistinct murmur of voices and canned television laughter drifted in from the living room. Footsteps creaked on the landing. Someone was coming.

She looked around for a hiding place, but the only space was the corner between the washer and drier and she hadn't fit there since she was Taylor's age. A loud thump shook the floor outside the laundry room. Lydia's heart pounded in her chest. The doorknob turned and the door opened. Lydia backed against the wall.

Her mother bent down to pick up the laundry basket she'd dropped to get the door. The breath caught in Lydia's throat. Hair, more drab than brown fell across her mother's forehead.

Her eyes were bloodshot, the skin around them lined. When had she gotten so tired? She tried to find a smile for her mom, but it felt stiff and awkward on her face. Her mother looked past her to the washer. Lydia shivered. The glamour. Her mother couldn't see her.

It took all of Lydia's willpower not to fling her arms around her. She had to find out what had happened here. How much time had gone by and where her namesake was. She watched her mother load the washer with clothes she recognized. Her clothes. No. Lydia's clothes. The real Lydia. The other Lydia.

She waited until her mother had started the washer and she slipped into the house behind her, hands shaking. Her father and Marco were sitting in the living room. Marco was watching TV. Her dad was pretending to read the paper, but his gaze was focused on something far in the distance. He didn't even glance at her mom as she walked past. Lydia wanted to yell at him to stand up and give her a hug.

"Dad?" Marco said, looking up from the flickering light of the TV screen.

"Hmm?"

"Can you practice kicks with me this weekend?"

It must still be soccer season.

Her dad put down the paper, took off his glasses, and pinched the bridge of his nose. "It depends on how Lydia is doing," he said.

A chill moved through her. What did that mean?

"Why couldn't she stay at the hospital?" Marco picked at one of the sofa pillows.

Her dad shot him a death-ray look. Lydia took a step back,

wilting under the second-hand glare.

Her mom knelt down beside him. "Oh, sweetie, I know this has been hard on you, but the doctors say that being in familiar surroundings will help your sister find her way back to us."

Lydia pressed her hand against her mouth. What the hell had Oberon done?

Her father sighed and folded the newspaper in exact creases before he stood and squeezed her mom's shoulder. "I'll tuck Taylor in. You sit for a while."

Her mom nodded. "Will you check in on Lydia?"

A flicker of pain passed across her dad's face before he nodded.

Lydia followed him, her glamoured passage ghost-silent. Her legs were as thick and heavy as tree trunks as she forced herself up the stairs. Her dad paused in the hallway and sighed before ducking into her room.

"It's okay, Lyds, you're going to get better soon and then you can take me trick-or-treating, just like you promised!" Taylor said.

Lydia felt her heart lurch. She stiffened at the threshold to her room and swallowed against the dryness in her mouth. It was just one step. One step. That's all. And she would come face-to-face with herself. She took a steadying breath and stepped into her own room.

Taylor was snuggled against a mound of blankets on her bed.

"It's time for bed, Taylor," her dad said.

"But I want to sleep here with Lyds."

Lydia gasped as the body beneath the blankets shifted.

"Not tonight, sweetie."

As Taylor pouted, Lydia grabbed the door frame to steady herself. She was afraid to look too closely at the body under the covers.

"You have to let me tuck her in, Daddy." Taylor stood up and put one dimpled fist against her hip. "You just have to."

Blinking back tears, she fought the urge to gather her little sister up and give her a fierce hug.

"Give your sister a good night kiss, Tails. It's my turn to tuck you in." Her father looked so tired, but he still had a smile for Taylor.

"Night, Lyds. Mom says we can bake cookies tomorrow." Taylor leaned over and kissed the bundled-up girl. Lydia's hands shook. She took a step closer to the bed as her dad swung Taylor on his hip.

"That's my girl," he said.

Lydia inched her way across the room. She looked back at her father and sister silhouetted in the hallway light. Anger heated her face. Oberon had a lot to answer for.

Taylor pointed directly at her and Lydia nearly walked into the desk.

"Daddy, look. It's Lyddie's guardian angel." Taylor looked her in the eye and smiled. "You'll help her, right?"

"Shh, Taylor, it's time for bed," her dad said, hugging her to his chest.

Lydia's whole body stiffened. Her little sister waved as her father carried her out into the hall. She looked down at herself, dressed in a sweatshirt and blue jeans. An angel? Not hardly.

Chapter 21

The only light in her room was the hallway light filtered through the partially closed door. Lydia kindled the memory of brightness in her mind and set a glowing lantern down on the desk. Using magic here, in the place where she had lived her whole boring, ordinary life, was the final proof that she could never belong again. She hung her head and listened. Water ran in the bathroom down the hall and the kettle whistled on the kitchen stove. The normal sounds of a normal night at home. Too bad this was anything but normal.

Wiping her damp palms on her pants, Lydia shuffled over to her Mortal twin. The girl's brown eyes glittered in the soft light. They followed Lydia's movements without any hint of recognition. Her hair spilled in a messy braid across one shoulder. Taylor had probably braided it.

"Lydia?" she called softly. There was no response. Looking into her face wasn't exactly like looking at herself. Without a living expression, the girl looked younger, more like a life-sized doll than a person, at least until she blinked. "What did Oberon do to you?" she asked.

She could send the girl back. Opening the door would be simple now that she had done it once already. She could send the girl back and be home. And this Mortal changeling would return to the only world she understood. It would be a mercy, really. What would she do when she woke up all the way, any-way? Her family would be left with a shell of a girl who looked like Lydia, but wouldn't know them at all. The doctors would call it amnesia or a head injury. Everyone would pity her folks. And everyone would learn to get on with their lives without the person they once knew.

Lydia let power spill down her arms. The edges of the door waited for her to draw it into being.

Taylor's voice echoed in her mind. *You'll help her, right?*

She couldn't send her back to Bright like this. Taking her hands from the ghost shape forming in front of her, she reached out to the girl. Magic trailed from her fingertips in tight spirals. She felt for the shape of Oberon's binding and picked apart the tight knot of his glamour. It was far more complicated than what he had woven the night of the mas-querade.

It would have been simpler if she could have just torn through it with her anger, but she didn't want to hurt the girl any more than she already had been. As she untangled magic strands, Lydia watched her face, a face that was almost famili-ar. A face that completely freaked her out. It wasn't everybody who got to look at themselves without a mirror.

The more layers of magic she pulled from her, the younger and more vulnerable the girl looked. There was no way she was almost eighteen. It shouldn't have surprised her. One of the first things Clive told her was that time moved differently in Faerie.

Of course she had to send her back. How would her family cope with a Lydia suddenly twelve or thirteen years old? But what if she didn't want to go back?

Lydia froze, her hands hovering over the girl, Oberon's glamour nearly completely unraveled. She swallowed hard. If she simply shoved the girl through a door back into Faerie, she would be doing just what she condemned Oberon for doing. No. She wasn't like that. And she wasn't vindictive like Titania, either.

If only Clive had never shown up in her life. She closed her eyes. But it wasn't really his fault. They were all playing out something that had started a long time before she was born. It sucked, but that's what it was. And now she had a chance to make it all right again.

If only she knew exactly what right was.

The last of Oberon's glamour fell away. The girl's eyes blinked slowly, the pupils constructing as she focused on the things in the room. When she got to Lydia, fear replaced the blank look and she scrambled back against the wall, clutching the blankets.

"Who are you?" The girl's voice was high-pitched and tight. She looked down at the bunched fabric in her hands. "How did I get here?"

Lydia had to grip her hands to keep them from shaking. "What's the last thing you remember?"

The girl fell silent, frowning. "I don't. I can't." She swallowed hard and tried again. "There's nothing."

Lydia recognized the panic rising in her younger self's eyes. She created an illusion of silence and of a sleeping girl that would fool anyone who might come to the door. This wasn't something her parents were equipped to handle. Hell, Lydia didn't think she could deal with it, either, but it wasn't like she had much of a choice.

She forced herself to sit on the edge of the bed and tried to reassure the girl with a smile. It didn't change her rigid posture or her wild, wide-eyed look. "I want to try to help you." She closed her eyes briefly, trying to figure out what to say. "Your name is Lydia." Her voice broke on the word. "Lydia Hawthorne."

"Who are you?" she asked, frowning as she studied Lydia's face.

"It doesn't matter right now," Lydia said. "You don't remember Bright court? Oberon?"

The girl shook her head.

Sighing, Lydia reached out with her magic. Maybe there was something she missed. Something more subtle that Oberon had done. If he had dammed up her memories somehow, maybe she could release them.

Moments ticked by as Lydia struggled to find any evidence of remaining Fae glamour, but it was as if Oberon has just wiped her mind clean of her lifetime in Faerie, leaving behind a blank shell. Now what? She closed her eyes.

"I'm scared," the young Lydia said.

"I know. Me too," she answered. She couldn't just leave her like this and she couldn't send her back to Oberon, either.

Peeling away the glamour had just made things worse.

The girl's shoulders quaked as she cried. Lydia's hands shook as she reached out to touch her. She half-expected they would both disappear in a puff of Faerie paradox. At least that would solve their problems. A moment passed and nothing weird or cosmic happened. Only that the girl flung herself into Lydia's arms, sobbing.

She stiffened, and then felt a pang of guilt for pulling away. It wasn't much different from comforting Taylor when a bad dream sent her fleeing into Lydia's room. "I'm sorry. I don't know how to fix this." Her sister expected her to help, but nothing in her life either before or since her time in Faerie gave her any answers.

"Who am I? I want to remember."

Lydia covered her face with her hands. She couldn't come up with a good answer for either of them, but if she didn't send the other girl back, she couldn't stay here.

"You can't remember, either?" The girl stopped crying and dried her face with the corner of a blanket. "Maybe we can help each other."

Guilt made her heart heavy in her chest. "I remember," she said. "I remember too much." Blinking away tears, she looked at the mementos of her childhood around the room. Scrap-books and photo albums, a bulletin board covered with movie ticket and concert stubs, cross-country trophies. Each item practically vibrated with a memory.

"There's no place here for someone who can turn into a tree."

The girl stared at her, her expression totally blank.

"It's going to be okay. I promise," Lydia said. "It's late. Lie down and close your eyes. I'll stay with you until you fall asleep." It was what she had told Taylor many times after a bad dream frightened her sister awake.

She nodded her head and slid down under the sheets, curling on her side, facing Lydia.

The girl would have memories, only not the ones she lived through at Bright court. With tears sliding down her cheeks, Lydia called to her power, building a glamour to rival the one Oberon had created. Ribbons of bright and shadow magic twined around one another in what looked like the DNA double helix she had studied forever ago in science class.

She pulled threads of memory from the photographs in her albums and scrapbooks, images and stories from the books in neat order on her bookshelves, the movies and the friends she had seem them with. From deep inside her, she formed a core of Lydia-ness and wound one long, unbroken strand of woven recollections around it, until she held what looked like a ball of variegated yarn that pulsed with color and light. Sweat dripped off her forehead and down her back. Her breath came in quick gasps and her hands trembled. She turned to the girl. Her eyes were wide open and unblinking.

"Sleep," she whispered and the eyes closed, the fear on her face easing.

Lydia touched the ball to the girl's heart and then to her forehead. She pushed gently, and it disappeared, briefly lighting the girl's face from within. Frowning, Lydia stared at the young body. "I'm sorry," she whispered. As distasteful as it was, she had to use something like Oberon's original glamour to convince the girl's body it was seventeen.

Tears dried on her face. It was easier than she had expected. Easier even then turning into a tree and that had been almost as natural as breathing. More than anything else, that told her how much she didn't belong here.

"Goodbye," she whispered, and leaned over to kiss the sleeping Lydia's forehead.

Chapter 22

CLIVE STARED INTO THE EMPTY space Lydia left behind, long after she had stepped out of Faerie. Now what? For the first time since Oberon had sent him into the Mortal world to collect her, he had no obligations left to fulfill. Callie was waiting for him, sitting alone on a low bench under the shelter of oak and elm trees. She looked up as he walked into the clearing. As much as he still didn't trust the Unbound, he still wished he had some hope for her. Or for himself.

"Where is the Changeling?"

"She has a name, Callie."

She nodded, conceding the point. "Where is Lydia?"

He fixed his gaze on Callie. "She went home."

Her eyes widened and a mix of emotions flickered across her face—fear, anger, resignation—before she replaced them with a placid blankness he knew was illusion. "So she has left us to our fate."

"I'm sorry." And he was, even though they would have taken what they could from Lydia. They had lost and at least had been gracious in failure.

She opened her mouth to speak, paused, shook her head, and tried again. "I believe you, Clive Barrow of Bright court."

He bowed his head. Absolution was the last thing he'd expected from her.

She placed a hand on his arm, as light as a dragonfly's touch. Warmth spread out from her fingers. He held his breath. "Will you fight with us?"

He closed his eyes. "Perhaps now with Lydia gone, there will be nothing left to fight over."

"You believe so? May you gain comfort from such naive imaginings." Callie slid her hand away and looked off into the distance. "Your Changeling has already shifted the balance. Whether she intended to or not no longer matters. Oberon and Titania will go to war."

Callie was right. Faerie was gathering itself to fight. And over what? He hoped Lydia, at least, had found her peace.

"We would make a place for you here, Clive."

He rubbed his hand lightly over the place she had touched him. "I am Oberon's. He still claims his tithe from me."

"Stay. We will shield you."

Clive smiled, shook his head. "You will need all the magic you can gather." And still, he knew it wouldn't be enough. Not to stand against Oberon and Titania.

"What will you do?" she asked.

The stillness of the grove pressed down on him. It was as if all the Unbound were waiting for him to declare himself, as if they were listening through Callie's ears. "I'm not sure." All of Clive's promises had revolved around Lydia. He had done what he could, kept his oaths, each one of them, to the best of his ability. There was nothing more he could do for her. And little he could do for Callie's people. "At the very least, I must return to Oberon." He shrugged. "Perhaps he will banish me after all."

"Perhaps," Callie agreed, struggling to smile. "If it comes to that, we would welcome you."

"Even after I let her go?"

She matched his gaze for what seemed like a long time. Her eyes held sadness, but not the anger he expected. "Even so," she said.

"She deserved to have a choice."

Callie winced and turned away. He knew that wasn't what she wanted to hear, but it was the only truth he had. Would he have refused Oberon at the beginning if he'd known what Lydia represented then? And if he had, would it even have mattered? The Bright King would have sent someone in his stead and nothing would have changed. Well, maybe not nothing. He had changed. Lydia had changed him.

"By her choice, she condemns us," Callie said.

"Do we not deserve condemnation? Look at what we have done to you and tell me you would have chosen any differently than Lydia." Perhaps his grandmother had the right of it, after all.

She turned to him, a half-smile on her face. "What glamour is this? She has turned you into an Ephemeral, Clive."

"I am tired, Callie." He pushed his hair from his brow. "All I have managed to do is to hasten the war that will destroy us all. How can I not feel regret?"

She placed her hand against his cheek. Her touch sent his

heart racing. Her eyes were the color of new spring grass. A soft breeze stirred strands of her hair. The air filled with the scent of peonies. He looked down at his hands and thought of Lydia's ragged cuticles and bitten off nails, her adopted Mortal frailties so at odds with her Fae grace. He stiffened and Callie pulled her touch away.

Laughing, she tried to smooth over the awkwardness between them. "What? No comfort for a distant kin?"

"I'm sorry," he said again. Regret was an unfamiliar and uncomfortable language. "I have no comfort for anyone."

"Go. Do what you must."

"Callie . . . "

She shook her head. "Go, Clive. Know that I hold you blameless."

"You cannot absolve me of this," he whispered. "Not when I do not forgive myself."

"But are we not Fae?" she said, lifting her chin up and staring directly at him. "Guilt is as Mortal as the limits of time. We do not concern ourselves with it."

Her eyes were bright with tears. He shifted closer and brushed his hand across her cheek. "You are right. We are Fae and none of this matters." Leaning down, he kissed her forehead, weary beyond all imagining. She tipped her head toward his and met his mouth with hers. Bright magic tingled across his lips before the kiss ended and she was gone.

He stood up. The bench they had been sitting on faded. A haze obscured the air between the trees and Clive couldn't see more than an arm span around him. The Unbound had gathered to prepare for the war that threatened to roll over them all like a summer thunderstorm. Behind the wall of mist, Callie and Isidore were helping their people share their meager magics. It was a futile act of defiance against the courts that had rejected them.

Even his Bright magic added to theirs would be like a droplet of water next to the torrent of Oberon's massed power. At best, one court or another would claim the Unbound's magic for its own, taking in extremis what it had once scoffed. At worst, the two courts would use this place as a battlefield, leaving nothing unscathed.

He had to go back. Oberon's summons plucked at him. It was a call he was bound to answer, regardless of his own desires. Even as he knew his own life would be forfeit to the Bright King's folly. This was as it had always been in Clive's memory. The Fae sought favor with their ruler using the only currency that mattered. In return for that slim chance of status and its rewards was the unspoken agreement—the pledge of power to be given at need.

He should have known it would come to this; that the stalemate between Oberon and Titania couldn't have endured forever, but it had endured. Until he met Lydia, he had never seen past his constant irritation at court and the petty slights of Oberon's courtiers. That, too, was as it had always been. Perhaps Aeon, with his life trailing back to the very roots of Faerie, would have seen more clearly than Clive had.

Aeon.

Clive jerked his head up. Perhaps the mad gardener could help him find his way through guilt and obligation. After all, wasn't that just another kind of maze?

*

Trailing her fingers across the rainbow wallpaper she had chosen in second grade, Lydia took one last look around the room that had once been hers. In the morning, the girl in her bed would awaken from her mysterious twilight sleep to a familiar world. A world Lydia had just made sure she had to leave forever. Maybe deep down, she had known it would come to this. From the moment Clive upended her normal, boring little life, it had been too late for her.

She tiptoed down the hallway to stand outside Taylor's room. Hesitating at the threshold, she placed a trembling hand on her sister's door. She would certainly be asleep by now.

Taking a deep breath, Lydia pushed open the door and slipped inside. The warm glow of a night light illuminated a mosaic of brightly colored shells, stones, and polished glass they had collected last summer at the beach. Stuffed animals filled nearly every bit of shelf space that wasn't crammed with storybooks. Lydia picked a book up from the floor, its spine splayed open. It was one she remembered from her own childhood. Actually two books in one. An illustrated version of *Peter Pan* on one side. Turning the book over, she flipped through the story of *Alice in Wonderland*. Shaking her head, she slipped the volume back on Taylor's bookshelf. She was no Alice following the white rabbit down the rabbit hole and the Fae were no deck of cards she had dreamed up one sleepy spring day.

Taylor was curled up in the center of her bed, nested on a

collection of little bean bag animals. The covers had fallen from her, leaving her arms bare and fragile in the dim light. Lydia tucked the blanket around her sister, her hands lingering on the thin shoulders. "I love you, Tails," she whispered.

Taylor's eyes blinked slowly. Lydia held her breath, afraid to move her hand away.

"I love you too, Lyds," she said, her voice thick with sleep, her eyes unfocused.

Lydia couldn't keep her sister in focus through the tears. "I have to go away for a while, sweetie."

"You're the prettiest angel I ever saw."

"Not as pretty as you," Lydia said.

"Why don't you have wings?"

"I don't know. Maybe you can draw a picture for me the next time . . . " Lydia's voice caught in her throat. "The next time I come and visit you."

"Okay," Taylor said, smiling. She burrowed down deeper into the covers and slid her eyes fully closed. In an instant, she was asleep.

Lydia wanted nothing more than to curl up with her little sister and forget everything from the past two days. But that wouldn't keep her family safe. Staying here was no longer an option. Neither was returning to Faerie. If either Oberon or Titania claimed her, the other would use her family as leverage. So she had to find a place neither of them would ever find her.

"Goodbye, Taylor," she said, and opened a door into a memory of rainbows, impossible trees and a dizzying horizon. Taking one last look at her sleeping sister, Lydia slipped Between.

Chapter 23

Clive followed Oberon's call to the edge of Bright court, a fish being reeled in on an invisible line. He wouldn't be able to deny it, but he could delay for a time. It would be what Oberon expected, anyway.

At the threshold between the forest of the Unbound and lands that owed allegiance to Bright, Clive searched for a path that would lead him into the maze. It was of indeterminate size and shape. Even Oberon, who had commanded it and who had bound Aeon within it for some infraction no one but the gardener and the Bright King remembered, didn't know its exact boundaries. It intersected every part of Faerie. Certainly it had grown far beyond the small formal plot that used to demarcate the entrance to Bright court itself.

Clive closed his eyes and called out to Aeon. He hoped the gardener would be intrigued by a Fae who wanted to get lost inside his maze, rather than discover his way out of it.

The quality of the light changed. Shadows swept across his face and closed lids. A cool breeze rifled his hair. The scent of honeysuckle vines wafted in the air.

"I think you have done a fine job of getting tangled all on your own," Aeon said.

Clive opened his eyes to the gardener's shining eyes and wrinkled face. "I have tangled more than myself."

"So you have," Aeon said, his expression solemn. Vines stretched and wriggled from the hedges surrounding him. Clive watched them warily. "The trees of Faerie will drink blood like water before long."

The finality in Aeon's voice chilled him. "I know," Clive said. "There is nothing I can do."

The laugh surprised him. "Perhaps if you had done nothing . . ."

"Then others would have acted in my place. It would have made no difference." It was the truth, but it didn't make Clive feel any better about his choices.

Aeon winked at him, beckoning him closer. Clive leaned in toward the little Fae. A thin vine fragrant with mock orange looped around his ankle. He forced himself not to jerk away. "Someone else wouldn't have been Lydia's friend."

He couldn't imagine that had made any difference. "I let her go," Clive said, looking past Aeon into the blur of greenery around them both.

"I know."

"How?"

Aeon shrugged. "The trees whisper their secrets to me."

"Do they tell you who will survive the coming war?"

"That is beyond the skills of even my garden."

They fell silent. Leaves rustled as a flock of sparrows burst through the walls of the hedge. Clive traced their trajectory up and out of sight. "They have the sense to flee."

"They have freedom we do not."

Clive looked down at the tangled vines rooting Aeon to the ground. His tie to Oberon was no different. He could only delay his answer for so long before the Bright King would extract his tithe, with or without Clive's consent. "The Unbound ready themselves for war."

Aeon twirled a leaf around his finger.

"They cannot survive this," Clive said.

The gardener made no response. Clive wanted to grab his shoulders and shake him. "Have they not suffered enough?"

A smile flitted across Aeon's face. "Haven't we all?" He spread his arms wide and for an instant, Clive saw thorns glittering with drops of blood encircle Aeon's body. He blinked and they were gone, replaced with fragrant boughs and flowers. The vine around his ankle had retreated and Clive shivered, wondering if the sweet scent of honeysuckle had masked his own blood.

"Can you help them?" he asked, though he didn't hold out much hope.

"Even if my power were not bound into the maze, I could not act against Oberon directly." Aeon sighed, his face aging centuries in its expression of regret. "I will not even be able to ward my own garden, should the monarchs bring their fight to me."

"Then I may as well stay here until Oberon drains me by force."

"I think not, Clive Barrow." Aeon was laughing at him. He

glanced up. The little man's eyes were almost completely covered in wrinkles and his round body shook.

Clive swallowed against the anger rising in his chest. It wasn't the gardener's fault. If he had been trapped in this maze for the centuries that had claimed Aeon, he would be crazy, too. "Is there nothing you can do?" Callie and her people wouldn't stand a chance.

Aeon shook his head. "The small magics Oberon have left me can cause mischief, but no real harm." The ancient gardener wiped his eyes and got himself under control. "Wrong question. You and Lydia, always asking the wrong questions," he said, still chuckling.

"What is the right question?" Clive asked. It was nearly impossible to avoid getting tangled in Aeon's garden or his riddles.

"Is there something *you* can do?" Aeon said.

"What?"

"The question. The question you need to ask." Aeon beamed broadly. "So ask."

Clive rubbed his throbbing temples. He had to leave soon. "Is there something I can do?"

"Not by yourself," Aeon answered.

If he hadn't known that war was coming, Clive would have been tempted to kill Aeon himself. He forced his jaw to relax. "Then how?"

"Ask Lydia."

Clive shook his head. He should have known better than to pin his hopes on this tortured Fae. "I'm sorry, Aeon. She's already made her choice." He wasn't going to drag her back into this. "I should never have forced her here in the first place. We were better off leaving her in the Mortal world."

"That's what she thought, too."

Clive brushed dirt and small twigs from his pants. "Well, at least she'll be well out of this."

"Would it surprise you to know she is no longer in the Mortal world?"

"What?" He grabbed Aeon by the arm. The outline of an invisible thorn pricked his hand before he jerked away.

"The trees do not deceive."

Clive looked all around him. "Where? Where is she?" What would convince her to return to Faerie? And on whose side?

"Not here, Clive. Not here, either."

"If she's not home and she's not here, then where?" He didn't wait for Aeon's answer. "The Between. She's gone back to the Between," he whispered.

Aeon tapped his nose with a long finger and winked at Clive. "And you can follow her there."

Clive shook his head. "I cannot." Even if he could open the specific door to the space she imagined, he had promised her a choice. A way out.

Aeon grasped a section of the vine around his arm and yanked it free from his bronzed skin. The trumpet-shaped flower flared with power and reshaped itself into a curved thorn, wet with a single drop of blood. "Give this to her. Tell her a friend requests aid."

Clive reached for it with a tentative hand.

Aeon shivered. The vines tightened all across his body. Something placed a hand at Clive's throat and began to squeeze.

"Tell her war will despoil the garden."

Struggling to breathe, Clive gasped the words out. "It's too late." The Bright King had run out of patience.

"Not yet. Soon. But not yet," Aeon said. His eyes glittered with malice and laughter. "Mischief, remember?"

Colors dimmed. Clive couldn't figure out if this was Aeon's doing or Oberon draining the power from him.

"Go. Find her. Quickly."

Aeon's voice came from everywhere and nowhere. Clive was lost in featureless dark, his breath coming in ragged gasps. Then the pressure in his chest eased and he hit the ground hard, rolling to a stop against the base of a peach tree. Aeon had thrown him into the heart of the maze. It wouldn't take long for Oberon to fight his way through, no matter how Aeon tangled the way. Clive stood, swaying with a rush of dizziness and grasped the tree trunk to steady himself. Power pulsed from its roots, feeding him.

"Thank you," he whispered, though he was sure Aeon wouldn't hear him. How was he going to find Lydia? The Between wasn't a true place, only a physical manifestation of power and thought. Clive had created the space using elements from Lydia's everyday life. Then he set his name to it and pushed open a space at the margins between Faerie and the Mortal world. But he had borrowed her magic to help him. He didn't have enough power or control to do this alone.

But Aeon did.

He hesitated for a moment, the tree trunk buzzing beneath his hand. What he was planning was little different than what

Oberon had done. But Aeon had tasked him to find Lydia. This was the only way. A deadly quiet fell across the orchard like a storm shadow. His throat burned. He had no other choice. Taking a deep breath, Clive pressed both hands and his forehead against the peach tree's trunk. "I need everything you can spare," he said.

Power flowed into him, a cool drink of water on a hot day that soothed his throat.

"Where are you, Lydia?" he said. Holding an image of her in his mind, he traced the unruly lines of her wavy brown hair. Her eyes, the color of polished walnut, radiated hurt and confusion. Even from the first, she had surprised him, insecurity in her sarcastic responses, her endless capacity for denial, and her ragged cuticles. Yet she had challenged Oberon's own glamour at the heart of his court and won. And she had the strength to wield iron in the Between. Would she go back to that same place? She couldn't know any other way. He had to hope she'd returned to the rainbow grove or he would wander in and out of the Between and never find her.

The tree shuddered beneath his hand. Branches swayed in the absence of a breeze. The taste of ashes filled his mouth.

Oberon was taking his tithe from the maze. Soon the garden would be a grove of blighted trees and dried grasses. Clive couldn't wait any longer. Aeon's magic bubbled up inside him like rising sap in a spring maple. Pushing his body from the tree, he tore a gash across the fabric of Faerie.

*

THE LANDSCAPE MADE HER JUST as queasy as she remembered. Somehow, even with all that had happened to her, it seemed ridiculously unfair. If Clive was right, and this was a place her own mind created, why couldn't she have created something that didn't make motion sickness feel like the better option?

She knelt down on the wavy sea anemone grass and lowered her head between her knees, taking deep breaths through her mouth. Her stomach took its own sweet time settling.

Time. The more time that passed here, the better. Especially if Oberon and Titania kept themselves busy searching for her. Maybe if she waited long enough, Taylor would have a chance to grow up and out of danger. She squeezed her eyes shut. It was easier seeing Marco as a teenager or even an adult—he was already less of a baby brother. But Taylor all grown up was something she didn't really want to think about.

"I did the right thing," she whispered. Then why did she feel so crappy?

Thunder grumbled in the distance and the air around her buzzed with static charge. "Great, just great." It was going to rain, too. Why should it? This was her place and if she didn't want it to rain, it damn well better not rain. She stood up, keeping her eyes fixed on a distant line of trees that stood at least close to perpendicular with the ground and sky. The nausea didn't come roiling back. That was a start.

Fae magic was all around her; the Between was really just a glamoured space, if she understood it correctly, so this should be pretty simple. Lydia lifted her head up to the sky and envisioned it clear and sunny. Clouds boiled off like steam blown from a hot cup of tea. She smiled. Good.

The ground vibrated again and the trees nearest to her shivered. The clouds rushed back, thickening as she watched. Crap.

"Lydia! Stop!"

She whirled around, the blood pounding in her ears, her body poised to run.

Clive stood, balancing on the balls of his feet, one hand curled into a fist.

"What are you doing here?" She couldn't even lick her wounds in peace.

He was out of breath, his face was pale and clammy.

"Don't. Don't use glamour here."

She put her hands on her hips. "Why the hell not?" This was her space. She didn't remember inviting him in.

"The Between's not stable. If you push the boundaries too hard, it will recoil."

"And you came all the way here to give me advice? How perfectly thoughtful of you," she said, struggling to keep her voice level. "Now leave." She didn't want anyone to see her this miserable, least of all him.

He bit his lower lip. Why would he be uncertain? His agitation must have been contagious. Lydia had to stop herself from picking at her cuticles. "I came here to be alone and no, I don't want to talk about it." It came out snippier than she intended.

"Lydia . . . " He took a step closer.

"What. You going to punch me or something, Clive?"

"What?"

She pointed to his curled hand.

"Lydia—no—I mean—I need . . . "

"Spit it out, Clive."

"The courts have gone to war."

The blood rushed to Lydia's face. "But I left so they wouldn't fight." With her gone, there should have been nothing left to fight over. "I can't. It's not. . . " *It's not fair.* But she didn't say that part out loud. "I already did everything I could." How could he expect she'd be able to stop the Bright King and the Shadow Queen? She couldn't even push the clouds away in the Between.

He unfolded his hand. A single thorn had cut into the flesh of his palm, leaving its imprint in blood. "Aeon. He needs your help."

It was as if someone had swapped her blood with ice water. "Where did you get that?"

"He tore it from his own arm, Lydia." Clive couldn't completely suppress his shudder. So he had seen the truth of Aeon's relationship with the maze.

As much as any Fae could be, Aeon was her friend. Clive, too. He may have taken her to Bright, but he certainly hadn't started this. Lydia picked up the thorn between her thumb and index finger. It was as sharp as one of her mom's sewing needles. "What does he think I can do?" Bound or not, the gardener was a powerful figure. More powerful than Lydia could ever be.

"He cannot act directly against Oberon." Clive shivered again and Lydia wondered what frightened him. "The monarchs have chosen the maze as their battlefield. Already, they are fighting over the latent power in the garden. Aeon's power."

"It's no use." She hugged her arms around herself. "I can't save anybody. I can't even save myself."

"Lydia . . . "

"Why do you think I'm here?" She turned her head and watched the ridiculous carnival colors drip and bleed around her. At least she was getting used to the place. "It's not for the ambiance. There's no other place for me to go. Oberon made sure of that." She wasn't going to slink back into Faerie like a dog with its tail between its legs.

"What are you going to do? Stay here until everyone and everything you loved is dust and memory?"

Lydia had thought she was past crying, but Clive still found a way to make the pain fresh. "Haven't you done enough?"

He winced and turned away. Good. He was feeling as crappy as she was.

When he spoke again, she had to strain to hear him. "You can hide here and feel sorry for yourself or you can try to help someone who trusts in you."

"Well, that's his mistake, isn't it?" Lydia hated herself for snapping like that, but she couldn't take the words back.

Clive was silent for what felt like a long time before he turned back to her and stared directly into her eyes. "I wasn't talking about Aeon."

She closed her hand around Aeon's thorn and let it bite into her palm. "I'm sorry, I'm so sorry," she said, though she wasn't even sure what she was apologizing for. The truth was, she ran away. It didn't matter that she thought she had good reasons, she ran away. Aeon and Clive had helped her. She owed them. It was that simple.

Wincing, she thought about her family. Going back would give Oberon another reason to hurt them. But as long as he controlled the doors between the worlds, he was a threat to them, anyway, and to anyone or anything else he wanted.

She couldn't stay here.

Lydia nodded and opened her hand. Clive's eyes widened. The thorn tumbled out, glistening with fresh blood, hers mingled with Aeon's and Clive's. The ground drank it eagerly. The air around them trembled; the sky shook free of clouds. She clasped his scored hand to hers and the shock of power nearly sent her to her knees. "Help me. The heart of the maze. Hold it in your mind."

"Hurry, Lydia."

The Between was degrading, but Lydia halted its decay, letting the rainbow colors slowly melt like sidewalk chalk in the rain as she opened a door into Aeon's garden.

Chapter 24

THEY SLAMMED INTO THE GROUND. Lydia got the wind knocked out of her. She struggled to get to her feet. Something was wrong. This wasn't the maze. At least not the maze she remembered. The lush carpet of moss was burned away. What was left was cracked clay and dried yellow grass that crumbled to dust in her hand. Where the hedge walls had been were bare and twisted twigs. She grasped her pendant. "Aeon, where are you?"

"Look!"

She followed Clive's pointing finger. A patch of green retreated as they watched, the color leaching from every growing thing. The maze turned into desert with the speed of one of those time-lapse films her science teacher loved to show. "What's happening?"

"Come on, Lydia," Clive said, yanking her arm and pulling her toward the last tinge of green.

They stumbled over splintered tree trunks and blighted hedges that looked bleached as bone, her eye starved for any sign of life. Dust coated her skin. Her tongue tasted of ash. She sent her magic deep into the ground, searching for water.

There was nothing but death as far as she could probe. Death and hunger.

"Lydia! No!" Clive's warning brought her back to herself. "Don't let them know you're here."

"What?"

"Oberon and Titania. We have to get to Aeon first before they drain him and his garden dry and start looking for more."

"More? More what?"

"Power. This is what war looks like, Lydia."

"I don't understand." War was tanks and troops and bombs.

"Did you think we would arm ourselves with bows and arrows and march in orderly rows to battle? If we don't stop them, they will lay waste to everything in Faerie." He swallowed hard. "Everything and everyone."

"But that's crazy," she said. This was the Fae version of nuclear Armageddon. And she was right in the middle of it.

"Come on."

They ran ahead of the spreading blight and into the heart of what was once Aeon's orchard. He sagged against a peach tree in the center of the grove, breathing heavily. No hint of the earlier, softer illusion of his captivity remained. Vines strangled his body, pressing their thorns into his skin. Aeon bled freely from dozens of small wounds.

Lydia ran to his side and fell to her knees next to him.

"I'm afraid I cannot offer you the hospitality of my garden," he said, wincing as a vine scraped across the front of his throat. He made no move to touch it, only pressed his back more firmly into the tree trunk. Lydia lifted her hands. Aeon's eyes widened. "No!" he said. She stiffened and jerked her hands back. "Oberon will only entangle you also."

"What can I do?"

"Will you mourn for the dead? Else my trees will have no one to remember them."

"No, there has to be something. Anything."

"We're too late. Look," Clive said.

A ring of apple trees framed the entrance to the small orchard. The tips of their leaves were white as if tinged by an early frost. As she watched, all the green leached from the leaves until only dull brown remained to crumble in a rising breeze.

"No!" Lydia cried.

"Be at peace, child. You are here. That is enough," Aeon whispered. He was rigid in concentration, sweat beading on his forehead. Lydia followed the trail of his magic as he poured his own self into the ground and into the trees through their deep roots. The encroaching desert slowed against Aeon's blockade, but the little man wouldn't last for long.

"Why doesn't he attack Oberon directly?"

"He cannot. He is of Bright, as I am."

"But I'm not," she said, squaring her shoulders.

Clive gripped her arm. "If you set your power directly against him, you will lose. He has the magic of the entire court to draw on, and of Faerie itself. At least whatever piece of it Titania has not claimed."

Lydia shook out of his hold. "I did it before."

"You surprised him at the masque. He will be ready for you this time. And if you do attack him, Titania will take the chance to move against you."

"I can't leave him like that," she said, staring at Aeon. He was one more thing Oberon was stealing from her life. She wasn't going to give him up without a fight. "I'm supposed to be here to help. That's why you came for me."

Aeon cried out as he lost another row of trees. Desiccated cherries lay on the ground, so shriveled, likely even the birds wouldn't eat them.

She stepped back, closer to Aeon and the few remaining living trees. Once the last one died, so would Aeon. He was too much a part of the garden now to live without it. She couldn't free him and she couldn't go after Oberon or Titania directly. But maybe she could add her strength to his.

A shield worked on the darklings. Maybe she could use it to help Aeon. Closing her eyes, she wove her magic as she had once before. It shimmered in her mind, thin and supple as silk. She wrapped it around them both, enclosing the peach tree, as well. A wind rose up, flapping the ends of her glamoured cloth.

"Oh, no you don't." She gripped the edges more firmly. "There, that should be better," she said, turning to Aeon. He was as pale as frostbite, his wounds still oozing their sluggish red. "I don't understand." She felt for her shield. It wound around them in an unbroken circle. They should be cut off from Oberon's assault, Aeon free of the choking thorns.

"I shouldn't have called you here. You would have to dig down to the very beginnings of Faerie to free me, child." He shook his head, wincing as a cut opened on his face. "Oberon bound me with his own name and I think I am too long tangled with the roots of this place." Moving slowly, he tugged one hand clear of thorns, hopelessly snarling the other. He reached over to Lydia and touched her cheek. "Do not despair. I will be free soon."

"No! Not like this! There has to be another way."

"I am an old tree, Lydia. When old trees fall, they cause the most damage."

She stared into a face creased with years and fresh pain. An anger she didn't know she could hold flooded her chest and face with a rush of heat. "No," she said, "Not going to happen."

"Lydia, you can't fight them both," Clive said.

"Watch me," she said, glaring at him. She let the magic held in her glamour spill back into her. She was going to need everything she had. And there wasn't much time left. Oberon and Titania had just about blighted Aeon's orchard, sucking every bit of Fae magic from the landscape. Everywhere she looked was more than winter drab; the only color left shone from the peach tree Aeon lay against. The peaches shined with desperate luminescence.

Lydia took great, deep breaths through her mouth, filling her lungs the way she did before a cross-country meet. This was a race of attrition. And she didn't want to think about what her opponents were capable of. Power swirled around her as if she were in the center of an invisible tornado. The air crackled with static. Her hair fanned out from her head.

"Lydia, be careful," Clive said.

"No time for careful." She grinned and Clive stepped backward. "Come out, come out, wherever you are," she sang out. They wouldn't get the Oz reference, but she stamped the ground, setting her name to the pulse of power that traveled outward from her in a spreading ring. Now they would know she was here.

"You want me? Come and get me." She stood still and tall, even as she had no idea what she was going to do. One thing she did know. She was through running.

Her ears popped in a sudden pressure change. Oberon stood in front of her, his gold-threaded tunic garish against the dull browns and grays of dead wood. Lydia's heart beat double-time.

"You have refused my hospitality and defied the dictates of Bright court. Submit to me now and I will spare your foster family."

She struggled to swallow the lump in her throat. "You have no right."

He laughed. Aeon's eyes flared in anger even as he shivered, pressing against the last living tree trunk.

"And you," Oberon said, fixing Clive in his gaze, "you already belong to me."

Clive sagged to his knees, but Lydia couldn't worry about him right now. Oberon towered over her, even larger than she remembered. His movements were clumsy, his voice booming. It was almost as if he were drunk on the power he had ripped from the Fae and from the land.

Lydia bounced up and down on her toes, not sure what she was getting ready to do. She stepped between Oberon and Aeon. "Let him go," she said.

Oberon raised an eyebrow and took a step toward her. She stepped back.

"It would be a shame to waste your magic on one old, dead tree," he said. "Honor your Fae heritage. You will have the satisfaction of knowing you have helped unite the courts."

He laughed as he kept advancing, and she was running out of room. Another step and she would be against the tree. "Why would I want to help you?"

"Your Mortal upbringing has kept you refreshingly vulnerable. I knew there was a reason I left you there so long." He raised his hand and Lydia pulled her magic around her like a cloak.

"Let the child be," Aeon said. "I will cede the garden to you."

"No!" Lydia cried.

Oberon laughed again. "I hardly need your concession, gardener. Look around you." The tips of the peach tree's leaves were tinged with blight. "You are already mine." He gestured with his fingers and the vines pulled tight around Aeon's neck, drawing a fresh necklace of blood.

*

CLIVE COULDN'T BREATHE. OBERON HAD pinned him to the ground with the force of an invisible tree trunk. He struggled to turn his head, to at least witness Lydia's stand. He didn't blame her for any of this. She had done what she could, foolish as it was. Aeon's life was draining from his wounds. The Bright King would use the power of the garden to destroy Shadow court. Finally, the stalemate broken. Perhaps Oberon would be merciful and Clive would be dead soon. The guilt of failing Lydia would die with him.

*

LYDIA JUMPED TO AEON'S SIDE, struggling to free him. Thorns pierced her skin and she pushed away the pain. Her fingers, slick with their mingled blood, slid from the vines. Aeon's eyes bulged and his body thrashed.

"Let him go! I'll help you," she said, tears blurring Aeon's distress.

"Too late for mercy, child."

She dug frantically in the soil, looking for something to pry Aeon loose with. There were only dead twigs that snapped at her touch. Aeon's struggles had stilled. His chest barely rose and fell against Oberon's stranglehold. A shower of ripe peaches thudded against the soft ground. Their scent rose in the air, a cruel reminder of summer and Aeon's kindness. She had to save him. She had to cut through the vines. Now.

Cut. Knife. Metal.

She dug through her pocket for her keys. The cool metal fob slid comfortably in her hand. Gripping it carefully, she sawed at the living noose around Aeon's throat, wincing as her hand slipped, the metal raising blisters on his already broken skin. Where the fob touched the thorns, the vine burned away with a high-pitched hiss.

Aeon sagged to the ground, his body rag doll limp.

Please be alive. Please.

Lydia whirled to face the Bright King, the sharp, double v-shape of the key fob pointing outward.

Chapter 25

THE WEIGHT RELEASED FROM HIS chest so suddenly, Clive's head swam. He rolled to his side and scrambled to his feet, panting heavily. Oberon swayed, his face pale and sweating. Lydia advanced on him, the sun glinting off the metal of her key fob. Clive felt the wrongness of the metal, a splinter in the heart of Faerie.

"Lydia," he whispered, "be careful."

She didn't hear him; didn't even glance his way. She was an arrow, loosed at the Bright King. Clive wasn't sure anything could deflect her anger or her roiling power now. She was as beautiful as she was deadly. He backed away, reveling in the sudden and unexpected reprieve.

There was nothing he could do to help Lydia now. This was between her and Oberon. But maybe he could help the Unbound ward themselves from the fallout. At least until Oberon remembered the tithe Clive owed him. "Luck and light, Lydia Hawthorne," he whispered, taking one more glance back to the withered grove before running through the dying and silent maze. He didn't have Aeon and his trees to help guide him this time, but he held to an image of Callie; her passion, her drive to protect her people. He followed the memory of green, searching for her.

He burst through brown branches into a living wood. The low buzz of darklings filled his mind. He raised a glamour of stillness and silence, meeting their hunger with emptiness instead. They swirled around him several times before streaming off into the sky.

"Clive." Callie's face was lined with fatigue, her shoulders sagged. "Titania seeks to open a breach in our defenses."

"Oberon has taken the maze."

She nodded, her eyes full of resignation. "So the Shadow Queen looks to our meager stores to bolster her reserves."

Clive nodded.

"Will you add your strength to ours?"

"Yes." For as long as it would do any good. At least he would spend his power on something other than the Bright King's folly.

"Come," she said, taking his hand in hers. "Welcome to the Unbound." She led him past a small grove of scrub pine that looked lush and vibrant after the blighting of Aeon's maze. The gathered Unbound were massed at the border to Shadow court's holdings. A wave of darklings, thicker than Clive had ever seen, formed a wall just in front of the ragged line of Fae. Isidore spared a tight smile for him before concentrating on the darklings again.

"Look to the border," he said. "We cannot cover it all. If you see a breach, raise the alarm."

Clive traced what seemed to be personal ley lines stretching from each of the Unbound toward Isidore. "You're directing their magic," he said.

Callie nodded. "It's the only way to create and control the darklings."

"The more power Shadow flings at the border, the stronger the darklings will become," Isidore said.

It was the same trap they had set for Lydia. He couldn't imagine it would hold Titania for long.

"At least until they discover what we have created." Callie shrugged. "We all know it's only a matter of time, but none has elected to leave." She trapped him with her direct gaze. "Are you willing to stay through the end?"

"As long as my life remains," he said. It was just as likely he would die by Titania's magic as Oberon's.

A shout rose from the line of tired defenders. "Titania." Callie sighed. "We knew it would come to this."

Their small pooled magics couldn't hold long against the Fae Queen. It was only a matter of time. How funny that it came down to something so Mortal. Well, at least he wouldn't survive to nourish Oberon. He studied the Fae around him. Men and women with lined faces, resignation in the slumps of their shoulders. They knew they were doomed. But they had always been doomed.

The darklings were a clever idea. If he believed in luck, he might even believe it could really work. Clive shivered, despite the bright sunshine. A ribbon of fog wound around his ankles and slithered up his legs. The buzz of the darklings slowed.

One of the Unbound cried out. Clive looked up. The group

of defenders stood staring at one another as the darklings thinned around them. Uncertainty was written on their faces. The shared magic sputtered and died. Isidore, white and shaking, stepped back from the border.

"Clive Barrow, how perfectly unexpected," Aileen said, forming from the cold mist.

*

OBERON STEPPED BACK, SNARLING. "WHAT have you done?"

Lydia's hand curled around the cool metal with a death grip. "Leave." She desperately wanted to look to Aeon, lying on the ground behind her, but she didn't dare take her eyes off the Bright King. His fury was like a blast of heat from a furnace.

If she showed any uncertainty, his magic would break over her like a wave and she would drown. She took a step closer to him, her hands rock-steady. "Leave. This garden is mine." Her heart ached for Aeon. If he was dead, she would choke Oberon in his own thorns.

Oberon narrowed his eyes. "This garden and its gardener belong to me. They were mine long before your mother even dreamed of betraying her own court with your birth. She was a fool to think she could overcome me and so are you."

With her free hand, she pulled out the pendant Aeon had given her. She had sworn him an oath. Had sworn to help him. The power of her promise, repeated three times and sealed with her name bound her, even if he no longer lived. "I am not my mother," she said. "You know nothing about me." She took another step toward him, the sharp metal prongs of the key fob dark with vine sap mingled with Aeon's blood.

Oberon scowled. Bright magic stirred beneath their feet as he gathered power against her. She held her ground, listening to the pulse throb in her ears. "Nothing. You know nothing about me," she repeated, clasping the golden peach stone and calling on threads of Bright and Shadow magic. "You figured my life in the Mortal world left me weak and helpless." She took another step closer to Oberon, smiling as he furrowed his eyebrows. Thoughts of home filled her with strength and sadness: the warmth of her mother's smile, her father's quiet confidence teaching her how to drive, Taylor's hand squeezing hers, even Marco's muddy soccer cleats littering the front steps. "You're wrong. I'm stronger than you think."

The warmth of green and growing things flooded through her.

This time Oberon took a step back.

The ghost of apple blossoms tickled her nose with their sweetness. Deep beneath her feet, Aeon's garden stirred. It was fulfilling a promise made when the old Fae had given her his sigil. It was answering her need. Or maybe its own need. Without Aeon to tend to it, it had turned to her.

Oberon jerked his head up. Lydia followed his gaze, but there was nothing she could see other than dead trees and empty sky. He turned back, focusing his amber eyes on her face and smiled, glancing at the weapon in her hands. "Impressive, but wielding iron alone will not be enough, child. I will deal with you once Shadow has fallen to me."

Lydia took a breath to answer, but Oberon had already vanished from the heart of the dying maze. Lydia stumbled backward, the release of tension like a rubber band suddenly snapped. Her hands shook. The metal key fob flaked away to powder and sifted to the ground. What the hell just happened?

Oh, God, Aeon.

Lydia whirled and ran back to the peach tree. The old Fae hadn't moved. Moisture gathered in her eyes, blurring her vision. She couldn't tell if he was breathing. "Aeon, I'm so sorry," she said, leaning over his broken body. Tears rolled off her face and splashed onto his cheeks, smearing the blood. She placed a tentative hand on his chest, feeling for a heartbeat. Nothing.

She mourned the strange little man who had been her friend. Wind moaned through dry branches, chilling her to her core. There was nothing she could do for Aeon, but at least she could bring back life to the things he loved.

Lydia leaned against the peach tree's trunk, searching for the spark of green inside it. The tree was hurt, but still very much alive. Taking a full, deep breath, she drew on all the sources of her power: Bright magic, Shadow magic, and memory, both of her family and the fragile peace of Aeon's garden. Glamour rose up like winter sap and she guided it through the roots of the sentinel trees at the heart of the orchard. She couldn't risk trying to repair the whole garden or any of the maze. Besides, it would only leave Oberon and Titania something more to fight over. But maybe she had given the orchard enough of a spark that it could renew itself. It was the only fitting tribute she could give her friend.

As she watched, buds swelled on the tips of the trees' outermost branches. It was a start.

Now it was time to find Clive. This war was not over by a

long shot and she couldn't fool herself into thinking she had frightened Oberon off. Well, not entirely, anyway. She wished there was some way to bury Aeon, but even if the ground were soft enough, Lydia had no shovel to dig with. And it was long past time to go.

Lydia looked back one last time to say goodbye. The earth at the base of the peach tree was dark and churned up as if someone had tilled it. His body was finally free of thorns and vines, the deep brown skin unmarked now. No blood smeared his clothes. The hint of a smile spread across his still face.

He was sinking into the rich loam. She watched, helpless, as the gardener disappeared, the earth drinking him in like cool water. His garden had taken him home. She bowed her head for a moment in tribute before slipping the pendant beneath her shirt. "I need to find Clive," she whispered to the tree, letting her fingers trail along now living bark. "What do the trees elsewhere in Faerie tell you?"

Branches swayed, creaking in the breeze. Where would he go? Lydia closed her eyes. She didn't know if it was the garden answering her call, but she thought about the group of Fae outside the courts. The Unbound. Even if Clive wasn't there, it was a space free of Oberon or Titania, at least for now. She needed somewhere neither of them had the advantage. After the way she disappeared, Callie wouldn't welcome her bringing the war to her doorstep, but it wasn't like any of them had much of a choice. War would come to the Unbound sooner or later, no matter what she did. It didn't make her feel any better, not that she expected it to.

Calling on her magic once more, Lydia opened a door directly from the heart of the orchard to the grove where Callie and Isidore had first taken her. She stepped through.

The war had already beaten her there.

Chapter 26

CLIVE BOWED TO HIS SHADOW court counterpart. Aileen was alone, but that didn't mean he and the Unbound could hold against her. Not this close to the court and Titania herself.

"Always the gallant, even now," Aileen said. Her words mocked, but her face was a mask of perfect calm.

"This is not our war, Aileen. It never was." She wouldn't meet his eyes.

"Give us your Queen's message and leave," Callie said. "Unless you have come to join us."

"Swear fealty to Shadow and Titania will welcome you in her court."

There wasn't a sound among the assembled Fae. Titania was offering them what they wanted, even if many wouldn't admit that even to themselves.

"The mighty Titania, granting the likes of us a place in Shadow?" Callie laughed. "When so many of us were rejected from her graces in the first place?" She glanced around the circle of tired defenders. Not all of them would meet her eyes.

Isidore clamped his jaw closed so tightly the muscles in his temples bulged.

"My Queen is not without sympathy for your plight."

Callie snorted. Aileen ignored her.

"But you cannot hope to survive this conflict. Titania offers you safety."

"And at what price?" Callie asked.

"Your tithe."

"No," Isidore said and the quiet certainty in his voice held the strength of any sworn oath.

"You ask us to cede our power, meager as it is, to protect us from a war of your design." Callie laughed. "How perfectly ironic."

Some of the older Fae muttered their agreement.

"Don't do this," Aileen said. She was staring at Callie, her eyes pleading.

Clive cocked his head, studying her. Aileen was uncomfortable. What had Titania really sent her here to do? She had already offered the caress. Where was the slap?

"Your Queen must be desperate to make such an offer." Callie stepped forward, her eyes flashing. "If we choose to side with Oberon, she will be well and truly crushed."

"Is that what you want? Faerie utterly controlled by Oberon's whim?"

Callie shrugged. "It has been thus for a long time. Besides, it matters little to the Unbound which court oppresses us."

Aileen's nostrils flared and two spots of color highlighted her sharp cheekbones, but she held herself still.

"Aileen, let them be," Clive said.

She shook her head and her black hair swung freely around her. "I cannot. I speak for my Queen in this." Sighing, she turned to Callie. "Are you certain?"

Clive studied the Fae. Fear and fatigue marked their faces. Callie closed her eyes briefly before looking to the Unbound, one by one. Isidore nodded and she took a deep breath. Most followed his lead, some more reluctantly than others. A few looked away. Clive couldn't blame them for wanting to find a way out.

"We are resolved." Callie said.

Aileen winced, her gaze sliding away from Callie toward Clive. "And you?"

There was little Clive could do but shrug. "When Oberon calls his debt, I will pay my tithe in blood."

She nodded, her expression blank, as a quiet settled on them like the silence before a heavy snow. Clive's steady heart-beat counted off time. "Aileen." Clive didn't know what to say, but he needed to break the oppressive quiet.

His head throbbed along with his pulse. Fatigue weighed his shoulders down with bone-crushing force. Callie was right. It didn't matter which court held power. They both just sought to bleed the life from the Fae, anyway. War would only speed up the inevitable. He looked at the rest of the Unbound. How could he ever have imagined that defying Oberon or standing up to Titania was possible?

He was so tired.

Clive turned to Aileen, wondering if she, too, was weary of this conflict. When she caught Clive looking at her, she winced and turned away. He forced himself to think through the fog numbing his mind. The Fae who had been arrayed in watchful lines along the border were stumbling away from one another, as if they couldn't bear to admit their hopelessness. It felt like his body was mired in mud. What was wrong with him?

Callie was standing with her hands covering her face. Isidore was sitting under the cover of a hemlock tree, his eyes red rimmed. A dense fog rose from the Shadow side of the border. Clive didn't have the energy to raise the alarm.

The fog thickened and rose, coalescing into the size and shape of a cloaked Fae. He balled his hands into fists. The thorn print bit into his palm with the memory of pain. Of Aeon and the garden. Of Lydia defying the Bright King.

Slender hands with fine, tapered fingers slowly lowered the hood from her face. Dark hair shook free. Aileen bowed and offered her hand to the Shadow Queen. Titania stepped into the Unbound's realm.

This was her doing. The subtle glamour of the Shadow Queen had sapped their strength and their will. Clive's heart hammered in his chest. He squeezed his hand harder, welcoming the sharp distraction.

"You have struggled enough," Titania said. "Tithe to me and I can give your pain surcease."

"No," Clive said, stepping back from the Shadow Queen's gaze. "I cannot grant you what is not mine to give." It felt like the fog filled his head, too.

Titania's voice was utterly cold, her eyes the blue of the sky's reflection off ice and snow. She laughed. "No. You are Oberon's lost plaything."

He moved further away from her and bumped into Callie.

She didn't stir. Gripping her arms, Clive pulled her hands from her face and shook her, calling her name. Her eyes slid past him, staring off into the distance. "Stop it. Let them go," he said.

"This is war, Clive Barrow," Titania said. "And you are on the side of my enemy. I could crush you here and now."

Aileen placed a hand on Titania's arm.

"But I can be merciful," Titania said.

Clive turned back to Callie. "It's a glamour. You must fight through it. Your people need you."

Titania's cloak rustled in the absence of any breeze. "Aileen, hold him until Oberon comes to claim him."

"Please, Clive," Aileen said. "Just step away."

He glared at her and drew his hand back, slapping Callie's face as hard as he could. She was as white as her hair and she shuddered once before her eyes swiveled to focus on him. One hand came up to touch her reddened cheek. "Clive?"

Titania was shaking with fury.

Callie shifted her gaze between Clive, Aileen, and Titania. Clive could see her pulse quicken through the translucent skin of her throat. "No," she said, "no."

Aileen placed her hands on Clive's chest and he was rooted to the spot. He couldn't speak. He almost couldn't breathe.

"Too late," Titania said.

Clive watched, helpless as mist twined around Callie's legs. Her eyes widened. She shuddered as the air itself thickened, climbing her body like a vine on a trellis. Color leached from her already-pale face. Her green eyes dimmed, the red of her lips fading to pink and then white. When the mist cleared,

Callie's lifeless body slumped to the ground.

There was nothing Clive could do with his rage. It squeezed around his heart and throat until he thought the pressure would make his head burst. He had known the Unbound could not win. Yet he still returned to them. And he gave Callie false hope. He shouldn't have come. Aileen had left his eyes free and all he could do was watch Titania take by deception and by force what the Unbound had refused to give willingly.

Aileen met his gaze and he would have killed her on the spot had he the strength to break her hold.

Flushed with power, Titania stepped as close to Clive as a lover. She ran a sharp fingernail down the side of his cheek. "When Oberon comes for you, we will be ready."

Clive had no anger to spare for her. So he was a pawn. He had been a pawn his whole life. At least now it would end, one way or another.

The crisp taste of ozone tinged the air and Clive felt more than heard the thrum of thunder in the distance. Someone was crossing. Either between the worlds or within Faerie. The opening moves had been made. The pawns were fully engaged. There were other, more powerful pieces shifting on the board now. Titania stiffened, her body eager and alert. Aileen stared at Callie's body, her mouth in a tight, thin line.

"How gracious of you to safeguard my kinsman," Oberon said.

His smooth voice sent chills up Clive's spine. The hair on the back of his neck tingled. The Bright King was right behind him.

*

LYDIA FROZE, THE OPEN DOOR TO the orchard behind her. Death had already taken the Unbound. Callie lay twisted on the ground, her white hair like an early frost over the pine needles.

Oberon and Titania turned to her, their faces wearing twin expressions of eagerness and hunger. Lydia fought the urge to retreat through the door. There was no place to hide anymore. She met Aileen's gaze with her own. The Shadow Fae inclined her head toward her in an almost invisible bow. Clive stood with his back to her. She didn't have time to figure out what his game was.

The monarchs were saturated with Fae magic. It beat against her in a pulse that formed the heartbeat of Faerie. She had no idea how she was going to fight them both. Against the two of them, her command over glamour was laughable.

"Cede Shadow to me and I will spare your kin," Oberon said.

Titania's laugh was as brittle as the sound of breaking ice. "I think not. Perhaps once you could have threatened me, but no longer."

There was a grim finality in Titania's words. She must have stripped her people of every shred of power to be able to stand here against Oberon. Lydia shivered, easily able to imagine the whole of Shadow as silent and dead as Aeon's maze.

"You cannot hold against the Trueborn's magic."

Lydia stared at Oberon. What was he talking about?

"She has not sworn to you," Titania said, shrugging. "Why would she fight me?"

"Oh, she will ally with me."

His smug assurance made Lydia want to gag.

Aileen gasped and Clive sagged to the ground.

"Lyddie?"

Lydia whirled, the blood thudding in her ears. "Tails!" she cried.

Taylor was standing across the clearing, holding Deirdre's hand. Fear and anger warred for space in her chest. She felt dangerously light-headed. *Oh, God, Taylor. He has Taylor.*

"She said we could play in a magic place. You and me, Lyds." Taylor smiled and it almost cracked something inside her.

"You see? You cannot win." Oberon turned his back on Titania and took a step toward Clive. "And you have toyed with my patience long enough."

He was going to kill Clive. Right here. In front of Taylor. "No," Lydia whispered.

They all turned to her. Deirdre's smug smile made Lydia want to slug her, but the Fae courtier was literally holding the trump card. Oberon licked his lips. Titania was gathering Shadow magic. Fog coiled around her legs. Clive slid his gaze past Oberon as if he weren't there to nod toward Taylor. She winked and waved at him. Lydia wanted to lie down and weep.

"You have my vow," Oberon said. "I will never hurt her."

He would keep her alive, a pet of his court, and consider his oath fulfilled. "You have no right," she said, her voice steadier than she had any right to expect.

"I have the power."

"I will fight you."

"I think not."

His smile filled her with enough fury to drive out the fear. If she did nothing, Taylor would remain in Faerie, at least until Oberon got tired of her. "What do I have to lose?"

Oberon laughed. "Can't you guess?"

Lydia shook her head, afraid to look back at Taylor.

"She will have a lovely life here with me, but she won't remember you."

"No!" Clive shouted. She met his gaze. He understood.

"Your time in the Mortal world has erased a lifetime of our Fae influence, Clive Barrow," Oberon said, his mouth twisting in a wry smile. "But why should I be surprised?" He took another step closer to Clive. He scrambled to his feet. Oberon nodded. "It is through my hand and will that you belong to the Bright court. It is right that you stand to face me at the end."

"I would say farewell to Lydia."

Oberon nodded.

"No, you can't do this!" she shouted.

"Lydia. He can," Clive said quietly. "You have been my friend. I am in your debt." He took a deep breath. "As is the Bright Court." He glanced at Taylor, back at her, and then to Taylor again. "Fare thee well, Lydia," he said, never taking his eyes from her little sister.

As far as debts owed, Bright court could never repay what they had stolen. Not in a million years.

"Come, Lady Titania, when I have disposed of our problem changeling, you and I will dance."

Titania stood, rigid as a marble statue, Aileen by her side. Clive and Oberon faced one another in pressured silence. Taylor frowned as Deirdre gripped her hand, only understanding that something was happening. Something that frightened her.

The bodies of the Unbound lay where they had fallen among the trees. Lydia hoped that Taylor wouldn't remember this.

Oberon leaned toward Clive, his hand cupping Clive's chin with eerie gentleness. Lydia didn't want to watch, but couldn't tear her gaze away. Clive's face was a mask of calm as he stared past the Bright King at Taylor.

What was he trying to tell her? She tugged at her hair, struggling to think. Bright magic streamed out of him in a wide ribbon, coiling around Oberon. Pain bloomed in Clive's eyes. His dark hair silvered as if he'd aged decades in an instant.

"Please, don't do this!" Lydia cried.

Oberon made no response.

"Lyddie? What's happening?" Taylor's voice shook, her eyes wide, shining. Her sister was on the verge of tears.

She had to do something. She had to make it stop.

Taylor was hostage for her cooperation. She couldn't save Clive with power. There had to be another way. His words echoed in her mind. *I am in your debt, as is the Bright court.*

Debt.

The Bright King owed her. And he would be bound by his promise. It was the boon Clive had given her.

He wanted her to use it to free Taylor.

Or she could save Clive's life.

He was helpless to stem the magic hemorrhaging from him. This was the tithe. A promise to offer individual power to the court at need. But what Oberon was doing was a perversion of that trust. She glanced at Taylor. Her little sister was trying to tug free of Deirdre's hold. Lydia squeezed her eyes closed.

Taylor trusted her.

Clive was dying.

Lydia snapped her eyes open and used Fae magic to paralyze Deirdre's hand. Taylor almost fell as she slipped free. She ran over to Lydia and practically jumped into her arms. Lydia set her sister on her hip, burying her nose in the silk of Taylor's hair.

She knew what she had to do.

"Oberon, Lord and King of the Bright court, I have an un-answered boon."

He turned on her, murder in his gaze. Clive fell to the ground like a puppet with his strings cut.

"Lyddie, I'm scared," Taylor whispered.

"Shh, Taylor, I'm here." She gripped her sister even tighter.

"What do you desire, Lydia Hawthorne, Trueborn of Bright and Shadow courts?" He practically spit the formal words out.

She kissed Taylor on the cheek before staring up into the smoldering fire of Oberon's amber eyes. If she freed Taylor, then they were back at stalemate. He would have no hold on her cooperation. And Clive would be dead. "Release your kins-man, Clive Barrow."

Oberon's eyes widened.

"Lydia, no," Clive whispered.

The Bright King looked down at Clive and began to laugh. "He is less than a drop of water to an ocean. You are welcome to him."

Lydia hugged Taylor to her chest, tears gathering in her eyes.

Oberon shook his head. "Fool, you could have ensured your sister's freedom." He glanced back at Clive. "Think you that anything has changed? I did not need his paltry tithe to conquer Shadow. But you? You I will have." He beckoned Deirdre to his side. "Take the child back to court. Lydia and I have a task to complete."

Taylor gripped Lydia's shirt in her chubby fingers. "Lyddie, no! I'm staying with you!"

Oberon took a single step closer to her. "Will the child cooperate? Or shall I ensure that she does so?"

The blood drained from Lydia's face. "No," she whispered, setting Taylor down on the ground and kneeling in front of her. "Tails. I need you to go with Deirdre." Taylor pressed her lips closed and hugged her arms tight to her chest. Lydia recognized that look. "Please, Taylor. Just for now. I promise, I'll come back for you. I need you to do what I tell you. It's important."

Fat tears dropped from Taylor's eyes. She sniffed and nodded, taking three steps toward Deirdre before she ran back and threw her arms around Lydia. "Don't forget. You promised."

She nodded, not trusting her voice. As Deirdre led Taylor away, Lydia swallowed hard, wondering if she would see her sister again.

Chapter 27

"TAKE HIM THEN. HE BELONGS to no court now." Oberon smiled, turning to Titania. "Now will you yield?"

Lydia rushed to Clive, ignoring the two of them, and the magic roiling over them all. He hadn't moved since Oberon freed him and if he were gone like Aeon, Lydia didn't know what she was going to do.

"Why did you waste your boon on him?" Aileen was standing in her way.

"Let me past."

Aileen frowned, her forehead wrinkling in concentration. "But why? You could have had what you desired."

"The price was too high," she said, pushing past Aileen to kneel by Clive's side. Placing a shaking hand on his chest, she had to wait until she calmed her own breathing to feel he still lived. "Clive . . . Clive, wake up."

Aileen knelt beside them. "I don't understand."

Lydia brushed the strange, white hair out of Clive's eyes. "I couldn't let him die for me." She squeezed her eyes shut. "Not when I could help him." Aeon's warm brown eyes haunted her. Maybe if she'd been faster or stronger, she could have saved him, too.

"But your sister . . . "

"I'll find another way."

"Lydia." Clive gripped her wrist. Her eyes sprang open. "You should have let me go."

She shook her head.

"So there will be one court," Aileen said. There was no anger in her voice.

"I'm sorry," Lydia said. A shadow fell over her.

"Come, Trueborn. You will stand with me." Oberon yanked her to her feet

Her arm was hot where Oberon held her. She swallowed the saliva flooding her mouth. This wasn't how it was supposed to end. Didn't Faerie tales have a happily ever after? Lydia curled her free hand into a fist. Aeon's mark throbbed.

Aileen placed herself between her Queen and the Bright King. What was she trying to do? "Milady, pledge to free the Mortal child and Lydia will ally with you," she begged.

Titania laughed, never taking her eyes of Oberon. "The time for alliances is more than past."

"Then send me after her," Aileen said.

"I need your strength by my side," the Shadow Queen said.

Lydia shivered. She knew what that looked like.

Aileen set her shoulders, confronting her Queen. "Will you consign the Trueborn to the same loss you have mourned all these years?"

Titania turned to Aileen, her eyes cold, blue flame. "How

dare you?" Aileen took a stumbling step backward as if she's been struck. "I lost a child. She is but a child. We have nothing in common."

"She is not your enemy, Milady," Aileen said.

"The Trueborn has chosen. And so, it seems, have you."

Oberon shifted his grip to Lydia's shoulder, his hand a vise keeping her still. He drew on her power. It rushed through her, flowing from her body and into his arm. She struggled to break free.

Titania turned her back on Aileen to face Oberon. Mist swirled around her as she called on her own power.

The ground lurched beneath Lydia's feet. Oberon tore magic from her to feed his own. Her head throbbed and her vision wavered. Aeon's pendant pulsed in time with her panicked heartbeat. Trees swayed as if the gathering power was an onrushing storm. Clive called her name, but she was powerless to answer. His hair, now completely white, reminded her of Callie. She wished she could apologize to them both.

A high, thin scream came from a place far away, or maybe only deep within her mind. Tremors shook the grove. Leaves tumbled to the forest floor.

Oberon and Titania were ripping the fabric of Faerie apart. They would destroy everything and everyone because of their own selfish hurt. She and Taylor were nothing to them beyond tools they could use. Even Faerie itself mattered less then lifetimes of slights and loathing. Tears moistened her eyes. "You're nothing but a pack of cards," she whispered. Cards with egos and vindictive power to match.

The peach stone spread a distracting warmth across her

chest. She rose above the pain the way she could run through the burning of a stitch in her side. Aeon was gone, but his influence still spread the length of breadth of Faerie. She could hear trees in both courts crying out in protest. Across the barriers that separated the two worlds, even the trees in the Mortal world felt the echo of Faerie's agony.

Oberon dug his fingernails into her shoulder. "What are you doing?"

Lydia clenched her jaw as he tore magic from her even more quickly. He was taking everything. Bright magic, Shadow magic, and her stubborn love for her family. Home felt thin and far away.

She clutched the pendant. "No! You can't have them."

Faerie itself answered her, pouring magic into her faster than it gushed from the hole Oberon had ripped open. She had to seal the breach or it would flood straight into him, first destroying Titania and then Faerie in the process, before sweeping her away.

"Fight me and you will never see your sister again," Oberon said.

She had to stop this. Regardless of what happened to her or her family. Grabbing at memories and the ragged remnants of Bright and Shadow magic, Lydia furiously wove a patch and slammed it against the continuing outflow. It slowed to a trickle.

Oberon growled and threw her to the ground. "No matter. I already have what I need of you."

He glowed, his eyes burnished copper against Titania's silver-blue. The two stood facing one another as close as lovers, their gazes locked.

Lydia lay panting, her muscles twitching as if she'd run a marathon. Magic saturated the air with electrical potential. The sky thickened and lightning flickered cloud to cloud. Faerie was like an overfilled balloon, ready to burst, its walls pressing against the barriers between the worlds.

Something had to give or the pressure would destroy them all.

Lydia struggled to her feet and pushed back against it, against Oberon and Titania. It was like trying to break through a brick wall. She needed a bulldozer.

Her ears popped. Her lungs were being squeezed. The storm was almost on top of them. A wall of rain swept across the sky. It was three days ago that she left her house for a run in the rain. A house she would never see again. All the doors between the worlds wouldn't help her get home now.

The doors between the worlds.

She knew what she had to do. Lydia gathered all the power Faerie had left to offer. It filled her with alternating waves of cold and warmth so intense she couldn't tell the difference between them. The storm Oberon and Titania struggled to control lashed the Unbound's grove. Lightning struck down the tallest pine and it toppled behind her with the force of an earthquake as an endless peal of thunder reverberated through her bones. Lydia fell to her knees, blinded, the scent of scorched wood rising around her. Even through closed eyes, she could see the glare from the lightning's afterimage.

Fae magic seared her from the inside with an intensity that matched the storm. She struggled back to standing, reaching out with tingling hands to find the glamour that formed the separation between Faerie and the Mortal worlds.

The boundary was as sharp as a blade and it sliced across her fingertips. Blood dripped from her hands. The barrier pushed her away. Oberon's laughter burned in her ears. Tendrils of fog slithered around her ankles, spreading cold through her body.

Oberon and Titania were too strong. There was nothing she could do. It was hopeless. It had always been hopeless. She slid to the ground.

"Lydia, you have to fight!" Clive shouted. She had no energy to answer him.

"Milady, no!"

Lydia heard Aileen's yell from a long way away. The sluggish fog shredded in a cold breeze. Lydia looked up to see Titania backhand Aileen across her face. The Shadow emissary crumpled at her Queen's feet.

The darkness lifted from Lydia's thoughts and she could breathe again. Aileen lay unmoving, her eyes staring up at the sky. Lydia forced back tears. The Shadow Fae had bought her the gift of time and she wasn't going to waste it. Lydia pushed herself back to her feet and slammed her hands across where she knew the barrier had to be hidden.

This time it took on weight and shape. Forming her magic into a wrecking ball, Lydia pulled it back, aiming it square. She released it at the top of its swing and dropped to the ground, letting it whoosh overhead to slam into the boundary.

The earth beneath her shifted and groaned. A rush of wind plucked at her hair and drenched her clothes as the storm was sucked out of Faerie and into the Mortal world. Clouds streamed through the breach. Distant flickers of lightning reminded her of summer nights and fireflies.

Silence stilled the grove.

Titania and Oberon stood stunned. The Shadow Queen's face was deathly pale and her hands shook. The Bright King had been scorched, a burn scar traveling the length of his face and jaw, disappearing down his neck. The embittered monarchs turned to her. They were joined now, if by nothing more than their hatred of her.

It would never stop.

Lydia scrambled back, almost falling over the ancient tree trunk. One hand scraped the rough, wet bark and Aeon's mark throbbed with power. Strands of Bright and Shadow magic twisted together as Oberon and Titania advanced toward her.

This wasn't how it was supposed to end. Taylor taken. And all the dead. She had accomplished nothing. Other than finally uniting the courts. Lydia laughed then, the sound reminding her of Titania's mad giggle. It went on and on, echoing in the Unbound's grove. The King and Queen stood over her, looking down. Lydia breath came in ragged gasps.

"Peace, child. Don't you think you have done enough?" Oberon said.

She curled her hands into fists and forced herself to look around, acknowledging the bodies of the dead. "Peace," she said, shaking her head, thinking of the peace that once lived at the center of Aeon's garden. Something of the place filled her panicked heart with calm. "There is no peace here."

Peace. Faerie needed peace in order to heal. She lifted up

both her hands in warning and Oberon and Titania stopped. Pulling strength and magic from the tortured earth, she built a glamour out of memory and the quiet of the forest. A place of remembered peace.

"You cannot hope stand against us," Titania said.

Lydia didn't answer. She was in a moment beyond fear, beyond hope. Titania smiled and fog whispered along the ground, reaching for her. She curled it back on itself with the illusion of a breeze, returning it to Titania. The Queen gasped and bowed her head as the mist spiraled around her.

Oberon struggled against the force of Lydia's rising glamour, hurling sparks of magic at her. They fell to the ground in a rain of ash between them. "What are you?" he asked, his eyes widening in shock.

"I don't know anymore," Lydia said, as the magic swirled within her. She released it in one soft outbreath, holding an image in her mind of ancient trees, one oak, the other elm. The quiet of green and growing things enveloped the shocked monarchs, thickening their legs into sturdy trunks. Roots pushed from their feet to sink into the ground. A soft wind tugged at their hair, fanning it around their stunned faces. Titania blinked once before her eyes disappeared beneath spreading bark. The breeze died and in the sudden silence, two sentinels stood at the open gates between the worlds. Lydia collapsed beneath their joined shadows, her anger and her power spent.

Perhaps in a few hundred years, they might be ready to let their hatreds rest.

Chapter 28

LYDIA PUMPED HER LEGS, WORKING the swing higher and higher. The flicker of light and shadow was peaceful through her closed eyes. The wind streamed her hair from her face. It was a temporary peace. She knew that. Letting her legs dangle, Lydia leaned her head back as the swing flew forward and back with its stored momentum. She knew she could use power to push herself even higher, but for now, she wanted to remember what it had felt like to revel in such ordinary magic.

The trees began to whisper. They were on their way.

When the swing finally stopped on its own, Lydia got off and walked toward the stand of trees her childhood fantasies had called the woods. Clive appeared through the slanting light, Taylor holding his hand and chattering nonstop.

When they got to the edge of the playground, Taylor pulled away from Clive and practically threw herself into Lydia's arms.

"Are you ready to go home, Tails?"

She pouted and would have stomped her feet if she were on the ground. "Why can't I just stay with you?"

"I told you. Lydia needs you."

"But you're Lydia, too," she said.

Their mom and dad were going to have a hard time with that one.

"I promise, I'll come see you often and we can play."

"Clive too?"

He smiled and the corners of his eyes crinkled. "Yes, me too," he said.

Taylor struggled in her arms and Lydia let her down. She immediately grabbed Clive's hand and joined the three of them, with her in the middle.

When they got close to her house, Lydia stopped. Her dad and Marco were laughing in the front yard. This was as far as she would go.

"Tails?"

Taylor tugged on her arm. "Come on!"

"Wait. I have a present for you."

Taylor's eyes lit up.

Lydia pulled Aeon's pendent from beneath her shirt and placed it over Taylor's head.

"It's beautiful, Lyddie!"

"It's magic. If you hold it and whisper my name, I'll hear you." Lydia placed a glamour on it so no one but Taylor could see it.

The sounds of laughter wandered closer. Clive touched her arm.

"Love you, Tails." Lydia cloaked the two of them in tree shadows as her dad and Marco crashed through the trees looking for their soccer ball. Her dad scooped up Taylor in his arms and spun her around as she shrieked her laughter.

"It's time, Lydia."

"I know." Fae magic was still flowing between the worlds, but it had slowed down to a trickle from the wild flood when she had first broken the barriers. For good or for ill, no one controlled the doors anymore. It would take some time for the Mortals to rediscover their way into Faerie and it would take even longer for the Fae to recover from what Oberon and Titania had torn from them.

Maybe by then, Lydia would figure out exactly what she had become.

* * *

About the Author

LJ Cohen is the writing persona of Lisa Janice Cohen, poet, novelist, blogger, local food enthusiast, Doctor Who fan, and relentless optimist. Lisa lives just outside of Boston with her family, two dogs (only one of which actually ever listens to her) and the occasional international student. She is represented by Nephele Tempest of The Knight Agency. When not doing battle with a stubborn Jack Russell Terrier mix, Lisa is hard at work on her seventh novel, a ghost story.

Connect with LJ online:

Homepage: http://www.ljcohen.net/
Blog: http://ljcbluemuse.blogspot.com/
Mailing List:
http://www.ljcohen.net/mailinglist/mail.cgi/list/bluemusings
Facebook: http://www.facebook.com/ljcohen
Twitter: @lisajanicecohen
Tumblr: http://www.ljcohen.tumblr.com
Google+: http://gplus.to/ljcohen
email LJ: lisa@ljcohen.net

Want to read more?

Sign up for Blue Musings, an occasional email newsletter complete with free, original, short fiction offered in a variety of drm-free formats. (http://www.ljcohen.net/contact.html)

If you enjoyed *The Between*, stay tuned for news about the sequel in progress and how you can become a supporter through a planned Kickstarter campaign and enjoy special access to the writing process and other perks. News will be posted in Blue Musings, the website, blog, and social media outlets.

Acknowledgments

The Between is a reality because of the support and encouragement of an entire tribe of people.

Thank you to my family and friends for believing in me and pushing me to believe in myself.

I am grateful for the honest critique and commentary from my various writing groups, including the wonderful peeps in part 1 and part 2 of The Ultimate SF&F workshop, taught by Jeffrey A. Carver and Craig Shaw Gardner. My reader extraordinaire and dear friend, Diane, whose honest feedback made *The Between* a far better story than it would have been. My online community of readers and writers, including the Novel Club at Forward Motion for Writers, as well as David, Aimee, Sue, Cat, Susan R., and Karla for help with the story arc in general and the opening chapter in specific.

A huge debt of thanks to my patient and talented agent, Nephele Tempest, who went not one but two editing passes with me on this one. I am grateful for the support of Nephele and of The Knight Agency as I explore a non-traditional path for *The Between*.

My editor, Lisa Hazard, of Hazard Editing kept me from making a fool of myself with commas and other assorted grammatical issues. Any errors remaining are here due to my own stubborn insistence.

Thank you to Eric M., who was so helpful at the 11th hour with typography assistance.

Last, but certainly not least, my heartfelt thanks to Jade E. Zivanovic, whose stunning artwork graces the extraordinary cover of this novel.

10842842R00188

Made in the USA
Charleston, SC
09 January 2012